THE
PHOTOGRAPHER'S
SECRET

BOOKS BY ELLIE MIDWOOD

The Violinist of Auschwitz
The Girl Who Escaped from Auschwitz
The Girl in the Striped Dress
The Girl Who Survived
The Girl on the Platform
The White Rose Network
The Wife Who Risked Everything
The Undercover Secretary
The Child Who Lived
I Have to Save Them
When the World Went Silent

ELLIE MIDWOOD

THE
PHOTOGRAPHER'S
SECRET

bookouture

Published by Bookouture in 2025

An imprint of Storyfire Ltd.
Carmelite House
50 Victoria Embankment
London EC4Y 0DZ

www.bookouture.com

The authorised representative in the EEA is Hachette Ireland
8 Castlecourt Centre
Dublin 15 D15 XTP3
Ireland
(email:info@hbgi.ie)

ISBN: 978-1-83618-334-1
eBook ISBN: 978-1-83618-333-4

To all survivors of sexual abuse and assault.

CONTENT NOTE

This book contains sexual assault, including references to the assault of minors. If this is potentially sensitive to you, please read with care.

ONE

THEN

Berlin, Germany. 1920

Gunshots are echoing from the depths of the city, but Grete isn't afraid. Silent and alert, her big eyes, like those of a doe, follow her mother's stealthy movements. She's long grown used to gliding through their apartment like a ghost, her *Mutti*. Grete is only four, but she, too, knows to keep quiet so as not to awaken the twins. *Mutti* is not taking them. She's only dressing her, Grete, in great haste, all the while listening to the sounds coming from the street outside.

Grete heard the door slam earlier on; heard the heavy steps of Papa's hobnailed boots recede in the distance. Sometime after —but not too soon after—*Mutti* slid through the door and pressed a finger to her lips, still swollen and bruised after the latest quarrel with her husband. Grete nodded, her small hands and feet turning to ice in an instant. Too afraid to believe and too afraid not to.

Red-tinged, infernal clouds begin to billow just above the roofs of the tenement buildings across the street—their personal, poor-man's horizon. Grete acknowledges it with a degree of content. If the fighting is bad, Papa won't return unexpectedly. Won't return until the last communist's skull is bashed in.

Still, *Mutti* shoves Grete's only winter coat and boots into a worn satchel as fast as she can, retrieves a change of underwear from the ugly, green dresser left from the previous tenants, and presses it all down with two heavy tomes of Brothers Grimm fairy tales. Grete's only doll, half-sewn, half-knitted by *Mutti*'s skillful hands, she keeps hold of while *Mutti* pulls a dress over her head and puts Grete's sandals on her bare feet.

In the hallway, Grete holds tight onto her mother's neck as *Mutti* slices through the darkness like a blade, avoiding the boards that make a noise. By the front door, another satchel is already waiting. As Grete's mother hoists it onto her free shoulder, Grete catches a whiff of soap and potatoes. *Mutti*'s clothes and foodstuffs. They're really going then. Really leaving, just like *Mutti* promised they would.

Outside, the air is thick with smoke and vague danger, but Grete doesn't mind it in the slightest. As they run through the streets, just another couple of shadows mixing with the army of night dwellers in the midst of an unannounced civil war, cordite smells like freedom to Grete. She wonders what it smells like to her unborn sister, the growing shape of which is still concealed by her mother's low-waist dress.

"The twins, they'll be fine," *Mutti* says in her breathless voice.

Grete can't tell if her mother is trying to persuade her or herself. Leaving her other two children to the monster's mercy must feel like tearing a limb off to the distraught woman, but if that's what she needs to do, then that's how it has to be.

"He won't harm them."

Grete nods once again. She already knows that much. Father will likely ship them off to the countryside, to his mother, who'll take care of them until the school takes them off her hands.

"In the country, there's still food to be had, unlike here, in Berlin," *Mutti* adds, as if reading her thoughts. In her eyes, the anguish shines like a shard of glass. "They'll be fine."

Grete's own cheek is wet with her mother's silent tears.

In her small chest, Grete's heart is beating like a wounded sparrow against the glass, but she forces herself not to cry.

Never again will he make them cry.

Never again will he see them.

TWO

NOW

Somewhere in Belgium. Winter 1944

"Sullivan!" Sergeant Foster's voice travels through the raw morning air. "Are you in a rush to meet your maker? I told you that we haven't checked the perimeter yet! Those Krauts haven't gone far."

Frank, Maggie's ex-husband, used to say that she was just like a cat: hearing someone calling her but ignoring it with an infuriating nonchalance.

The marriage didn't last long. They'd met in the thirties in France, where Maggie was freelancing for *Mademoiselle* and Frank was writing "a great American novel." Well, attempting to write, which mostly meant he spent his days in artistic Montmartre in search of ideas and survived by writing copy for different advertisement agencies he never hid his contempt for. He was tragic and tormented and wonderful with words and Maggie loved him for that "otherness," for his rejection of the *petit bourgeois* mentality, so prevalent among Brooklyn immigrants of the first and second wave, in favor of pursuing his dream on foreign shores. The proposal was spontaneous;

Maggie said yes in the same manner she plunged into the dark waters on the rocky beaches of Italy—drunk, reckless, and headfirst.

As an engaged couple, they traveled a lot—at Maggie's expense, but that mattered little to her. At home, the Depression was still raging and lines for soup kitchens were never-ending, but here on the continent, expats were living it up and even freelancers were ridiculously overpaid. They stayed in different hotels and took photos of themselves drinking cocktails with umbrellas in them and sunning at the Riviera to send home.

Upon their return home, they had a simple courthouse wedding and moved into Maggie's apartment—Frank with only a suitcase to his name. But the honeymoon quickly came to an end.

Maggie wrinkles her nose at him popping unexpectedly into her thoughts and puts a fresh roll of film into her camera.

"Sullivan, I'm talking to you, damn it!"

"I hear you," Maggie replies without turning to face the man, her teeth clenching the glove she pulled off her hand.

"Then haul your tail back here right this instant!"

At last, the film is in. Maggie feels her dry lips crack as they stretch in a triumphant grin and wipes her runny nose with the back of her other, still-gloved hand.

Through the camera's lens, the pristine, almost pastoral expanse in front of her instantly transforms into a graveyard. It's invisible to the naked eye, but armed with her Kodak, Maggie sees it all: a head buried in the crook of a frozen elbow, a hand reaching out from the snowdrift as if begging for mercy that never came, a mouth opened in a silent scream.

Each snap of the camera echoes through the wintery expanse like a gunshot.

Foster's battalion stumbled upon the massacre by sheer chance. For several days now, they've been chasing the scattered

Panzer divisions which have run out of steam (or gasoline, as Foster correctly observed), gradually pushing the Germans back toward their own borders. A war correspondent for the *New York Times*, Maggie Sullivan rode in the back of a mud-splattered, olive-green jeep, her camera slung around her neck like a talisman. The engine's roar reverberated through her bones, drowning out the chatter of the soldiers beside her. The landscape of war-torn Belgium blurred past her tired eyes, a canvas of desolation painted with the strokes of conflict. The jeep bumped and jolted over the rough, frozen terrain, but Maggie's grip on her camera remained steady. Unlike the soldiers' machine guns resting casually on their laps, this was her weapon. Throughout the past year, she's held onto it as if her life depended on it.

For several days, all the action they'd seen was abandoned and torched German tanks and bundled-up villagers begging a few cans of Spam from the American GIs and grumbling about the damned Nazis who stole their last skinny chicken and a few rotten potatoes. And then today, suddenly, an abrupt halt of the jeep that threw Maggie forward and a strangled gasp of the driver, followed by, "I think I just ran over a body."

She caught herself, her heart skipping a beat as she looked up. At first, as her trained eye scanned the field through the windshield, she only saw snow and what looked like boulders but were in fact frozen masses of earth turned up by the Panzers as they had pushed through the Allied lines a mere couple of weeks ago.

"Nah." Sergeant Foster, too, seemed to doubt the shaken driver's claim. "Must have been a clump of mud. They feel soft under the wheels."

But the driver was adamant. He asked for permission to go and double-check.

As soon as he was out of the jeep, so was Maggie. Kneeling side by side, they reached for what looked like a twisted, mossy log in between the vehicle's wheels and recoiled at the same time as their eyes widened in recognition. This was no log and certainly not a lump of frozen mud. It was a mangled body with a uniform eerily similar to the one the driver was presently wearing.

"Sergeant, sir!" the driver called, eyes scanning the newly hostile surroundings, hands pawing at the holster on his hip.

In the meantime, Maggie was dusting off the corpse. Once the initial shock had passed, razor-sharp concentration replaced it. With the trained eye of a war correspondent, Maggie took it all in: the markings of a US Army GI, the dog tags spilling out from under the bloodied uniform, the bullet holes—far too many of them. An overkill. An execution.

Her instincts, so finely attuned to violence, sensed something and Maggie ventured further away from the jeep, her boots crunching over the frozen ground.

"What's happened here?" she heard the driver ask no one in particular, his voice cutting through the stunned silence that had befallen the troops.

"Damned if I know," Foster's voice replied. "Where's he from?"

"285th Field Artillery Observation Battalion, sir."

"What was he doing here alone?"

The question hung in the air tinged with metal as Maggie advanced further into the field, a sense of unease coiling in her stomach. With her eyes trained on the sparse woods around, she didn't see what caught her foot, only felt herself falling, falling and then instantly scuttling back—away from yet another corpse.

Issuing a curse under her breath, Maggie forced her emotions under control and dusted the snow off the dead man's uniform to reveal the identifying patches on his sleeves and lapels: 285th Field Artillery as well—same battalion.

Slowly, she rose to her feet, unraveled a scarf from her neck, and began dusting off the snow-covered mounds surrounding her. The scene that gradually revealed itself to Maggie's eyes was one that would haunt her for the rest of her days. Partially concealed by the recent blizzard, bodies lay strewn across the peaceful countryside, their lifeless forms contorted in grotesque shapes. Heads, uncovered. Belts missing off jackets thrown wide open, soaked in blood.

"He wasn't alone," she called over her shoulder. "There's many more here. Unarmed, from the looks of it."

Instantly propelled to action, Foster began issuing rapid commands. "Men! Everyone out. Guns out and look out for the enemy. Those Krauts may still be here somewhere. We'll need to clear the area before we begin collecting the bodies. Briggs, take one of the vehicles and shoot straight for Malmedy. Our men are stationed there. Call for reinforcements and the investigators while you're at it. Nobody touch anything. Including you, Sullivan. Looks like an execution to me."

Execution.

Once uttered, the word hangs in the air like an ax.

It feels like seconds have passed since the first gruesome discovery yet hours at the same time.

Maggie feels a chill run down her spine, not from the cold but from the sheer brutality of what lies before her. Unlike Foster, though, she isn't surprised. There's a sense of familiarity to the cold-blooded slaughter, to the manner in which the bodies are left lying in pools of their own blood. She's not even thirty, but her body feels heavy with the exhaustion of it, witnessing all the torments that can be imposed on a human by another human. And all for what?

Because they can, that's what.

"Sullivan! Back in the truck, I said. It's an order!" Foster growls once again, reminding Maggie of her own father. Daddy, too, used to lose it over her antics every once in a while, but there was nothing but genuine love and concern behind those stern eyes, nothing but a heart full of desire to protect under his New York cop's uniform.

Just as with Daddy, Maggie talks back to Foster more than she should.

"If it's an execution, documenting it is the first thing to do," she replies.

"You shouldn't be here, near the frontline, in the first place. There are specific orders for you womenfolk. But do you listen? No, you don't." Just like Daddy, Foster waves his hand at her in exasperation and leaves Maggie to her own devices.

It's far from the first time she's heard the same sentiment. Ever since her army-issued boots touched the ground on the continent, Maggie zeroed in on the advancing troops and stuck to the vanguard, despite all of the commanders' attempts to send her back where she, in their opinion, belonged. She flirted her way shamelessly into the jeeps carrying officers to the combat zone and into the cockpits of pilots flying back to London, so she could be the first to break the story. If women's charms didn't work, she wordlessly carried her forty-pound equipment-packed duffel bag, with a helmet moved down to her eyes, blending in perfectly with the marching GIs—just one of the guys no one paid any heed to. In just a few short months, her reputation among her fellow foreign correspondents, depending on their own character, grew into that of either a legend or a shameless hussy. Maggie owned both titles with equal pride, signing off her articles "always first on the frontline, Margarete Sullivan."

As she clicks the shutter, the faces of the dead gaze back at her through the lens, their eyes frozen open in expressions of shock and agony. Such young boys, all of them, younger than her, younger than her sister even. How relieved Mommy and Daddy were when the war broke out that their two daughters at least would be safe at home. And then Maggie went to the

Times office, where she worked as a freelance photographer, and volunteered for the frontline.

If the editor-in-chief had known the real reason behind her request, he would have never signed her accreditation. If the SHAEF—Supreme Headquarters Allied Expeditionary Force —learned of it here in Europe, she'd likely get arrested on the spot, but she's willing to risk it, just as she's willing to risk her very life here on the frontline to document macabre history in the making. Because sometimes, the stakes are just much too high.

Methodically, Maggie moves among the fallen GIs, capturing the wounds, the absence of the helmets, the telling lack of guns.

"Did the Germans really just shoot them in cold blood?" a private's voice asks in the distance. The frigid air carries sounds far along the empty field.

Sergeant Foster responds through his teeth, "It wasn't regular army, it was the SS. This is their handiwork. Those bastards don't take prisoners."

Maggie stills herself at the mention of the elite Nazi unit. An old *what-if*—as old as Maggie herself—prods her like a red-hot poker and withdraws at once, leaving a fresh brand in an already restless mind pulsing dully with pain.

When Norma, Maggie's sister with her frank blue eyes and a cardigan concealing her fragile frame, sat her down and asked her why in the world she was going to "that hell of a place," Maggie claimed it was for the thrill and the fame. Lied through her teeth, bared them in a fearless grin.

But Norma saw right through it all. They grew up side by side, after all. They shared more dark secrets than anyone could fathom. Norma knew precisely why Maggie was going to Europe.

"Don't go, Mag. Don't do it."

"I have to."

"You'll end up in military prison if they find out."

"So I'll just have to make sure that they don't."

"Always liked picking scabs, you."

"Look who's talking!"

Norma's grim, sardonic grin comes to the forefront of her mind as Maggie continues to take pictures, each click a defiant act against the past. Norma is the way she is because of that very past, and Maggie will pick all the scabs she wants until she gets to the bottom of it all.

Ever the truth-seeker, Maggie picked up photojournalism at fourteen precisely because photos didn't lie. They documented the good, the bad, and the ugly with clinical indifference and that's all Maggie was interested in. God-honest truth.

And some damned answers.

THREE

The reinforcements arrive from Malmedy within an hour. Investigators are with them, with their own photographers. In silence, Malmedy GIs pass brooms to Foster's men. Together, with utmost care they begin to dust the snow off the bodies as cameras snap away. Leaning against Foster's jeep, Maggie watches them work as she pulls on a cigarette.

"Got another?"

It's Specs, Foster's driver, whose real last name is lost to the US Army tradition of baptizing its men with war names instead. He used to be a supply train accountant or some such; no commander in his right mind would put a guy with such compromised eyesight anywhere near the frontline. However, Foster's former driver caught a German sniper's bullet and Specs had the misfortune to be the only one with a driver's license in the small field kitchen where Foster's unit was restocking their rations. The rest is history, and a pretty damned sad one as far as Maggie is concerned, for Specs doesn't belong on the frontline. He's an excellent driver but a terrible soldier, certainly not one for killing. Just look at him, still looking the worse for wear after discovering a corpse under the wheels of his jeep.

"Sure thing." Maggie digs in her pocket and holds out a crumpled pack. "How did you manage to get them to come so fast?"

"I didn't." From the corner of her eye, Maggie notices his hands trembling slightly as he fights with his lighter. "They were already on their way here when I came across them. Apparently, there were a few survivors. They somehow made it to the town and alerted local command."

Maggie turns to him in surprise. "Survivors?"

"Yes." Specs nods and steals another quick glance at the wheels of his vehicle. "From what I was told, the survivors said they came across a *Waffen*-SS Panzer detachment. Fighting broke out, but the GIs soon realized that the forces were uneven and decided to surrender. Next thing they know, the SS assemble them in this field, strip them of their weapons and helmets, line them up and then..."

He doesn't need to finish the story. The ending is all laid out in front of their eyes.

"The survivors, did they run?" Maggie regards the open field doubtfully.

"Some ran, some pretended to be dead." Specs follows her gaze and explains, "It was still dark, you see. If it was daylight, like now... Even then..." Another glance at the wheels.

Against her better judgment—it's better not to form any personal attachments in a place where anyone can catch a bullet tomorrow—Maggie reaches out and wraps her arm around Specs's shoulders. He's a scrawny little thing; been here only for a month since deployment, counting rations mostly before joining Foster's merry band of Kraut-killers. He's still not used to it all. "Don't blame yourself, kiddo. He was already dead."

Specs looks up at her with honest, startled eyes behind the

steel-wire glasses. "What if he was only injured?" he whispers after a lengthy pause, voicing the fear that must have been tormenting him ever since the fateful stop. "Like the others, who just pretended?"

"No, he wasn't. He was cold and stiff. I touched him. I know."

Maggie squeezes his shoulder once again and pushes off the jeep.

Summoned by the commotion, local villagers have begun emerging from their dwellings. They hover at the edges of the field, shift from one foot to another as they watch the Americans line the bodies side by side.

After thoroughly documenting the positions of the bodies and their wounds, the investigators collect makeshift numbered markers from the snow.

Her hands in her pockets once again, Maggie approaches Foster.

"That's not how I imagined them."

Foster half-turns to her, as if just noticing Maggie. "Who?"

"The investigators."

"Don't look like your daddy?"

"Daddy's not a detective, he's a beat cop. He was never interested in rising in the ranks." Maggie shrugs slightly. "I thought they'd wear some distinguishing marks. Like the military police or some such."

"They're relatively new; I reckon that's the reason." Foster offers a shrug back. "Before the Nazis began doing this"—he indicates the slaughter in front of them with a disgusted jerk of his chin—"there was no need for them. And now they're talking war crimes and crimes against humanity." He shakes his head. "Whatever happened to good old one-on-one combat? There's no honor in men anymore."

Maggie never considered even "good old combat" to have

anything honorable about it, but she keeps her opinions to herself.

"What will they do now?" she asks instead.

"Who the hell knows? Collect evidence, I would guess. I don't know how they'll go about prosecuting anyone for it, but from what I heard, that's what they're here for."

Maggie nods very slowly at some inner thoughts of hers. If these investigators are compiling evidence against war criminals, perhaps it would pay to stick with them for a while. Probe them for information, look through the names on their lists... She's a journalist; it won't even look suspicious.

For a few minutes, there is nothing but silence between them.

"Do you still need us?" Foster finally calls to the investigator team. He's never been one for patience, Maggie thinks with a faint smile. She'll miss him... "I'd like to get on the road sooner rather than later. If it happened only a few hours ago, we can still catch the bastards."

"As soon as we write down your testimony," the man in charge responds. "And yours too," he adds in German, startling the local villagers lingering nearby. "Quit crossing yourselves and looking all mournful. I'll bet my service pistol you were the first ones to cheer when your SS friends laid these boys down."

He's the complete opposite of Foster, who's stocky and brimming with restless energy. No; this one reminds Maggie of dried jerky, all angles even under a bundle of winter uniform and eyes sharp as daggers.

She feigns nonchalance as she moves closer to him, but he stops her in her tracks before she gets a chance to get a single word in.

"Margarete Sullivan, isn't it?"

Maggie produces a smile, refusing to be caught unawares. "Guilty as charged, sir. May I ask why you addressed the locals in German? We're still in Belgian territory and I happen to speak decent French. I can translate for you if you like. In exchange for a short interview, if it's all right with you."

Not a muscle moves on the chief investigator's face. "Your geography may be correct, but your history is obviously lacking. These aren't Belgians. They are ethnic Germans, who were more than happy when Hitler marched his troops here. Feel free to interview them yourself to your heart's content after I'm done my job here."

Maggie takes an exaggerated breath through her teeth. "Would if I could, but I'm afraid I don't speak German."

"I recommend you learn it. We're in Kraut land and it'll only get progressively Kraut-ier." He's about to turn his back on her when he suddenly pauses. "You took photos, I assume?"

"That's what I'm here for, sir." Maggie smiles more warmly.

"I ought to confiscate your film," the investigator says, his eyes on her Kodak. Maggie can't quite decipher the emotion behind his words.

One thing is certain, he's not Foster.

Maggie drops her act as soon as she sees its futility. He doesn't want the nice-girl? Fine by her. She has many more options available.

"Why would you do that, sir? Your men took the exact same pictures. Besides, it's very frowned upon, interfering with journalists on the frontline."

"First, you're not supposed to be anywhere near the frontline, Miss Sullivan. How vulgar, employing your womanly charms to trick honest soldiers into giving you a ride to explicitly forbidden territory. I ought to report you to the head of the Associated Press so he can disaccredit you for violating your travel orders."

The investigator steps closer to her, leveling his gaze to Maggie's. She thought they were brown, but now, up close, she realizes they're darkest gray. Gray, cold, and very unforgiving.

"And second, you're not a journalist, always-first-on-the-frontline Miss Sullivan. Miss Carpenter of the *Boston Globe* is. Miss Carson of the International News Service is. Miss Stringer of the United Press is. They are respected war correspondents, whereas you are an adventuress and a fame-seeker. And these fallen men deserve better than being exploited on the pages of your newspaper just because you so desperately want attention."

"Attention is not what I'm after, sir. And I didn't catch your name." Unfazed, Maggie flips the notebook hanging from the string on her neck and pulls the stub of a pencil from behind her ear.

"What do you need my name for?"

"So I can quote you on your next steps. I'll share the information with the local *Stars and Stripes* before I telegraph it to New York." She offers him this little bribe like an olive branch. "All army units read it. They'll know who to be on the lookout for."

He narrows his eyes at her until they're mere slits—a silent question as to where she gets her audacity from—parts his thin lips to throw something vile in her face, but then thinks better of it, scoffs, and stalks off on his long legs.

"Harlow."

Maggie turns on her heel, brows rising in surprise at the newcomer. He's younger than the investigator but older than most of the GIs. Her age, if she were to venture a guess. Swarthy looks reminding her of their Italian neighbors from Williamsburg, Brooklyn, but polished off, with purpose no doubt, to better fit in. Maggie knows all about that shameful desire—to fit in. Daddy was born in America to Irish immigrant parents and even he still carries that inexplicable inferiority about him. And there's not a chance in the world the newcomer's name is Harlow.

"I beg your pardon?" Maggie's pencil is hovering over the notebook.

"You may quote me, if you like, for your article. Harlow and I, we're of the same rank, but he isn't quite a people person."

Maggie smirks. *That's one way of putting it.* But Harlow is the furthest thing from her mind now. A sense of familiarity and longing swells in Maggie's chest at the newcomer's unmistakable drawl.

"And your name is?" she prods, wondering if she knows his family.

"Orso," he supplies and nods somewhat embarrassed. "An odd one, I know."

"Not odd. Just... not that usual for an Italian."

Now he recognizes it in her speech as well. His eyes crinkle in the corners knowingly. "You're from Brooklyn, aren't you?"

"Born and raised." The lie slips easily from her lips. A tiny lie, but a girl must protect her secrets.

"Bensonhurst?"

"Williamsburg."

"That's why I don't know you."

"I bet you do have your share of Sullivans though. More than you would like."

"Hey, I personally have no truck with the Irish. I was a copper myself before I volunteered for the front."

"My father is one too."

"I was going to say a firefighter."

"Now you're being plain racist."

They laugh about it good-naturedly, the shared experience of being second-generation immigrants in the city that prides itself on being a melting pot and yet reminds their Brooklyn communities daily that they shall never be good enough for Manhattan's Lexington or Park. They chat about their families and Junior's bakery on Atlantic and summers on Manhattan Beach and Coney Island and reminisce on the amusement park's famous Nathan's hotdogs and argue if fresh oysters are better at Randazzo's or Gargiulo's.

"You can't possibly compare the two!" Orso exclaims empathetically. "Gargiulo's is a fine-dining establishment, while Randazzo's is just a bar on the water—"

"We aren't talking about white tablecloths, we're talking about the oysters," Maggie counters, unimpressed. "And I bet both of them get their oysters delivered from the same boat."

"That very well may be the case, but at Gargiulo's a waiter delivers them on a silver platter with a towel wrapped around his arm."

"And that makes them taste better." Maggie crosses her arms at the absurdity of the statement, even though she understands perfectly well that it's meant to be a joke.

"It does and you will never persuade me otherwise."

Specs suddenly materializes and the illusion of having been transported back home falls apart like a house of cards. All at once, they're back in the middle of war-ravaged Europe, surrounded by corpses neatly laid out nearby, with their boots sinking into the snow instead of hot Coney Island Beach sand.

"We're leaving," Specs says, gesturing toward Foster's men hopping into their vehicles. "Sergeant Foster hopes to catch up with *that* SS detachment."

For a moment, Maggie looks from Specs to Orso to Foster and back to Orso.

"You go ahead," she tells Specs. "I'll catch up with you in a second."

"Don't take too long," Specs grumbles and throws a look at Orso. "Foster said we're leaving now."

"Yes, yes, I gathered that much."

He trots away and Maggie quickly assesses Harlow's party, to which Orso belongs. "Are those your jeeps or the GIs'?"

"That one is ours." He points to the respective vehicle.

"Where are you going from here?"

"Back to Malmedy, to interview the survivors as soon as they feel up to it and compile the evidence against the SS detachment that did it. If Foster catches up to them, good. But my guess is that they're long gone and we'll have to find them later, when all of this"—he gestures vaguely around himself, meaning the war, no doubt—"is over with."

"And then what?"

"International court."

Foster's jeep pulls up at her side. Foster slams the side of the door with his gloved palm. "Sullivan, hop in. Gotta get going."

Maggie holds a hand up to Orso—*don't go anywhere*—and walks up to the jeep.

"Thank you so much for the ride and for looking out for me, sir," she says, cupping Foster's great paw in her two hands. "I'll go with the investigators' team from here. Have to talk to the survivors. You know, for the story."

If Foster is surprised, he recovers himself quickly.

"All right then." He nods and shakes Maggie's hand, throws a glance at Orso and smiles at her the same smile Daddy had when Maggie brought home her first boyfriend. "Maybe it's safer this way. I wouldn't want you in the line of fire. You stay with them, seem like nice fellows." Another knowing look directed at Orso.

Foster thinks he understands her reasoning, but he doesn't. Sometimes Maggie doubts that she understands it herself.

"Thank you for everything, sir." She reaches into the bed of the jeep and pulls out her backpack, weighed down with journalistic equipment.

"You take care of yourself, girl."

"You too, sir."

The jeeps speed off and Maggie gazes after them, feeling oddly empty inside. She could have gone with Foster and stayed a war correspondent chasing a story, not someone with a personal mission that all but spells trouble. Norma warned her against going after the past. She, herself, understands the odds are against her. If she opens this Pandora's box, the question of her being discovered is no longer *if*, but *when*. Is it really worth it, risking her reputation, freedom, and—who knows?—even her life chasing ghosts? But then the choice has long been snatched from under her and Norma's feet like a proverbial rug. It's only natural to see the matter through to its logical conclusion, whatever it may be.

Maggie slings her backpack over her shoulders and steps toward Orso—one step closer to why she came here in the first place—and fixes her gaze on him with her most winning smile as she speaks, "I guess you're stuck with me now, like it or not."

FOUR

THEN

"He's such a wonderful father," *Mutti*'s friends coo.

He is, helping her change Grete's nappies. Few women in Germany can brag of such help.

"He's such a wonderful father," neighbors say with a mixture of wonder and jealousy.

He is, bathing Grete all by himself in an aluminum basin in the communal bathroom so that *Mutti* can concentrate on dinner. No matter how hard times are, he always gets the soap somehow, and not the harsh one for washing clothes, but the one that smells of lilacs, the kind that only the rich can afford. They have no money for it and even if Grete's *Mutti* has her doubts as to where the soap comes from and by what nefarious means, she never voices them. And Grete, she loves the bubbles her father makes in the basin. They float around her like a cloud and shine with all the colors of the rainbow under the dingy light of the bare lightbulb hanging crookedly from the ceiling.

Only once did Frau Brunner make a remark to her papa, something to the effect of it being a shame, wasting so much of a good thing on a small child. Grete will never forget how Father's eyes narrowed dangerously, how his nostrils flared, silencing the noisy woman mid-word. Nothing is too good for his little princess.

Frau Brunner never butted into Father's business again.

Her papa is a handsome man. He isn't disfigured by gas like many of his former fellow soldiers and doesn't have to rely on prosthetics—again, like many of them do. Grete sees them almost daily, begging for coins or food near banks and pawn shops. His hair is black and naturally wavy, his eyes are piercing and bright, and his arms are so very strong—he easily lifts not only Grete but her *Mutti* as well and laughs at her attempts to free herself as he tickles her silly.

And yet, there is something about Father that makes people afraid of him, something almost animalistic that others sense, something predatorial. Grete senses it too, but he's always gentle with her, always permissive, much more than *Mutti*, always playful and indulging.

Grete loves her papa. For a short time, she fears that he'll lose all interest in her once *Mutti* gives birth to the baby she's heavy with, and particularly if it's a boy—and everyone insists having a boy is just the thing to do for every German woman and especially now, when the war has claimed the lives of so many of their young men. But when the time comes and *Mutti* produces not one but two boys, much to the delight of the entire tenement, Papa only grows closer to Grete.

Rather to Grete's surprise and relief, Papa, seemingly, wants nothing to do with the twins whatsoever and bristles at the first plaintive whimpers they issue in their shared basinet. *Mutti* always rushes to pick them up before the whimpers turn into full-blown cries. Papa doesn't tolerate them as well as he did Grete's. He shouts for *Mutti* to shut the brats up before he does, in the voice that makes the thin walls of the tenement tremble. He doesn't bathe them, nor does he help *Mutti* change their nappies. Grete does.

But whispers of "what a wonderful father" still follow them

around whenever Papa carries Grete on his broad shoulders along the civil war-ravaged streets of Berlin. He's in his paramilitary uniform and Grete holds onto his cap with her small hands. Papa's hands are always holding firmly onto her bare ankles, so she doesn't fall off. She's taller than anyone this way, and happier.

She's Papa's little princess and no one can tell her otherwise.

FIVE

NOW

It's a silent trip from the nameless village to Malmedy. Harlow, his posture ramrod straight, doesn't inspire any desire in Orso and Maggie to continue reminiscing about old times. They share a back seat but keep to themselves, Maggie scribbling the beginnings of an article and Orso staring straight ahead.

They pass through a few roadblocks manned by American GIs and enter the Belgian town just as the sun starts dipping below roofs with icicles hanging off them. Like holiday streamers, white sheets hang from the windows. As with most of the towns Maggie has passed so far, bullet holes scar the façades of the buildings. Anti-tank barricades turn the route into an obstacle course, but the investigators' team's driver manages it with the confidence of an old-timer.

"We don't have any accommodations for you," Harlow announces as soon as the jeep pulls to a stop next to a two-story building with an American flag hanging over its entrance.

"Don't trouble yourself on my account," Maggie replies with a mock-bright smile. "I'm used to accommodating myself."

"I'm sure you are." Harlow disappears into what must be a local Army detachment headquarters without a second glance in her direction, the driver following him. Though, at least the driver offers Maggie an apologetic salute with two fingers at his helmet before disappearing inside.

"I'm sorry." Orso shakes his head, wiping at his eyes with obvious embarrassment. "He overslept on the day God was giving out good manners."

Maggie smiles at the joke and shrugs it off. No skin off her back.

From the second army vehicle, the investigators' staff photographers climb out. They, too, give Maggie a cold shoulder as they pass her by. She's used to this attitude by now. It doesn't sting any longer. They consider themselves professionals and her, just some broad from the city who's after fame and the money that comes with it.

An odd place, the frontline, to search for fame, in Maggie's personal opinion, but there's no reasoning with them and so she doesn't waste her breath any longer. Not that she doesn't have an ulterior motive for being here, but that's her business and Maggie plans to keep it that way. Let them think what they like.

"If you don't mind waiting a little, inside of course," Orso says, calling Maggie's attention back to the present, "I'll ask around and see if we can find you somewhere suitable to stay while you're—"

"It can wait," Maggie interrupts him and scans the town with a trained eye. It's small but hasn't been bombed into oblivion at least. "Where's the nearest RCA transmitter? Got anything closer than the one in Brussels?"

Orso moves his shoulder uncertainly. "The troops use SCR-300 walkie-talkies when on the go, but that's all I know. We—the investigators' unit, that is—we don't have much use for radios. We gather evidence and build case files."

And there's no urgency in transmitting any of that. Maggie nods in understanding. The recording trucks housing transmitters travel with the army, but still not fast enough to catch up with its vanguard. If she wants the Malmedy terror reported as soon as possible, she'll just have to hitch a ride back to Brussels and pray to all gods the reception is good enough to transmit it straight to London. If not, she'll just have to record it, leave it in one of the curriers' hands and hope that the aircraft ferrying them across the Channel doesn't catch German flak.

"Where's the hospital where the survivors are? I'd like to speak with them."

Orso's dark eyes brighten. With that, it seems, he can help. "There are a few boys who got away with just a big fright and a couple of scratches. I'll take you there. In fact, I would be doing just that—talking to them, I mean—if we hadn't gone to see the crime scene."

The crime scene. The words sound alien to one's ear here, in the land of war and scorched earth.

Maggie wipes her runny nose with the back of her gloved hand and motions to Orso. *Show the way.*

In the dull, dying sunlight, they walk briskly side by side, the translucent clouds of their breath mixing together. A couple of times, local boys approach them and beg for cigarettes or gum with dirty hands outstretched. Maggie has no gum, but parts with her smokes with ease. They're of great value on the local black market. Cities and towns and even countries change as she passes through them, but the universal war currency remains the same. The gum Orso hands out, the children shove straight in their mouths. Maggie notices how it warms Orso's expression, seeing them beam at him in gratitude.

"Have you been here long?" she asks.

"Malmedy, or the continent in general?"

"The continent."

"Since July. We follow the army. They clear the territory of the enemy, we dig up the corpses the enemy has left behind. And the deeper into occupied territories we go, the more corpses we dig up," he finishes with barely concealed emotion.

"In your opinion, is it only the SS that perpetrate the crimes or the Wehrmacht as well? Some say those serving in the Wehrmacht are ordinary Germans conscripted against their will, unlike the SS men, whom most consider ideological soldiers and rabid Nazis, but are the Wehrmacht servicemen really innocent of the regime's crimes?"

Orso glances at her with the hint of a grin. "Is this an official interview?"

"You said I could quote you," Maggie responds evasively.

Orso's budding smile fades away, melts into the gathering twilight. "I did say that."

He did say that but hoped that she was still asking in a personal capacity rather than a professional one. Maggie curses inwardly. *Life's a bitch as it is*, as Norma is fond of saying. She picked up the phrase from a Langston Hughes' book she immediately shared with Maggie, knowing exactly how much her sister would appreciate the story of a lost soul looking back on his past and still reeling from his father's abuse, all the while suffering from systematic racism both home and abroad. Hughes was Black and the Sullivan girls are white, but not the right kind of white to be spared anti-immigrant rhetoric, and certainly not the right gender. The point is, the book resonated, and very soundly at that, just like its infamous catchphrase which Norma instantly adopted. *Doesn't mean you have to be one.*

"I'm sorry." She reaches out and touches his arm fleetingly. "Sometimes it's hard"—she pauses, searching for the right word—"to switch. And especially here."

"You don't have to apologize. And you're right, it is hard." He looks straight ahead. "To switch. It haunts you, what you see almost daily, no matter how prepared you think you are. Back home, I saw my share of murders, but..." He, too, seems to struggle with a fitting explanation. "They're different there. Mafia clans sorting their own affairs, sending messages to each other; husbands strangling their wives in a jealous rage"—Orso doesn't notice Maggie's jaws clench tight as he goes on— "someone stabbing someone for a wallet with seven dollars in it. They're *regular* murders—if there's anything regular about any murder. Here, on the other hand..." He trails off once again, chewing on his lip, and Maggie allows him that moment without interruption.

She matches her step to his, all attention, but doesn't rush him. One shouldn't be pushed during such revelations; Maggie knows this much, from her own example.

"Here, on the other hand," Orso picks up where he left off, "it's cold-blooded and methodical, almost clinically dispassionate, and yet so very savage and brutal, as though it's personal, a thousand times over."

Maggie feels the chills lifting the thinnest hairs at the nape of her neck and along her arms under layers of sweaters and a green army jacket. Somehow, her fellow Brooklynite put in just the right words what she's been experiencing since she first stepped onto this accursed land.

"Why do you think that is?" Maggie asks quietly and adds with another quick tap of Orso's arm, "Asking as a fellow human being, not a war correspondent." She smiles.

Orso hides his own grin at the clarification and contemplates his response for some time.

"I don't know," he says at last, with almost endearing honesty. "I'm still trying to understand it myself, but for the life of me, I can't. How the refined, highly cultured nation of Goethe and Schiller could suddenly turn into bloodthirsty savages. How such duplicity is even possible in someone. They're husbands and fathers in most cases and yet they slaughter entire families as if they don't see the reflection of themselves in their victims. Of course, I'm not talking about those dragged into this entire rotten affair or those fellows from high ranks of the Wehrmacht who tried to blow Hitler up this past July, but those who went into this willingly, singing their brassy march songs as they goose-stepped over the corpses. Not all Germans are like that—"

"—But still enough of them to turn Europe into a blazing ruin," Maggie finishes for him, staring grimly at her boots.

"Precisely." It's Orso's turn to look at her as if she's just voiced his very thoughts. "One can't help but wonder what happened to them."

"A man came to power who allowed those ordinarily contained by the societal and criminal code's norms to act upon their darkest fantasies. They've always been there, those men you're talking about. Hitler simply unleashed them. Let them show their true face without any consequence."

"Well, there will be consequences now," Orso promises her in a voice tinged with well-contained cold fury. "Plenty of them. We're here to see to it."

Something stirs in Maggie's chest, some long-slumbering, aching desire for vengeance. But life's still a bitch and her sister is proof enough that justice isn't always served, and so, Maggie strangles that hope in herself before it becomes too overpowering, too painful to bear.

"You do that," she says instead. "You make them pay for everything. For every single thing."

The hospital welcomes them with drapes drawn over its windows, according to the blackout regulations, and the pleasant warmth of its heated quarters. The GI manning the entrance glances at Orso's papers and Maggie's press pass and motions them through, returning to his steaming mug of army-issued coffee and *Time* magazine almost at once.

Their helmets off, Orso stops a local nurse and asks her, in very passable French, where to find the massacre survivors. The woman, thin and harassed-looking like most of the locals

Maggie has met throughout her travels, still goes out of her way to help the liberators. Without being prompted, she escorts them to the second floor—"we keep our people on the first and the soldiers on the second, it's warmer here"—and pushes the door open to the ward, tucked all the way into the corner by the staircase.

Maggie thanks the nurse and pauses as she catches her reflection in the mirror hanging by the ward's entrance. What a mess! She ruffles her dark short curls, flattened and matted by the heavy helmet, but it does little to mitigate the damage. She needs a bath and a month of uninterrupted sleep. She has never been anything remotely close to the GIs' ideal of a pin-up girl with lustrous locks, an upturned nose and an hourglass figure barely contained in bright, cutesy clothes, but the creature that now stares back at her is a whole other level of hideous. Pale lips with a bluish tint to them, sharp nose and cheekbones reddened by the frostbite she sustained by sleeping in the open for days on end in the absence of accommodation; circles under her eyes so dark, they look drawn on with charcoal. Only her eyes, dark and piercing, are more alive than ever, alert and shining with a purpose that's been driving her relentlessly, like a motor, for the past year.

And they accuse her of using her womanly charms to get her stories. What womanly charms? Have they seen what she looks like? A scarecrow with a jack-o'-lantern for a head looks more attractive.

And yet, as she enters the ward, several pairs of eyes stare at her, instead of Orso, and uncertain smiles blossom where mortal fright took hold not even twenty-four hours ago. Maggie counts eight of them to one ward, the lucky American boys that got away with their lives by sheer chance from the hail of German bullets.

Survivors. Witnesses.

In her chest, Maggie's heart clenches. Outwardly, she smiles so brightly, the room itself looks momentarily lighter.

"Is this where they keep the sprint winners of the Belgian Winter Olympics?"

Orso turns to her. *How can you jest about such things?* his accusing eyes read, but Maggie knows what she's doing.

She remembers how Norma reacted when the psychiatrist, called by Norma's physician after her sister's first suicide attempt, established a relationship with his patient in the very first minute. Instead of shaking his head and tutting at the thirteen-year-old—"Now why would you do something so idiotic, a good girl from a good family like you are?"—he lifted his brow and whistled after reading the list of medications they had pumped out of Norma's stomach. "Must have been some migraine you were trying to get rid of, Miss Sullivan." And suddenly, Norma, so very small and fragile in her big hospital bed, was fighting not to smile.

"How did you know it would work?" Daddy asked Dr. Colbert later, in the hospital's hallway—the same question that was on the tip of Maggie's tongue.

The psychiatrist fixed his glasses and folded his arms on his chest, hugging Norma's chart to it. "A person just went through something incredibly traumatic. In most cases, the brain is still stuck in the past, reliving on repeat the event that landed the patient here, like a train stuck in its tracks, hurling itself faster and faster until it gets derailed and crashes. What I try to do is to stun it out of its state and set it on a new track so we can move forward toward healing. It's my personal approach and many disagree with me, but I find it effective."

It is effective, even here, in war-torn Belgium. There's a stunned pause after Maggie's words, but then, suddenly, laughter. And she's a young woman on top of it and so they fight over whose bed she will sit on and surround her and talk to her, this strange lady from back home who wears the same fatigues and writes shorthand without once taking her eyes off whomever she's interviewing at that moment.

"It was dark and we didn't have any scouts—"

"Well, we were scouts ourselves, you might say, because we advanced so rapidly—"

"We thought the Krauts were all gone from the area as our troops were stationed here at Malmedy—"

"—That much we knew—"

"—So we were heading toward Malmedy from the south and literally crossed paths with them as they were retreating from the western direction—"

Maggie nods as she rapidly writes it all down. They were retreating from the west. Foster's detachment was chasing them for several days.

Maggie's blood chills as she can't help but wonder what would have happened if Foster's men caught up with the SS squad.

"It was the SS, wasn't it?" Maggie's hand hovers over her notepad.

Several shaved heads bob eagerly at that. The SS, to be sure. They saw their black uniforms and insignia after the Nazis disabled the vehicles at the head and the end of the American column, thus cutting off their means of retreat.

"Black uniforms?" It's the first time that Orso chimes in. Maggie only now notices that he's been standing outside the circle gathered round her, silent and yet sharply attuned to everything being said, a stub of a pencil also poised over his notepad. "Tank troops then?"

He exchanges a quick glance with Maggie.

Maggie gives half a shrug in response to his silent question. No, she doesn't recall seeing any tank tracks either.

"They weren't driving tanks," one of the survivors supplies the explanation, his bandaged arm resting in a sling. "Regular vehicles—and just a couple of those, from what I remember.

The rest of them were on foot. But they did have those anti-tank launchers with them. That's how they got us, with those launchers."

"Shot from the sides, the bastards," another one says. "The vehicles in the middle couldn't budge, so we had no choice but to surrender." He lowers his eyes in shame, but Maggie will have none of it.

"Which was perfectly reasonable of you to do," she says firmly, reaching out to pat his knee in a sisterly gesture. "Do not, ever, apologize for surrendering to a superior force. Sometimes, it's simply unfeasible to fight someone off. The best one can do to survive is to rely on the aggressor's good graces. How were you to know you were dealing with someone who feels no compassion, who is rotten to their very core, who takes pleasure in intimidation, torment, and, ultimately murder? Such people, they don't let their victims walk free. They always kill them before moving onto the next one. They're the ones that are ought to be ashamed, judged, and spat upon by the entire world. Not you. You, hold your heads high. You did nothing wrong; hear me?"

Maggie doesn't recall the end of the interview. It's all surged up in her like in an abandoned well, the murky waters muddying her very mind. All she knows once she's outside the hospital is that her notepad is full, her hand is aching from furious writing, and she's shaking all over to such an extent that her very teeth are chattering. And through the ring in her ears, deep inside her mind, one single name is throbbing like a wound: *Grete*.

Grete.

Grete—

Orso steps into the night and approaches her with uncertainty. "Are you all right?" he asks in a soft voice, holding her jacket open for her. "You forgot this."

For a few moments, Maggie regards the army jacket as if it's something foreign. She still isn't all here. She hates them when they happen, moments such as these. There's no predicting what can trigger them and how she will react. Sometimes she bolts like a bat out of hell—the further from the situation, the better—and sometimes she gets into the trigger's face and snarls at it like an animal, seeing red, smelling blood, turning into something she has sworn to herself she would never become.

It's that bad blood in her. There's no ridding herself of it, no matter how much she tries to deny it.

"I'm all right," she responds in a voice that is flat and distant and entirely not hers. "I did take their pictures, didn't I?"

"You don't remember?"

Maggie only stares at him and Orso steps away for some reason.

"You did," he responds in that certain voice her own father used with someone ready to turn violent, when he was out of his uniform and with his family in tow. Maggie witnessed it only a handful of times but recognizes it now, that pacifying pitch in Orso's tone. She hates to hear it being applied to her. "You took quite a lot, in fact."

Without responding, she turns on her heel and walks away, into the night.

SIX

THEN

Something is wrong with her papa. Grete can't think of a moment when the thought first occurred to her, but the sensation is there, the *wrongness* of certain things like false notes slipping into the otherwise perfectly rehearsed concerto of her childhood.

The twins weren't born yet; it was dinnertime and *Mutti*, busy setting the table, asked Grete to call Papa from the bedroom where he was resting. Oddly, Grete found the bedroom door closed and innocently pushed it open, only to discover her papa swiftly shoving a bottle with some brown, revolting-smelling stuff onto the top shelf, behind the books. His eyes gleaming, he quickly recovered himself and, biting down a chuckle, wiped his wet mouth with the back of his hand and pressed his index finger to his lips: *Don't tell Mama. It'll be our little secret.*

Some of the brown liquid spilled down the shelf and left a whitish scar *Mutti* discovered the next day. She confronted Papa about it, but he flatly denied knowing anything about it or the faint smell of the cognac *Mutti* claimed was still there. The bottle had miraculously disappeared by then and *Mutti* was left questioning her own judgment without any physical proof. Grete could have told her that, no, *Mutti* wasn't imagining things as Papa claimed, but for some reason, she said nothing at all.

She was rewarded, in her own way. From that day on, Grete was worthy of Papa's trust. Papa sips brandy in front of her now, winking at the little girl, making her feel so very special. They have their own secret little world, just the two of them. He shows her trinkets "lifted off the communist scum" (Papa's words that Grete doesn't fully understand) and lets her play with them, but only for one evening as they have to be pawned the next day and only outside so that *Mutti* doesn't see the gold chains and signet rings.

Weather permitting, he takes Grete target shooting in Grünewald, his big hand wrapping around her small one holding onto the cold, well-oiled steel. Papa tries to teach her to shoot small birds and squirrels but doesn't get mad when she refuses, thoroughly appalled, each time; only laughs good-naturedly and lets her shoot cans and bottles they find along the way. In case *Mutti* asks, they were just walking, Papa reminds Grete each time. Grete hates keeping secrets from her *Mutti*, but she loves her papa far too much.

The feeling of choosing between her parents is something Grete doesn't have the vocabulary or enough life experience to name, but the ambiguous doubt and nagging shame is there all the same.

And the more Papa says that she's a big girl and can be trusted, the more it creeps into her innocent, unblemished child's mind, tainting it with its poisonous sprouts, putting down roots where they have no business to be.

Something is wrong with her papa.

Something's terribly wrong.

SEVEN

NOW

The night is as dark as pitch and one can barely see their hand in front of their face, but Maggie doesn't mind it one bit as she navigates the unfamiliar streets. She's fierce and unshakable once again, just minutes after swallowing amphetamines German corpses happen to have in spades in their pockets if one bothers to search. Maggie always does.

The name is different from the pills the American doctors prescribed to Norma, but Maggie has long ago discovered that they work the same. No wonder the German High Command is giving them out to their soldiers like candy. One can march for hours without tiring with their aid. One isn't afraid to take on the entire army with a single handgun. And one certainly can find a way to get to the transmitter in time to break her story— the first on the frontline, as always.

Her eyes gleaming like those of a cat, Maggie seeks out a jeep parked for the night and flirts her way into it with the smitten private for a driver. Driving at night, and through the same field where his fellow GIs were executed not even twenty-four hours ago, no less, is a suicide mission, but he sets off all the same, thoroughly bewitched by this siren with black eyes and wild curls in his passenger seat.

There's some restless, yet entrancing energy radiating off her. It's catching and deadly and irresistible at the same time; Maggie knows precisely the effect it produces on men whenever she chooses to use it, and she uses it tonight without a second thought. Though, her thoughts are quite elsewhere right now. All she knows is that the transmitting station closes at twelve and she needs to submit her report for the paper before the rapidly approaching deadline.

With the darkness, the temperature plummets once again, but Maggie's face is awash with heat. She clutches the jeep's metal frame with a bare hand and urges the driver to go faster, faster!—and laughs like a maniac when he sheepishly calls her crazy.

"Are you scared?" she demands, challenge in her voice.

"To crash?" he probes, unsure. His eyes are fastened on the darkness that lies ahead, as if expecting tracer bullets fired from an ambush to slash through it at any moment and end them both.

"To die." Maggie baits him on purpose.

These soldiers are all so very brave and boastful when attacking the outnumbered enemy with tanks and big guns and aerial support, and even braver later, when they invite themselves into the liberated towns' homes and their female inhabitants' beds, sometimes several at once.

Maggie hates those post-battle celebrations the most. There's always drunken singing on every corner, there's always a piano dragged into the street littered with gun shells, and there's always a merry band of GIs slamming its keys until they grow bored of it and stuff it with grenades or set it on fire just for the thrill of it. There's always souvenir hunting going on and a scramble to collect as many Iron Crosses as they can yank off the dead enemy's necks to decorate their respective vehicles later. There's always some SS corpse set alight near the public fountain, with a GI pissing on it to his comrades' delight, and prisoners of war being kicked about to drunken jeers. And the worst part, there's no escaping them. No matter how hard Maggie tries to stay out of their sight in moments like these, one—or, more often, a few—such reveler always makes it his business to engage her, one way or another.

It's not that they don't have the right to celebrate; they have just cheated death once again, avenging heroes, it's only fair to drink and sing to that until one is hoarse in his throat. Maggie just wishes they would go about it without all this... violence. Without shooting and smashing things and setting fires and gang-raping local women.

She's one of them, for God's sake, and they still grow suddenly emboldened by this seemingly unrestrained power of the victor fresh out of battle. They put their heavy arms around her shoulders and grope her legs and breathe stale brandy in her face until she yanks her service weapon, and puts it against the organ not a single one of them wants to live without, in a no-nonsense way. That sobers them up promptly enough to leave her well alone.

Yes, they're all so very brave when in a pack. But not in the middle of the night, all alone, in a foreign land crawling with detached enemy units. Maggie can't help but gloat just a little bit at this visible discomfort of his.

The young driver clears his throat and shifts in his seat, growing progressively uncomfortable. "I think everyone's afraid to die," he says, choosing his words carefully, not wanting to lose face. "It's natural to our species. It's not that I'm afraid, it's that I'd rather do something with my life first, you know?"

Maggie puts her legs up on the dashboard and lights up a smoke. "It's all right, you don't have to be embarrassed."

"Aren't you afraid?" he asks with a quick stolen look in her direction. "To die?"

"No." Maggie's response is as flat as the valley they're presently crossing. "There are things that are much worse than dying."

The boy clams up entirely at this cryptic response, frightening on its own.

Once in the town she passed with Foster a day ago, the driver waits for Maggie to transmit her report and leave two rolls of film for the local press corps and then takes her back to Malmedy in a silence so thick, it could be cut with a knife. When she steps out of his jeep, he bids her goodbye and disappears into the safety of his local army quarters, not wishing to have anything to do with her whatsoever.

Maggie shrugs, dry-swallows two pills of Luminal to counter the effects of the amphetamines, and finds her way back to the investigators' unit's lodgings. There, after showing her pass to the sentry on duty, she curls up on the floor and instantly falls asleep.

"Get up."

Maggie squints at the pair of boots in front of her face, rubs her eyes, full of grit and memories she wouldn't wish on her worst enemy. Gradually, Harlow's pinched face comes into focus. The morning is still gray and he's already fuming.

"Good morning, darling," Maggie mock-purrs, sitting up and stretching. "Is the coffee ready yet?"

"Very amusing, Miss Sullivan. On your feet, now."

Maggie sighs and picks up the backpack she used as a pillow. Her mouth is dry and her head is pounding and her lower belly pulls with a dull telling pain. Great. Just what she needs to be dealing with right now, on top of Harlow. "Didn't realize I was in the way. Don't get yourself in an uproar, I'll be out of your hair in two shakes of a lamb's tail."

Good thing they're in a town and not a camp in the middle of a field. GI camps only have communal showers, scarcely allowing anyone any privacy. To Maggie, climbing into an empty tank to put her sanitary napkin in place is more dignified than using one of those facilities.

"This is not about your sleeping arrangements, Miss Sullivan," Harlow interrupts her train of thought. "This is about endangering one of our US Army GIs for nothing but a shallow whim. What were you thinking, demanding a ride in the middle of the night, to God knows where?"

Maggie rubs her face. Too much on her mind, too little sleep for this conversation, and the wrong time of the month to have any patience for sermons. "It wasn't a shallow whim; I had to get to the transmitter before twelve. I had a deadline. Also, no one twisted his arm. I asked; all he had to do was to say no."

The callousness of her own words grates on her, but it's a defense mechanism that has a life of its own. With the best will in the world, Maggie can't retract the spikes the world has forced her to grow.

"Do you even know his name?" Harlow asks, very quietly, and something in Maggie surges to the surface, burns her cheeks with acid. Next to them, the fresh sentry on duty feigns disinterest in their conversation with all his might. "The name of the boy who could have died. Did you bother to ask?"

She did but didn't bother to commit it to her memory. He was a means to an end and she was in one of her states where something other than cold logic takes over. Like a bad hangover, it nauseates her now—her behavior last night, the irresponsibility, but, most of all, the heedless flirting with death.

Maggie takes another deep breath and meets Harlow's eye, sober and collected once again. "You're right, my conduct was inexcusable. You'll be perfectly within your rights if you bring it up before my superiors at the Associated Press. I fully deserve to be reprimanded and stripped of all of my credentials."

She won't be the first one, either. Maggie remembers very well the scandal surrounding Martha Gellhorn when she was arrested by the British military police for the crime of doing her job—reporting on the Normandy landings as the first woman correspondent, under fierce enemy fire.

Maggie was still in the training camp back in the US, waiting for her travel orders, when the news broke among her fellow reporters. No one blamed Gellhorn's famous husband, a certain Ernest Hemingway, for stealing her credentials from Collier's to cover the opening of the second front. Everyone somehow unanimously agreed that it was a perfectly reasonable thing for the scorned husband to do to avenge himself.

"Avenge himself? For what?" Maggie, also the only woman among their little troop, made the mistake of butting in. "Wasn't it him who was having an affair behind Martha's back while she was risking her life reporting from Italy, where the Nazis were still very much present?"

"Affair?" Several pairs of eyes stared at her as though she'd just blurted out something incredibly idiotic. "What does that have to do with anything? He's had enough of her playing reporter when all he wanted was a wife in his bed. The man has needs. She wasn't around, so he found someone who was."

"And in the process stole her credentials for a story that could have brought her the Pulitzer?" Maggie refused to surrender. They stared at her with infuriating, purposeful obtuseness like a herd of sheep that refused to see reason. "And not just that, he pulled all the strings he could, out of sheer spite, to block her from obtaining a new pass to get to Normandy to cover the landings—that also looks perfectly reasonable and justified to you? To kill a woman's dream to punish her for choosing it over warming his bed and tending to his desires?"

And then the answer followed, as condescending and

patronizing as they came, explaining precisely what they thought of her and her kind: "Come now, Maggie. What dream? He's Hemingway. And she's Hemingway's wife and that's all she'll be remembered for, if at all."

"She's called Martha Gellhorn and she'll be remembered for being the first woman who risked her life to hide away on a ship with explosives to travel across the Atlantic and cover the landings in Normandy, not because, but in spite of her sore-loser husband whose fragile ego couldn't take the competition. The woman is a damned hero and he's just a pig. You can quote me on this one."

Yes, she surely wouldn't be the first, but at least she'll be in good company. And if to begin with Maggie had doubted that Ms. Gellhorn would consider her, Maggie Sullivan, "good company," Martha was one of the first women correspondents stationed in London who greeted Maggie and made her feel at home.

Still, she's not heroic like Martha, but careless and sometimes mad, and if Harlow decides to report her, she won't even hold it against him.

Harlow searches her face and, when Maggie doesn't look away, shakes his head almost incredulously. "I don't know what's wrong with you, Miss Sullivan, but you have no business doing what you're doing."

He stalks off, disgusted, and Maggie has nothing better to do than ask the sentry for directions to the local mess hall.

No one talks to her inside the makeshift canteen and each piece of bread is more difficult to swallow than the previous one. Maggie washes the lump in her throat down with some ersatz coffee and goes to rinse her mess tin in the communal sink. The space around it empties as soon as she opens the faucet.

She can refuse to give a damn and choose to walk away like she often does, but that hasn't seemed to be working for her lately. It never has, if she's entirely frank. Maybe it's finally time to break the pattern, no matter how difficult that may be. Old foundations are notoriously hard to demolish, but if that's what it takes, Maggie will do her utmost to try.

Her heart in her throat, she swings round and scans the hostile crowd with her eyes. When she finally finds who she is after, she approaches him amid murmurs and stops in front of the young man whose life she so brazenly risked last night.

"I know words mean little in situations like these, but I would like to apologize for my actions last night. It was unfair from my side, to use your selfless desire to help to my advantage and put you in danger for no good reason. I can't express how relieved I am that no harm came your way. I understand that I don't deserve your forgiveness and I won't even ask you for it, but I just want you to know how sincerely sorry I am."

The mess hall is as silent as the grave when Maggie turns around to take her leave. It's only then that she notices Orso standing in the doors with an unreadable expression on his face. Less than anything, Maggie wants to see him now, but there's no avoiding him and so she squeezes past him with a quiet "excuse me," and welcomes the blast of cold air hitting her full force in the face.

"That was nice of you."

Maggie half-turns to Orso's voice but doesn't slow her steps. He still follows. The creaking of the snow under his boots is familiar and yet painful at the same time.

"Taking responsibility," he adds.

"Yeah, well." Maggie is annoyed—with herself—and hopes he doesn't dig deeper into the wound that is yet to scab over.

"You could have asked me, you know." The fellow doesn't give up, but that's a New Yorker for you, Maggie thinks with a smile. "I would have taken you to the transmitter."

Maggie stops so abruptly that Orso nearly stumbles into her; opens her mouth to explain that she wasn't in her right mind yesterday, that she wasn't thinking logically, but even in that state, her subconsciousness refused to risk his, Orso's, life and chose some poor innocent guy instead—

But then she says nothing at all.

"I waited for you at the hospital last night." Unlike Harlow, Orso doesn't look mad. No, his hazel eyes only betray concern. "Thought you'd come back."

"I'm sorry." Apologizing is easier than explaining the mess in her head and so that's precisely what Maggie does.

"I've read your article in this morning's paper."

"Which one? I sent two variations of it to be published: one to the *Stripes* and the other to the *Times*."

"I read the one in the *Stripes*, the *Stripes* travels faster here," Orso says. "It was..." He inclines his head slightly, searching for the right words.

"Hopefully worth risking someone else's life for?" Maggie supplies with a crooked grin full of remorse.

But Orso is kinder to her than she is to herself. "It was very stirring. Angry and raw and profoundly touching at the same time. You're a very good writer."

Maggie contemplates this for a few moments. She was hired at the *Times* as a photographer, not a journalist. All of her writing education came from high school and, later, secretarial courses, which didn't really teach how to write but how to type efficiently. Her very first written piece she submitted after hearing the story from her father. He was the cop on duty when the police were called to an apartment building to check on one of the tenants. In the poorly lit hallway stinking of cat urine, Officer Sullivan was met by the building's superintendent who'd made the call, and a man in his undershirt. Something was wrong with the man's missus. "Won't wake up to feed the baby, the lazy broad."

Instantly suspicious—the stench of old sweat mixed with cheap alcohol fumes coming from the husband must have had something to do with that—Officer Sullivan climbed the stairs to the couple's apartment. Doors opened and closed at the sound of their steps, heads popped from behind them, murmuring words to the effect that something finally would be done about the baby, crying his lungs out, and people had to be up in the morning, damn it!

"What d'you want me to do 'bout it?" the husband barked back. "I haven't grown tits to feed him, have I?"

To his doubtful credit, the husband had placed the newborn next to his sleeping wife's breast as Officer Sullivan soon saw.

"What's wrong with her face?" The angry red welt on the motionless woman's right cheek was impossible to ignore.

"Besides it being ugly as sin?" the husband tried to joke but dropped the act at the sight of Officer Sullivan's stern look. "Backhanded her to wake the broad up," he finally said, shrugging and scratching at his armpit. "Always used to do the trick." Another attempt at "manly" humor, again totally lost on Sullivan.

Lowering himself over the woman for a closer look, Sullivan didn't detect any odor of alcohol. Only something sharp and metallic, far too familiar after years of being on the force. At once, he yanked the cover off the woman's body and froze for a moment at the sight that presented itself to his eyes. The entire mattress under the woman's back and legs was saturated with blood.

Swinging around, he stared at the husband, who appeared to be just as stunned with the revelation. "She dead?"

"What do you think?"

Maggie still remembers the disgust on her father's face as he recounted the story itself and the trial that followed. He was the witness for the prosecution and the prosecution wanted to know what Mr. Chapman was thinking when he demanded marital relations from his wife two days after she gave birth to their first child. The second witness was the doctor who'd attended to

Mrs. Chapman and strictly warned the couple before discharging Mrs. Chapman home that no marital relations must occur in the next six weeks as Mrs. Chapman's labor was very difficult and the tearing so substantial, it required multiple stitches.

Posed with that question, Mr. Chapman had only shrugged and asked, "Well, what was I supposed to do? Go without for another month and a half just because the doctor said something? They go to medical school and think they know better than everyone else. I'm a man, I have needs."

The judge and the jury conceded that, yes, indeed, this was a good enough excuse to allow one's wife to bleed to death and dismissed all charges against the husband. That night, after learning the verdict from her father, Maggie pulled her typewriter out of its case and banged out an article she presented to the *Times'* editor-in-chief the following morning. He read it carefully, congratulated Maggie on writing a truly fine piece of journalism, and then returned it without meeting her eye.

He couldn't publish it. They weren't that kind of newspaper and they had a public image to uphold and their audience wouldn't be interested in something of this sort... Besides, she was a young woman writing about another young woman's death, which was unfortunate, yes, but there was really no crime committed, negligence at best, and what if that Chapman fellow decided to sue them for libel? He could, too, since he was acquitted by the court of any wrongdoing.

First, Maggie fumed to the point of shaking and hearing her own blood rushing in her ears. Then, she thought about it long and hard, and the next time, when she learned from her father that a middle-school teacher had got away with only a reprimand after molesting one of his students and blaming it on her and her eleven-year-old "seductiveness" she supposedly worked on him, Maggie wrote a scathing piece and signed as an anonymous father whose student was in the same school and who was extremely concerned that there was a child predator walking freely in the school's halls.

There was no claim to fame for Maggie, but the result was swift and impressive. The teacher was first suspended and then fired altogether, which was nowhere near what he deserved for ruining the child's life, but at least it was a step in the right direction and Maggie could live with that much.

From then on, she either wrote anonymously and claimed to be a concerned—male—citizen or signed with a generic male name. At times, she felt the beginnings of guilt tentatively reaching its tentacles into her mind, but this was invariably replaced with righteous fury against the whole rotten system. If the rules of the game are rigged, it's only logical to play dirty.

Orso's gentle shoulder tap—"where have you disappeared to?"—jolts her back to reality.

Blinking the memories away, Maggie grins feebly at him. "Just realized that I haven't published a damned thing under my own name until I came here," she says.

Orso cocks his head, confused. "How come the *Times* sent you here then as a war correspondent?"

Maggie's smile grows a bit warmer. "My editor-in-chief knew about every single article I submitted anonymously or as an op-ed penned by a man. He only told me about it when I volunteered to go. Apparently, like any serial killer leaving his signature clues for the detectives to find, every reporter leaves their own word trail as well: a certain style, favorite expressions, emotions, metaphors—the works. My editor, he's been working in publishing for far too long not to notice."

"Why *did* you volunteer to go to the front?"

Maggie gazes into the distance as she searches for the right words. The right words that are half-true and don't involve her sister, about whom Maggie is just not ready to talk to this man.

"You know in Williamsburg we have quite a German community," she begins at length. "We also have a Jewish community, and those two communities, most of their members still have family in Germany, Eastern Europe, you name it. Well, when the Jewish community began to lament family members disappearing, according to the rumors, into Nazi concentration camps, our gentile German neighbors began to accuse them of spreading lies and setting the entire neighbor-hood against them. Now, the family that lives in the house next to ours, they're also German Jews and were always very friendly with us. I personally saw letters their relatives wrote to them, until those letters stopped coming."

Maggie pauses by the intersection to take a photo of a freshly painted sign: "Malmedy men fought on German side. They consider you enemy, not liberators. Do not accept food-stuffs from them and avoid water wells—they may be poisoned. First Army Command."

Orso looks around as well, as if the town has suddenly changed shape. "I was wondering why so many of them speak German here," he mutters.

A civilian in a long brown overcoat shifts his gaze from the sign to the Americans and picks up his pace, holding onto his felt hat against the wind.

"Looks like they speak English too," Maggie notes with a nod at the prospective fleeing Nazi. "Wanna catch up and ask him a few questions?"

Orso gazes after the local but waves the idea off in the end. "Just a collaborator, most likely. These border towns are such a pain, frankly speaking. Half think themselves German, the other half—Belgian or Polish or Czech or whatever-the-hell. Turn into the wrong street, speak to the wrong person—get stabbed in the neck."

"Reminds you of home." Maggie prods him with an elbow.

"It does, doesn't it?" Orso half-laughs, half-coughs in his fist. "Speaking of. You haven't finished your story."

"There's nothing really to finish." Maggie shrugs. "It just got to the point where everybody had to take a side and we sided with our Jewish neighbors, which didn't go well with the German family, the Schenks, who had a grocery on the corner where we used to shop quite a lot before. The grocer's wife came over to our house and began to complain that they were losing customers because of this Jewish foolishness that wasn't even true. To this, my mother said that she couldn't possibly patronize a business that denied that anything wrong was going on with the Jews in Europe when all the facts were pointing to the contrary. If the Schenks just left it well alone and claimed ignorance, that would have been one thing, but openly denying the reality that our neighbors were living, that was just a step too far."

Maggie pats herself for cigarettes absently.

"Mrs. Schenk said that Dachau wasn't real and that she would only believe it if someone without a horse in the race proved it otherwise. And then my father said something that evening, at dinner. He said, imagine how many people there are like the Schenks all over the world, claiming the same? Long story short, here I am, someone without a horse in the race, on my way to Dachau with my camera to prove all those Schenks otherwise."

Orso regards her with a wandering smile for some time before finally uttering, "You're the only person I know whose answers are more confusing than the questions leading to them."

"I'm a very confusing person."

"Yes. That, you certainly are."

But, somehow, it sounds like a compliment instead of an accusation.

EIGHT

THEN

The doll in the window of the Wertheim is so very pretty, but *Mutti* tugs on Grete's hand and ignores her tears. They barely have money for food; does Grete really think she will buy her a toy? *Mutti* can be mean sometimes, particularly when money is tight.

"How did you grow out of this dress so fast?"

"Are you certain that the shoes really pinch? How badly? Can you wait it out until next season at least? There's only two months left and you can tolerate the pinch well enough, can't you?"

"Is that a stain on your good dress? Haven't I told you a million of times to be more careful? We aren't millionaires, you know! Your father isn't Rockefeller. We can't buy you new dresses every damned month."

When Grete emptied the shampoo bottle into her wash-basin and made herself a bubble bath like on the poster she saw on the Linden, she got a thrashing she would remember for her entire life. In truth, she was more frightened by *Mutti*'s tears than by the fact that her mother was spanking her soap-covered, bare behind and couldn't understand why the shampoo was such a big deal since the child was splashing in bubbles on that brightly painted ad. Bubbles were for children, weren't they? But *Mutti* sobbed as though Grete had taken something infinitely precious from her and, no, she didn't know how difficult it was to get shampoo; didn't really know what shampoo was, only that it made bubbles far better than any soap.

It's only natural that Grete comes to her father whenever *Mutti* is being mean. Papa always pats his lap for Grete to climb on and holds very still as she whispers in his ear, so that *Mutti* won't hear, about something very special she saw that day.

The doll. Such a pretty doll, and with blue hair, just like the Fairy with Turquoise Hair from the Pinocchio fairy tale! Grete has never seen a doll with blue hair before. If only she could have it!

Papa considers it for some time while bouncing Grete on his lap. At the Wertheim? Where all of the capitalists shop? Must be an expensive doll indeed.

Grete's eyes fill with tears, her small chest deflates with despair. If Papa can't get it, no one can. Her chin trembling, she tries to climb down, but Papa holds her fast.

It is expensive, very expensive, he repeats. He can try to go to some trouble to get it for her. Give some fat-bellied Jew a beating and take his wallet—and why not? It's because of them that honest Germans are suffering while they stuff themselves with delicacies.

No, Grete doesn't want that. A doll, even the one with blue hair, doesn't justify violence. And Grete doesn't want someone else's money. She'll make do without the doll then.

But Papa only laughs and tickles her ear with his hot breath. He's only joking. He'll just get himself some extra gig; it might be a dangerous job, the one in the quarries where they blast granite with dynamite, but he'll risk his life for her. He'll risk his life for the doll, he says nobly to an elated Grete, but then adds in a very soft whisper that she will have to show how grateful she is.

She'll have to give him a kiss. A real good, nice kiss for her papa.

NINE

NOW

Troops flow through Malmedy on their way to the German border and Maggie hitches a ride with one of the British reporters, waving a stunned Orso goodbye from the back of the open truck—"See you in Germany, hurry up and catch up!"

She doesn't look back and gladly shares the British chap's flask of whiskey that burns her throat but makes her forget things she doesn't care to remember. They laugh about both of them working for the *Times*—Maggie, the *New York Times* and Jack Knightley for the *London Times*—and make playful bets on who's going to score the main scoop of crossing the German border.

The troops stop by the Castle of Reinhardstein to regroup and allow the infantry and supply train to catch up. In the swiftly falling dusk, Maggie and Jack take photos of still-smoldering fires and a single disabled German tank on the side of the road.

"Ran out of the last of their gas. They're hoofing it from here," the captain in charge declares gleefully as he stares through binoculars into the distance.

"Can you see them?" Maggie asks, squinting at the blinding

blanket of snow sprawling in front of them as far as the eye can see.

"Sure can." He's in such good spirits, he even passes the binoculars to her and points at the Germans' location.

The captain isn't exaggerating. There they are, small like ants and just as diligent in moving in a single line through the knee-deep snow into nowhere.

Maggie hands the binoculars back to the captain and feels, oddly, nothing at all.

"We could catch up," his first lieutenant suggests, all restless energy and trigger-happy fingers.

"Whatever for?" The captain moves a lazy shoulder. "There's no more than twenty of them. No shelter here for them. We'll break camp here, inside the castle, away from the elements. Have dinner, have a good night's sleep, wake up, shave, have breakfast, and they'll still be plodding through that snow. Nah, I'm not budging from this good-looking spot anytime soon."

"Fair enough." The first lieutenant agrees surprisingly easily, seeing reason in the superior's words.

Knightley looks over Maggie's shoulder at the dog-eared map she extracted from her backpack. "How far are we from the border?"

"Double the distance we covered from Malmedy," she responds, tracing their progress with her finger. "But that's if we proceed straight ahead, across these valleys and forests."

"Like the Krauts are doing now?"

Maggie nods. All established roads are to the south. And it's the established roads that the Germans will be protecting from the skies and mining as they leave them.

"If the snow is only knee-deep for them, it should definitely be passable for our jeeps," Maggie muses out loud, but no GIs respond to her. They're finally off their feet, rekindling the fires the Germans were burning here mere hours ago and waiting for the chow to be distributed. They have rest on their minds, not tomorrow's prospective route.

The castle is not The Savoy hotel and its feather beds that Maggie's sorely missing, in which her fellow foreign correspondent lot must be resting their weary heads right now, but it'll do for the night. Reinhardstein's round turrets rise like silent ghosts of the past against the purple hues of darkening sky. Maggie wonders how many wars these sightless windows have seen as she follows the narrow path made by the departing German detachment away from the castle and aims her camera at the odd creature of bygone times. Where horses must have been hitched, US tanks and Army jeeps are now parked. Laughing GIs are waving at each other from the gaps through which muskets must have aimed at the approaching enemy.

Moved by some ancient instinct, Maggie looks down at the ground under her feet and wonders just how many people must have bled and died here, on this very spot where she stands; how many bones must have been stacked under the layers of this earth, both animal and human, and all because men like to subjugate instead of coexisting.

Inside the castle's walls, it's not much warmer. There's too much room and too much cold stone and all the carpets and animal skins have long been looted. Only a lone chandelier, a beast of cast iron and deer antlers, looks on at the young soldiers from its high perch, probably wondering what these humans were fighting over now.

Through her camera lens, Maggie looks on as well. War used to be a glorious affair, with knights and standards and horses in armor of shining steel. Kings roused their armies with fiery speeches and sounded their horns as they led them into spectacular battles. Now, world leaders sit in their respective offices (or bunkers, in Hitler's case) and make phone calls that send entire armies to their glory or death. And even the armies themselves, how soulless everything is! It's not the most skilled

swordsman who wins but whoever has more bullets and
machine guns and tanks and gas and planes and bombs that rain
from the skies across the enemy's land... How horribly busi-
nesslike and industrialized. And all for what?

"You seem awfully thoughtful."

It's Knightley again and he's offering her the same flask, but
Maggie isn't in the mood for banter any longer. With the
German border growing near and more real with every step, her
heart grows colder, as if she's slowly descending into a bottom-
less well. She wants to be alone, to allow herself to get her head
together, to let herself feel what needs to be felt.

"Come on, Mags, to our imminent victory." He stands much
too close, invading her personal space, and Maggie bristles
because this forceful closeness jolts something in her. She tells
herself that it's because of that one—and only—time, when
Frank got in her face, which almost ended in tragedy for one of
them, but she feels there's more to it, no matter how much she
tries to deny it.

"Thank you, Jack," she says, making an effort to smile
through the pain of the past, "but I'll take a rain check."

He doesn't take no for an answer. "Gotta drink for the
victory, Mags. It's the law." Knightley shakes the flask in front of
her face.

Without another word, Maggie hitches her backpack into its
place and walks out of the room, out of the castle, and into the
night.

The vehicle with the US Army star on its side catches up with
her within an hour, the astounded first lieutenant staring at her
as if he didn't expect to find her alive.

"Where have you run off to, sister?"

Sister. It suddenly occurs to Maggie that she is indeed his
big sister, in age and almost in rank. All foreign reporters are

sent to the front in gold-buttoned officers' jackets with a captain insignia on them, shirts and khaki slacks and a bright C, for Correspondent, armband around their sleeve. *Sister*...

"Just felt like a walk."

Liar, liar, pants on fire.

He's right, the first lieutenant. She ran off. That's what she always does, Maggie. Runs.

"Some walk, at night, in the middle of December."

"If the Krauts can do it, so can I."

"I have no doubt you can, but why would you?"

"Wanted to beat that self-important prick from the *Times* to the border."

The first lieutenant's face is barely discernible in the indigo light of the headlights painted blue—protection from whatever German planes are left rummaging the skies. He studies Maggie for some time. She tries not to shiver too openly. In the far distance, where the main roads lie, arches of fire rise from both sides and meet halfway in the black-as-soot sky.

If he doesn't understand what's behind a woman's seemingly illogical desire to set off into the frostbitten wilderness in the middle of the night, he understands competitiveness. "We'd still catch up with you before you crossed it."

"Your captain is very comfortable in that castle. He'll want to stay there for another day at least to allow the kitchen and infantry to catch up. I'll cross it by then."

"You'll walk without stopping?" he asks, incredulous.

"One can't stop anywhere here. That's why the Germans are walking. There's no shelter and therefore no choice."

"Except to walk."

"Yes, except to walk."

He contemplates her even longer. Then, suddenly, "Get inside."

Maggie remains where she is. "No. You go back. I'm not one

of your men, you're not responsible for me. They won't reprimand you. Just let me be."

The first lieutenant leans in and only then does Maggie see the same feral grin she often sees in the mirror on days—or nights—like this one. "Hop in, I said. I'll drive you there. We'll be the first ones to cross the border. You'll take a picture of me."

It's Maggie's turn to pull back. "Are you completely off your rocker? There's the matter of that Panzer detachment in front of us to consider. We'll catch up with them in no time. Then what?"

The first lieutenant only pats the machine gun mounted on the hood of the jeep with great affection and jerks a thumb at the bed of the vehicle. In it, under the yellow light of the moon sliced in half, gunmetal gleams dully. "Know how to operate?" he asks Maggie savagely.

Maggie nods and, not quite knowing why, jumps into the passenger seat. The engine roars to life as they speed off.

There was a shooting range in the training camp Maggie was sent to before boarding the former cruise liner RMS *Queen Mary*, retrofitted and aptly renamed the *GI Shuttle* by then, from New York to London. For Maggie's fellow journalist kin, attendance was voluntary, not mandatory. Just like the religious folk who were setting off to Europe as part of the American Red Cross, some of the reporters refused to touch weapons. They were going to Europe to document the war, not participate in it, they claimed. They didn't need to defend themselves; they were the press, easily identifiable and untouchable, according to the laws of international warfare. Maggie thought that they didn't know Germans all that well but said nothing, only took the courses, with all kinds of weapons available.

"Have you ever killed anyone?" the instructor asked on her very first day, a familiar condescending look on his face.

"No, sir." *Came very close to, though.*

"Do you think you could?" An even more familiar tilt of the head, almost pitying.

"Kill a man, sir?"

"Yes."

"Of course, sir."

There was no doubt in her mind then.

But there is doubt in her mind now, now that the lieutenant shifts the jeep into first gear and completely switches off the headlights.

"Reckon they noticed us yet?" he asks quietly, pulling to a complete stop.

"Dunno."

He puts the binoculars to his eyes, but even with the moonlight, the valley in front is a velvet of darkness. "I wish it was snowing. We'd sneak up on them easily then. Now, they'll be prepared, the cocksu—" He catches himself mid-word and switches to a much politer, "Bastards."

Maggie always finds it amusing, how they try to mind their mouths and manners whenever nurses or female press colleagues are present. They have heard worse, war girls. And they have uttered worse, working under enemy fire. No matter how un-ladylike, they have dropped their own f-bombs when the literal enemy bombs have pounded the earth all around them. In moments like these, "gosh darn it" just doesn't cut it.

"It's not too late to turn back, it's not like the Germans will tell on us." Maggie tries to smile, but even her lips are all pins and needles.

"No, I don't think they will, but do you want to? To turn back and just leave?"

Maggie thinks it over, then, looks up at him sharply. "No."

She doesn't even know his name and doubts he knows hers, but here they are, heading to their possible deaths together. There are twenty Germans, the captain said. There's only two of them. The odds are very much not in their favor, and still the lieutenant doesn't turn the jeep around.

"If they saw us, they'll try to ambush us like they did with the boys at Malmedy," Maggie warns the man next to her as her eyes peer into the darkness.

He doesn't respond, simply withdraws his gun from its holster and shoots in the general direction of the German detachment. They return fire, but not immediately. Maggie spots the cluster of flashes, all coming from approximately the same place. No tracer bullets, either, which means no machine guns to fear.

The first lieutenant sees it too. "You gave them too much credit, sister. They aren't ambushing anyone, they were running for the hills. Get your pretty head down, doll. I got this."

At once, he rises to his feet and grabs the machine gun. Without further ado, he showers the enemy with bullets—and not only the enemy, but everything around them as well.

From her half-crouched position, Maggie feeds the deadly ribbon of bullets into the mounted beast's maw and hears nothing but its deafening raw. From time to time, the first lieutenant holds his fire and crouches next to her, only to resume his indiscriminate shooting the instant a few bullets smash into the snow nearby or the hood of his jeep.

Maggie was right about one thing: it is an unequal fight, this savage annihilation the first lieutenant has unleashed on the lost German detachment. It soon becomes clear that not only do they not possess any machine guns, but their rifle ammunition is minimal as well. They try to ration it as much as they can, but soon stop firing altogether, realizing the futility of it. Their screams of surrender are weak and pathetic coming from the distance.

"Can you drive?" the first lieutenant asks, slapping the steering wheel like the rump of a horse.

"Yes, of course."

"Good. Switch with me, just in case they're up to something."

With Maggie behind the wheel and the headlights on once again, they approach the pitiful group of survivors. The first lieutenant needn't worry. They've long dropped their rifles and are holding their hands up high in the air as they stare at the approaching jeep with their childish eyes, all young boys still in their teens, drowning in overcoats made for the adults they're still growing into. Now that they're so close, Maggie sees that some of them are crying, frightened, no doubt, by both being caught unawares so close to the homeland and by the sight of their comrades lying dead all around them, fifteen out of twenty.

Before Maggie can say anything, the first lieutenant sends a short burst of machine-gun fire through their tiny ranks and drops them all next to their friends.

Maggie twists in her seat—"What did you do that for?"—but is met with a somewhat confused look of utter indifference.

"What? Didn't you write about this very tank detachment doing this to our boys first?"

"It couldn't have been them! The other unit was motorized."

"They were motorized, they lost their tank on the side of the road."

"Motorized meaning several vehicles and tanks that could successfully ambush a hundred people also in vehicles, not twenty sorry-looking *Hitlerjugend* riding on a single tank!"

The first lieutenant only shrugs and wipes his nose with the back of his hand, almost amused by her reaction. "Well... My mistake. Besides, we couldn't have taken them prisoner. We still have to make it to the border. Where was I supposed to put them? In the back, with all the weapons?"

"They were disarmed and exhausted. You could have left them where they were."

"So that one of those sneaky Krauts would shoot me in the ass with a service gun as soon as I turned it on him? No, thank you. I don't trust them as far as I can throw them. Do you?"

Maggie considers this for a moment and realizes that, no, neither does she.

"Could have searched them to make sure," she grumbles under her breath, just to satisfy her own conscience, and climbs out of the jeep.

"The hell you're patting them down for now?" the lieutenant asks. "They're deader than doorknobs, you can take my word for it," he adds with a certain pride.

"Souvenirs," Maggie responds without turning around. Her hands, stained with blood, reveal photos of parents and letters from home, hairbrushes and razors and a lone roll of aspirin, but no Pervitin. And her own stash is all but depleted, only a sorry coating of dust left in the cylinder after one of the pills got crushed. "Damn it," she mutters under her breath, burying her hands in the snowdrift to clean them.

"Too young to have any Crosses on them," the lieutenant says knowingly, never questioning Maggie's "souvenirs" claim. "Sorry, sister. Maybe next time. Hop back in and let's shoot for the border before my captain wakes up and has kittens on account of my going AWOL, together with his vehicle."

Once they reach the border, they pause in front of it and contemplate the underwhelming look of it—sparsely planted border posts painted white and black. Maggie parks the jeep next to one of them, so that the US Army star is easily visible, and directs the lieutenant to lean against it.

"Will it be visible though? On account of the night and all," he asks.

"I'll use a flash."

He doesn't even question the idea. There are no German warplanes here to take a shot at the insolent interlopers. They're in the middle of nowhere and so Maggie mounts the flash on her camera and snaps the lieutenant for yet another article that will bring her even more fame—or infamy—she didn't ask for. She can already see the headline: *First American to Cross German Border*.

It's only then that she asks him for his name.

"Boyle. First Lieutenant James Boyle."

Twenty German tank troopers had to die for this photo. Maggie knows she's supposed to feel some way about it but finds that she doesn't. All she feels is numb.

TEN

THEN

Mutti works now, cleaning rich people's apartments and doing their laundry, and Grete watches her twin brothers while she's gone. She's supposed to love them, but she's grown to resent them for their incessant crying and for being yelled at by the neighbors for not shutting them up. She tries, she genuinely does; she checks their nappies, but most of the time it's not a nappy problem, it's hunger. With *Mutti* and her breast milk gone, there's only bread that's left for Grete and her brothers to share. She soaks it in water and feeds it to the boys, bit by little bit, and they quieten for some time, but then start up again, even louder than before.

Frau Wilma says there's yeast in bread and that's what gives them colic and that's the reason they cry, but Grete doesn't have anything else and doesn't know what colic is and how to help it. So, one day, tired of rocking the bottom drawer in which the twins sleep, she covers the crying boys with a blanket and carefully pulls the drawer shut. Their cries are muffled and grow weaker as she eventually drifts off to sleep, still starved herself but in blissful silence.

Mutti's screams jolt her back to reality. She's cradling her sons in her arms and crying hysterically and soon they do too. Only Papa is laughing as he stands in the doorway, hands in his pockets. He tells *Mutti* to quit it with her hysterics. No harm done. Grete didn't know any better, she's a child herself.

"They almost suffocated!"

"And whose fault is that? You're their mother."

Grete is hiding under his arm because *Mutti* slaps her for lesser things and Papa never does and so it's safer here, clutching at his old army pants which smell of tobacco and sweat.

"You know I can't take them with me. I'm working. I'm the only one of us who's working."

There's a certain undertone to her voice that Papa doesn't like. Grete feels his arm stiffening where previously, it rested loose next to her shoulder.

"And I serve. Shall I quit my troop to babysit for you?"

"I'm just saying, they aren't paying you anything."

"There are things more important than money, unless you're a Jewess. Are you a Jewess? Go find yourself a nice Jew then. Go on. Take the brats with you—not Grete though, she's a good girl and will stay with me—and find yourself a Jew who will hire a nice German maid for you to clean your house. Like your current employer did for his wife."

Mutti doesn't say anything; only rocks her sons harder.

A few days later, on a Sunday, when Papa is away on one of his drills in the mountains and *Mutti* has her only day off, she sits Grete down and asks if she would like to stay with Papa if *Mutti* really leaves. Grete clutches at her and begins wailing at once, frightened by the prospect for reasons she can only feel but can't yet articulate. *Mutti* cries too, in half-hushed, suppressed sobs as she caresses her daughter's soft locks.

"I don't understand," she says and Grete feels that it's more to herself that *Mutti*'s speaking, not to her, "he loves you best of all and spoils you so. And I'm so very tired... I know... I know. Don't you cry now. I love you more than life and wouldn't leave you. I only thought that that's what you wanted: your father and to be away from me and your brothers. I know how hard it is on you. God knows, I do. And I'm trying so very hard for you all, but there's only so much that I can do. Don't you cry, though. I'm not leaving. If you don't want me to go, I'm not going anywhere."

She doesn't leave and Grete doesn't push the drawer closed again. She's only three but already knows that women often have to sacrifice something—just to survive.

ELEVEN

NOW

London. December 1944

After the nomadic chaos of the front, even bombed-out London is a feast to Maggie's eyes. She's glad to be back in the city that welcomed her, a greenhorn correspondent, just this past summer and whipped her into a weathered veteran in the span of just six months. It's wintertime and the night pitch-black, but inside The Savoy, where most of her fellow foreign correspondents are stationed, the walls are dripping with gilded opulence and the lights are as bright as ever, shining through the crystals of the chandeliers suspended overhead.

It takes some time for a newcomer to adjust to the blinding carnival greeting them just behind the tall Art Deco doors. Still squinting against the lights, Maggie stares at the floor under her feet, but even the marble is much too dazzling with its checkerboard pattern. Exhausted after a flight during which their C-47 had the misfortune of gaining a few German fighters on its tail, Maggie throws her bag at the foot of the nearest column and drops down next to it. She ought to report to the foreign editor of the *Times* before sorting her sleeping arrangements for the night, but her feet refuse to carry her any further, and there are no magic pills left in her pockets to raise her from the dead. Her stomach is also rumbling in protest, but Maggie's eyelids are much too heavy after the ordeal of the past few days. She'll take a short nap right here, and then—

"Look who the cat dragged in!"

Maggie unglues her eyes and can't help but grin at the sight of the familiar face that used to grace the pages of fashion magazines in the twenties, back when she was still a child. The woman squatting next to her is no longer a *Vogue* model but a colleague now, but still, Maggie wipes her hands down her face with a groan at the contrast between the two.

"Miller, do me a favor. Go away and pretend you didn't see me until I soak myself in a tub for a few hours, will you?"

As always, Lee will have none of this nonsense. "You just returned from the front, do you think I expected you to be perfumed and powdered?" Her full lips smile, while the big, expressive eyes remain deadly serious as she scans Maggie's disheveled form. "Heard you flew out from the German border."

"From near the German border. But I crossed it, took a picture, and went back to hitch a ride." Maggie pats her inner pocket in which the treasure of an historic film rests.

"Bitch," Miller quips good-naturedly.

"This is for covering the liberation of Paris while I was stuck here at the press center."

"Go take it up with Junior, I'm not the one giving out assignments there."

Maggie snorts at the mention of the London bureau editor who has promised several times to strip her of her accreditation and yet is still to act upon his threats. True, much like Martha Gellhorn, Maggie goes off on her own adventures more often than not, but the material that she brings back is much too good —just like this time.

"Speaking of, what are you doing lounging here in the lobby when you have an article to write?" Miller arches her wide, Scarlett O'Hara-like brow and taps her wristwatch to drive the point across.

"Well, I was going to rest for twenty minutes after barely surviving a goddamned dogfight, but seeing as you won't piss off—"

"You'll sleep when you're dead," Lee counters in her no-nonsense way and pulls Maggie up by her sleeve, simultaneously hitching her heavy kit onto her own shoulder. "Up on your feet and into the press center you go."

Maggie grumbles her protests but puts one foot in front of another as Miller escorts her out of the hotel and back into the night, with its biting cold and all-encompassing darkness. They trot to keep themselves warm and in no time burst through the doors of the London University building where the Ministry of Information is housed for the *war*-time being. There, with frightening efficiency, Miller grabs ahold of someone to develop Maggie's film and finds a free spot for the typewriter she has just wrestled out of Maggie's kitbag.

"It's seven, you still have time to write a piece to go with your photos if you want them to be published tomorrow. I'll go find Junior and tell him he has something special to squeeze into tomorrow's issue."

"You haven't even seen them yet."

And the article doesn't even exist, and Maggie honestly doubts she can produce anything readable in the next hour, but Miller gives her a certain look.

"I know you and I know your work," she says and adds, already over her shoulder as there's no time to be lost, in a put-on British accent, "it'll be bloody brilliant."

And just like that, Maggie is suddenly awake and chuckling.

She cracks her stiff joints and begins to pour the words onto the page; out of nowhere, a mug of strong-as-nails, bitter tea appears and Maggie slurps it without taking her eyes off the page and typing with one hand. All the while, Miller is hovering just over her shoulder despite having her own assignments to worry about, standing watch, just as Maggie did when it was Miller who was reporting on liberated Paris and Maggie was the one who kept supplying her with tea and mean English tobacco and slapping her cheeks to keep her awake just so her piece would be the first to break the very next morning. This is what they do for each other, these war sisters.

Back in The Savoy, just past twelve, Miller draws Maggie a bath and helps her into it with a sisterly care that Maggie hasn't realized she's missed so sorely in her adult life. It's always been her who has taken care of Norma, always the one who's carried all the weight on her shoulders. No wonder she feels like she's crumbling.

"Lee? Thank you for today," Maggie says, eyes shut against the soap Miller's working into the oily strings of her neglected hair.

"Don't mention it. That's what friends are for."

"I'm so grateful that you're here."

"Why, any of those fine gentlemen down in the lobby would be more than happy to give you a bath." Miller is back to her sharp-witted self.

"Yeah, I'd just have to put out right after."

"I bet they're thinking you're putting out for me as we speak."

Maggie giggles and holds her nose as Lee dunks her in the water to rinse her hair.

There is a measure of truth to Lee's joke: Maggie has lost count of all of the times she and her colleagues have been called lesbians. Sometimes, for ignoring catcalls; sometimes, for wearing army fatigues instead of a skirt; sometimes, for billeting together or not using makeup or cutting their hair much too short, or cursing or smoking in public—the list goes on. They used to be embarrassed and tried to be mindful of how they acted and were perceived until one of them had an epiphany: "And just what's so embarrassing about being a lesbian? At least, another woman would know what to do with my lady parts and satisfy me for a change."

They laughed about it then and stopped worrying altogether about such opinions soon after. Let them think what they like.

"Do you want me to wake you up for girls-only breakfast tomorrow or would you rather sleep in?" Miller asks, calling Maggie back to the present.

"Who else is here?"

"Rita, and Ann. Martha's gone back to the continent on assignment and so has Helen. There was some new girl—also Maggie, by the way—but she's abandoned us for her husband for the time being. He's on leave here, or some such. Wants her to play house."

It's Maggie's turn to arch a skeptical brow. "Like Hemingway with Martha?"

"Speaking of."

"Gah." Maggie makes a face. "Don't tell me he's here."

"Sure is, a bachelor once again."

Maggie sits up, her hands clutching the porcelain curves of the clawed tub. "Martha divorced him?"

"You sound surprised for someone who called it in the first place."

"I'm not surprised, I'm excited. Good for her!"

"We gave this new Maggie till the end of the year as well. Judging by the looks of it, it'll be the divorced women's club that'll be covering the war in the new year."

They both grow silent for a while, wistful expressions

replacing the hard, sardonic smirks used as protective masks. They never meant for this to happen—to pay for the professional life with their private lives. Nothing would make them happier than to do their job knowing that somewhere their husband was showing someone the morning news and pointing to their name and saying, "That's right, that's my missus's article, right here on the front page—isn't she brilliant?" But, unfortunately, women aren't allowed to be brilliant, lest they outshine their ordinary spouse or, God forbid, try to compete with an extraordinary one. That's how they've ended up alone in this gilded bathroom, two birds of a feather, wounded by the same hand that aimed to bring them down, yet free.

Sure, Lee has her lover, David, but lovers are much better than husbands. They mind their business and take each day as it comes, and for that very reason, Miller positively refuses to ever consider another marriage. As does Maggie. When her ex-husband was just a lover, they were also much happier.

"Wake me up." Maggie makes up her mind. "But let's have breakfast here, in my room, just us girls."

The morning dawns sunny and bright and they crawl into her bed, her war sisters, in their smart uniforms with sweaters underneath. The Savoy is all gilded glory but still no heat. Feathered beds offer the one source of warmth, but only if they nestle next to each other, wrapped in blankets around two big breakfast trays.

Between bites of toast, powdered egg, and C-ration biscuits, they indulge in gossip about the press frontline and heart-to-heart confessions meant only for friendly ears.

"Gotta give it to the German press center, their people think they're winning the war," Ann Stringer of the United Press declares, half-amused.

Her wedding ring is gone, Maggie notes without keeping

her gaze lingering on her counterpart's left hand. Ann doesn't like talking about Bill, whom she lost to the war last summer, yet she keeps his memory alive by picking up where he left off, by moving forward with the victorious army to write about things he no longer can. It must still hurt like hell, but at least the light seems to be back in her eyes and the hair Ann had shorn as though in mourning is growing out once again, brushing her shoulders in dark, glossy ringlets.

"To be fair, the Ardennes offensive was brutal," Rita Wandervert of *Time-Life* says. "I tried hitching a ride there, but the SHAEF promised to dishonorably discharge anyone flying us girls anywhere near the front."

"Speaking of: just how did you sneak your tail there, Sullivan?" Lee demands.

Maggie grins through a mouthful of thin toast. "Junior gave me an assignment on Nurse Corps in northern France. He didn't mention explicitly that I had to return to London after I submitted it."

Rita snorts into her teacup and puts it down with a loud clang, laughing. "Thanks for the tip. I'm doing just that next time."

"Martha pulled something similar, a little bird told me this morning," Lee says, her smile lighting up. "Went on the assignment in Paris and talked some pilot into taking her to the frontline. You just missed her, Mags. She's in the Ardennes, from what I hear."

In the harsh light of morning, the lines around Lee's eyes and mouth are prominent; her lips are so pale, they're almost blue, and yet to Maggie she has never seemed more beautiful, not even in her golden *Vogue* days. There's something unapologetically freeing in Miller's crossed legs and slumped shoulders and tousled hair and the way she holds her cigarette—the way she likes, instead of feigning something that looks good on glossy magazine pages.

None of them wear makeup. Rita's hair is still in pin curls and Ann's face is glistening with Vaseline—the only thing that saves them from cracked winter skin brought on by brutal cold and poor nutrition devoid of any vitamins. In their own little circle, unobserved and not subjected to constant scrutiny, they finally relax and curse all they please and laugh because they want to and not because a pilot who can give a ride across the Channel told some tired, flat joke.

"By the way, nice article on the border crossing, Mags!" Ann is waving the latest issue of the newspaper in the air.

It's been making the rounds; Maggie can tell by the smudged ink all around First Lieutenant Boyle's picture.

Her second front page. She smiles contentedly and almost persuades herself not to remember the German Panzer troop that had to die so that the picture could be taken.

"It's not an official one," she says, but her words drown in the ensuing protests.

"You're just like Martha." Lee gestures in annoyance, sending cigarette ash flying. "She storms damned Omaha alongside the guys, takes historic photos, but when we make her a cake to celebrate her return—"

"—After going through London with a fine-toothed comb to gather the ingredients, mind you," Rita adds with a knowing nod.

"—She looks all embarrassed and says, *well, those aren't really legal photos; I was arrested by the military police afterwards,*" Lee finishes in a voice that eerily resembles their daring comrade, sending the women around her laughing once again with the mock-annoyed tone.

"But it's so true," Ann says, reaching into the jar of jam Lee generously supplied from her own provisions. It's good American stuff, fresh from home. "Why do we always do this to ourselves? I look at the fellows toasting their articles at the bar downstairs every single night and yet when one of us gets a front page or photographs history like Martha did, blazing the trail for all of us to follow, we feel as if it's undeserved somehow."

"I toast all of your articles," Lee says, shrugging.

"I do too, but never my own," Ann explains and issues a moan after the first taste of real jam. "Strawberry. My God! I died and went to heaven. Where did you get it?"

"Family." A warm smile lights up Lee's eyes.

"Can they adopt me? Mine send me mittens and scarves. I love them, but how can I tell them that I can't quite butter my toast with mittens? But going back to my original point, why do we feel so unworthy of praise, even if it's well deserved?"

"I personally don't like attention," Rita admits with a small shrug. "I love the job, but not the scrutiny that comes with it. We're never the ones who just deliver the news; we are, somehow, the news. It began with Sonia Tomara, who had to model the very first uniform ever made for a woman correspondent instead of just packing her bag and going about her assignment, and it still goes on. That new girl, Higgins, they began photographing her as soon as she arrived. And all because she's young, blonde, and pretty."

"Mhm." Lee accentuates the point with a stab of her finished cigarette into a saucer. "There are plenty of handsome guys I see in the press center, but if I pulled out my camera on one of them, they'd look at me like I've got three heads. Even David; damn, I sleep with the guy and it's still him who photographs me, instead of me photographing him."

"Well, you *are* more photogenic."

An explosion of laughter.

"I was so happy Kotex buried my modeling career," Lee continues, alluding to the infamous magazine spreads that sent shockwaves throughout the United States, back in 1928. Maggie remembers her mother's shock very well, when, instead of designer dresses, it was sanitary pads that Lee Miller was advertising. It didn't matter that Kotex used her photo without Lee's consent, or knowledge for that matter—the damage was done. "Finally, I thought. I can be an artist instead of an art object. Only for the war to break out and to be in the papers again. I'm almost forty. I'm getting old, goddammit! Leave me alone already."

"I do love your photos," Maggie says, rubbing newspaper ink off her fingertips. "You have such an eye for what will have the most impact. I always look at them and think, damn it, I would have walked past the same exact thing and wouldn't look at it twice. And this bitch Miller goes and shoots it and—my God!—it just takes your breath away. You're a true artist. Some may say there's nothing artistic in war, but I disagree. Art isn't meant to be only something nice and pretty. The point of art is to move, first and foremost. And there's nothing more moving than a photo of a half-burned teddy bear next to a pile of stone under which, you just know, the bear's little owner is buried. It sends a message, a very powerful one. And you know just exactly how to photograph such things."

"Yes, but I can't write the way you do, Mags. I don't think anyone of us can. You don't take any prisoners, you just go straight for the guts, and I can't even tell you how much I respect you for it."

Maggie chews on her lip, growing pensive.

The women seize on that; grow serious and silent as well.

"Tell me to shut up if it's none of my business, but why are you here, Mags?" Ann asks and pushes the last tiny lump of sugar in Maggie's direction. "Most of the ladies, like Martha and Lee here, they've been in the business for over a decade, so it's understandable why they wanted to document the war. Then there's me, but, frankly, I wouldn't have even thought of coming here if that German tank didn't kill my Bill. You, on the other hand, popped like a jack from the box and jumped smack in the middle of action without anyone even knowing your name at first. You aren't a career journalist. Why, suddenly, the war? The front? Just felt the call?"

Maggie pushes the sugar back into the middle of the group, smiling softly to herself at this little game they always play. *You finish this. No, you. I'm already full. And I don't like sweets—so, you finish it.* Giving the last bit of their very heart so that a sister can feel a little warmer from this sliver of love in a world full of hate.

She can say, "yes, the calling," and leave it at that, but it feels inappropriate and ratty somehow, lying to their frank, sympathetic eyes. And yet she can't quite utter the truth, since she's unable to admit it even to herself, tiptoeing around the issue, waiting it out, hoping it'll all blow over somehow without her direct involvement. It's easier to slice open one's veins instead of slicing one's soul open in front of an audience.

Maggie pulls her sleeves down to cover the scars on her wrists and clamps the wool in her fists. "I came here to report on Dachau and Buchenwald and also, hopefully, to find someone," she finally says. "Norma, my sister, she's in Bellevue because of something that happened in the past and—" She stops there, suddenly unable to finish.

The other women, too, lower their eyes at the mention of one of the most renowned New York psychiatric facilities. It's not the second-hand embarrassment Maggie's used to encountering, but the silent promise instead: *You don't have to share if you don't want to. It's tender, personal, and sensitive. We understand.*

It's because of that shared silence that Maggie can speak. They make it easy for her, these seasoned press warriors. "It was self-admission this time. She didn't trust herself, thought she could harm herself again. Fall is a difficult season for her."

"I heard the doctors are very good there," Rita says with a sympathetic tilt of her head.

"They are. Norma once joked that she likes it there so

much, she keeps coming back." Maggie, herself, doesn't smile at that. "If everything goes well for me here, if I find who I'm looking for, she hopes it'll be her last stay there. She craves... resolution. Of one sort or the other."

"Do you need our help?" Lee asks.

Maggie's heart swells with gratitude for having such friends as Lee, Ann, and Rita in her corner. However, she can't tell them the full truth. Besides, this is her and Norma's own demon to exorcise.

"No." Maggie shakes her head. "I have to see this through on my own."

Lee nods, pulling back in respect of her friend's wishes. "All right, you go and take care of your business. Just let us know if you need anything."

"And we mean, anything." Rita nods.

So does Ann. "Anything."

Maggie looks at each of them with a gratitude that's beyond words and links hands with her war sisters. Between the four, a lump of sugar lies untouched.

TWELVE

THEN

After the stifling confines of Berlin's slums, Halensee Luna Park opens up before Grete's eyes like a majestic fairy land. As soon as they step off the train, carnival music envelops them in its cotton-candy cocoon and carries them toward the strings of multicolored lights and swirling attractions.

Grete is beyond herself, a dressed-up doll, and not just because *Mutti* pulled out her favorite dress, with pink ruffles and kittens embroidered on the pockets, that is only for special occasions. It's a tad too short now and pinches Grete in the waist, chest, and shoulders, but such trifles matter little now that she holds onto her parents' hands and they smile at one another and at passers-by, and all is well in Grete's little world. With the twins left in her grandparents' care, Grete soaks up all the attention until her cheeks are glowing with joy.

How beautiful *Mutti* is, also in her Sunday finest, her short hair curled and eyes darkened by shadows and mascara. And how handsome Papa is now that he's out of his old uniform, attired in pressed slacks and a new shirt his parents-in-law presented him with on his birthday.

"The world has moved on," Grete's *Opa* said as they toasted the occasion. "What's the point trying to hold onto the old glory when Germany can't even have an army any longer? Go find yourself a real job. You're such a fine, smart, strapping fellow. Any employer will be fortunate to have you."

Papa tossed the brandy down his throat, smiled, and put on the suit for the Luna Park instead.

Grete's mouth is wide open. She has never seen such finery. Everyone is a film star here, everything is shimmering, everything a delight. How pretty the carousel horses are, their manes all the colors of the rainbow. Grete picks the one with a pink tail and golden hooves and a pristine white body and holds onto the pole fast as the carousel begins to move and her steed picks up pace. Up and down she goes as she squeals in delight, her parents' smiling faces greeting her with each new circle completed as they look on from the crowd.

It's over much too fast, when Grete only began to develop a taste for it. She wants to go on something that goes faster, higher!

Mutti tries to object, but Papa will hear nothing of it—he'll hold Grete just fine.

They step on the stairs that begin moving up as if by magic and go past the swivel house that twists and turns in the air, mute screams of exhilaration issuing from inside. There's a water slide that leads straight into the lake, but none of them brought their swimming things to change into. Instead, Papa steps into the line for a racing car ride. The sign next to it says that one has to be this tall to ride it, but Papa hoists Grete onto his shoulders and she's taller than anyone in the crowd now. Boys older than her look on with visible envy as she's admitted inside, carried on her father's wide shoulders like a princess.

Cars go round on their own, connected to the base by metal poles, but Papa still lets Grete turn the wheel as he, himself, hoots in delight like a child and makes racing noises that make

Grete shriek in ecstasy as she delivers them across the finish line time and again.

Grete wants *Mutti* to join in the fun with them for the next ride, but *Mutti* only smiles and shakes her beautifully coiffured head. They don't have enough money for all three of them, and adult tickets are more expensive. It's all right, she's happy to just watch from the sidelines.

Papa is already dragging Grete into the fun house, but Grete keeps looking back at her mother. This was supposed to be for all of them. It's no fun when one is left behind. And Papa can skip the funhouse and let *Mutti* go with Grete instead. But Papa suggests no such thing. Instead, he takes the money out of her velvet purse and pays for the funhouse, and then for beer, and then for more beer, and then to enter the arena to spar with a carnival boxer.

Grete holds his new shirt stained with beer and smelling sharply of sweat and looks up at her mother, who's holding Papa's new jacket. Papa is drunk and is making a fool out of himself and the people around are laughing at him and the magic is suddenly gone from the air.

"I want to go home," Grete says and reaches for her mother's hand.

"You don't want to watch the fireworks?" *Mutti* asks.

"No, I want to go home."

Mutti smiles at her weakly through all that lipstick and mascara. "Let's see what Papa says."

Grete already knows what Papa shall say. He'll want to stay and for them to remain by his side and he'll want to drink more and get into a real fight this time, and Grete doesn't want the day to end this way.

It won't do any good to just ask him to leave and so Grete lies—lies before the time most children even learn what a lie is.

"I'm sick to my tummy, *Mutti*."

"Sick to your tummy?"

"Very sick, yes. I have to go *now*."

Before it gets bad enough—with Papa, not with her imaginary illness.

When he gets down from the arena and sees genuine suffering in his daughter's eyes, he lets them go. Reluctantly, with just enough money for the train tickets back, but he does.

THIRTEEN

NOW

The Battle of the Bulge, as it was christened by both the military and the press, fizzled out faster than anyone expected. Hitler promised the great counteroffensive that would turn the tide of the war by the new year of 1945, threw half of the troops from the Eastern front to the Western one, supplied them with whatever leftover gas was to be had from already fuel-drained Germany, and ended up standing with his manhood in his hands, according to General Eisenhower. Maggie chose not to directly quote on the matter.

"Don't underestimate them though," Eisenhower added in the same press conference. "They still have fight left in them. The most zealous of them, that is."

That, Maggie did put in the paper, warning the troops to be on their guard even when entering the towns which had officially declared surrender and were hung with white sheets as far as the eye could see.

It's the end of February now and most of the towns they passed through were indeed happy to give themselves up, and to the Americans most of all, since the Amis weren't as personal as the Europeans in their revenge and harbored their anger mostly for the Japanese and not the Germans. Besides, they had gum and chocolate and seemingly limitless Spam they didn't mind sharing.

But then there are the so-called "werewolves," of which the German press boasts in the same vein as it does of new miracle weapons, and unlike the latter, the former turn out to be very much real.

"A mighty big name for a bunch of gun-waving kids," a commander of the detachment Maggie is accompanying from across the Rhine sneered just a day ago. To be fair, that's precisely what the "werewolves" are: German civilians, most of them from nationalist youth organizations, who wage a guerilla war at the Allies and their fellow Germans if the latter make the mistake of welcoming the former into their homes.

Now, his attitude is much less blasé as he's crouching together with Maggie near the pockmarked wall. The shooters are holed up two stories above them in the school building which they likely attended just weeks ago. They threw a hand grenade at the first US Army jeep passing through the narrow street and killed all four men aboard, disabling it in the process. The other three vehicles following it pulled back at once, narrowly missing being blasted by several more grenades raining down from the second-story window. Shrapnel got them, though; even Maggie, despite riding in the very last jeep together with the commanding staff. They scrammed at once, even before the commander's order to do so, and took cover in the doorways of the houses lining the street and around the corners.

Pushed back out of harm's way by one of the GIs, Maggie checks her camera first. It's in one piece, thank God. Only then does she examine her shoulder. Grenade or cobblestone shrapnel sliced it in several places, but that's about it. The bleeding will stop on its own.

Without wasting any more time, Maggie picks up her camera and begins clicking away.

"Red!" the platoon sergeant shouts into the black smoke rising from the disabled vehicle. "Where you at? Your crew OK?"

"I'm all right! The boys are too," the voice responds from behind the smoke curtain. "Busted my ear, I think..."

"You still got two hands though, so start shooting before I bust your other one!" the sergeant yells back, crouch-walking closer to the windows where the teens are holed up. "Boulder! You alive?"

"Yessir!"

"Can you see those lil' suckers up there?"

"Sure can!"

"Give me cover while I'm making it across to you, can't see shit from here!"

Maggie's eardrums, still ringing from the explosions, are assaulted anew as several blasts of machine-gun fire pour into the second-story windows on her side of the narrow street. Half-crouched, the platoon sergeant makes it across quickly and takes cover behind one of the vehicles. Maggie snaps his progress under the hail of tracer bullets. It always surprises her how surreal and seemingly harmless shootouts appear through the lens.

She gradually moves from under her cover as well and runs from one entryway to another, following the soldiers' progress, documenting their every step.

Snap. A rifleman taking aim at the gunman in the window, who aims at someone different in turn.

Snap. The German rifle is mid-fall as the young blond boy's head explodes in a fountain of red haze and skull fragment.

Snap. The cool expression of a girl with two long braids as she looks out of the window, a hand grenade in her slender palm.

Snap. The platoon sergeant's face distorted as he calls for cover.

Snap. Bodies torn open, a leg only half-attached by ligaments.

Snap. A soldier clutching his intestines with a look of surprise on his face.

Snap. The same window but the girl no longer there, only plaster exploding with bullets showering it.

Snap. Soldiers kicking the school door open.

Maggie doesn't follow them inside. With the armband with the bright-yellow letter C on it, she walks along the side of the street that is open to fire and approaches the disabled first vehicle.

Snap. A driver who looks as though he's sleeping despite the blood streaming down his face, his helmet torn off by the explosion.

Snap. The GI in the passenger seat thrown against the mangled frame of the windshield, what's left of his head resting atop his shredded arms.

Snap. A GI's leg with a bone broken protruding at a sharp angle as his body rests against the jeep from which he was thrown.

Later, as Maggie taps away at her typewriter in the local press center, a secretary calls her to the phone. It's her foreign section editor, all the way from Paris, where the new European press headquarters have just been established.

"Sullivan, what is this you're sending?"

"What?"

"The photos, they're gruesome. You know perfectly well I can't print them."

Maggie works her shoulder, which keeps getting numb from the recent wound. She forgets all about it when she types, but it flares up right after, as it does now. "What do you want from me? I'm at war, aren't I?"

"Fair enough, but kindly don't send me photos of body parts. Send me something nice and uplifting, like that Boyle fellow crossing the border, or those French Resistance girls you interviewed last fall. Both readers and troops want something uplifting, something to celebrate."

It takes a lot for her not to resort to screaming. "That's all you send us women correspondents to report on. French Resistance girls and Allied nurses. Wartime recipes and fashion. How to bake bread without flour and how to make spring stockings out of last fall's scarf."

"That's what our women readers are interested in."

"Who told you that? Because last time I checked, with the French Resistance girls you sent me to interview, they were more interested in how to sabotage enemy communication lines and how to fashion portable radio parts from ordinary items that can be found in any household."

"So you remember there are actual assignments I send you on from time to time?" Sarcasm is audible in his voice. "Kindly remind me of the one you're supposed to be working on."

"Foodstuffs distribution in the newly liberated cities," Maggie grumbles into the receiver and shifts it to her other shoulder.

"I thought, perhaps, you'd suffered a concussion and forgot and that's the reason why I'm getting the report on werewolves instead."

"I'm documenting *the war*," Maggie repeats slowly, articulating every word. "And, in my humble opinion, the recent werewolves' attack is a bit more important than the number of Spam cans in the local soup kitchen. And if you think this is gruesome, go through the Soviet press on the Auschwitz liberation. That's where you should send us with assignments—to the camps, not supply-train headquarters."

"Keep your tone in check, Sullivan. I'm not an idiot. Get off your high horse. You're not the only reporter there and certainly a replaceable one."

"I'm sorry, sir." She isn't.

He knows it but lets it go surprisingly easily. "It's not me, Sullivan. It's the censors. We can't publish something like this. You want to report on the werewolves' attack—fine. Wait for the fight to be over, find the most good-looking GIs, line them up next to the grateful German townsfolk, and tell everyone to smile. *Another German Town Liberated!* A nice byline to add to your extensive résumé."

"I'm not here for the résumé," Maggie says and rubs her eyes. They're stinging again, from typing at night and the harsh chemicals in the makeshift developing rooms, and not washing her face properly for days on end.

"What are you there for then?" He sounds tired—of her.

It's all right—she's tired of herself as well.

"I'm here to document the war."

One of two reasons, but the second one isn't his business to know.

"Good, and I just told you how to document it properly."

"No, you want me to document celebrations of liberation. There's a difference. You want people to see glory, smiles, and flowers. They'll see it and frame it and put it on their walls and in the next twenty years their children will look at those photos and will want the same—glory and flowers and smiles, without realizing they only come after spilling guts, torn limbs, and faces burned to a crisp. And once we get to Buchenwald and Dachau, what do you want me to do? Line up whoever can still stand on their skeletal legs and make them smile for the camera with whatever teeth they have left after the Nazis kicked the rest in? No, sir. You want to celebrate the end of the war and genocide, I want to prevent the start of a new one."

"Very noble of you, Sullivan. Call me back when you do

that, and in the meantime, send me photos I can actually use or I'll recall your marching orders and quickly send someone there who will."

He hangs up and Maggie remains by the dead phone, brooding.

After some time, she signals one of the operators with the receiver, which is still warm in her hand. "Can you connect me with a facility in the United States?"

"Where?"

"New York."

"City or state?"

"City."

"Phone number?"

Maggie rattles it off from memory and waits for the reaction she's grown accustomed to.

The operator doesn't disappoint. His brows shoot up as he looks at Maggie in confusion. "It's a sanitarium."

"Yes, it is," she confirms. "Ask to speak with Norma Sullivan. She's a patient there. Tell them it's her sister, from the front."

The operator's eyebrows remain arched, but he dictates Maggie's request into the receiver.

"They asked for you to wait."

Maggie nods and takes the phone from him. She'll wait.

Ordinarily, the medical staff are very strict when it comes to phone calls. Only the fact that Maggie is on the frontline allows her such perks. Not that she uses them all that much.

"Mags?" Norma's painfully familiar, slightly hoarse voice clenches Maggie's heart in a vice. "Is everything OK?"

"Everything's all right," Maggie confirms and hates herself for the tremor in her voice.

"Doesn't sound like it. Spill it."

"Nothing to spill, really. Just wanted to hear your voice."

"You found them yet?"

Maggie's breath hitches in her chest. For some reason, a wave of guilt washes over her. "No. Not yet."

"Have you been looking, though?"

"Not actively," she finally admits after a pause. "But I will. I promise, I will. Then, you'll be all right again."

"It's not me who ought to be all right, Mags. It's you."

Maggie's throat contracts in spite of herself, but she bites into her lip—hard—and tells her sister about the editor who gives her a hard time, the GIs who are all such fine lads, and the Germans who seem like nice people.

In turn, Norma tells her about the art she's been making, the Natural History Museum's new exhibit they just visited with her group, and how she got to spend Christmas with their parents on a two-week leave before checking herself back into the Bellevue.

And between them, for thousands of feet, for the entire length of the phoneline, all the things unsaid stretch.

FOURTEEN

THEN

It's summer and with *Mutti* always at work, Papa takes Grete and the twins to the countryside. His parents live there, keep livestock, and there's plenty of food to be had, unlike in the cities all over Germany, where a loaf of bread goes for a billion marks.

Opa Klaus addresses Grete in formal *Sie* for some reason and always offers her stale marmalade with breakfast. *Oma* Maria keeps talking about the neighbors' daughter who married a Negro who was taken prisoner during the war and used to work on the neighbors' farm, and had a child by him, and keeps insisting, with a degree of glee, that said child is more white than black.

Despite her reservations, Papa encourages Grete to run around naked, both inside the house and outside. It's natural, being at one with the elements, he says. But when she asks to go see the Black Baby, he prohibits her from going anywhere near him. Mixing of the races is *un*natural, he says, unlike the running-naked idea.

Grete doesn't understand any of that, but there are plenty of things to keep her mind occupied and so she feeds the chickens and sets off on "expeditions" with her grandfather to collect cow dung for fertilizer and climbs the ladder to the hayloft, where the air is hot and stuffy, and lies there with her new dolly, in her own secret place, imagining herself to be a character out of the Grimm Brothers' fairy tales.

The dolly is not the blue-haired one Papa promised to buy and never did. *Mutti* made it for her just before Grete's departure after she couldn't take Grete's silent, suffering glances stolen at their neighbors' daughter's doll. Grete likes *Mutti*'s dolly even better than the store-bought one she used to dream of. It's half-knitted and half-sewn, with buttons for eyes and even real hair—*Mutti*'s hair she's sewn into the doll's head. It smells of her mother and is so soft to snuggle with when Grete's missing home and cries herself to sleep.

There are no bathrooms here, only an outhouse made entirely out of wood and crawling with spiders. Papa never says no when she asks him to take her there. Armed with a broom, he always swipes all the spiders and other critters away as Grete looks on. It's still much too dingy in there and Grete is always apprehensive of spiders, that are far too conniving in her opinion and could have stashed themselves in some crevice just to crawl out as soon as she's inside and jump on her. But Papa only laughs at her quietly and tells her not to fret: the spiders are more afraid of her than she of them.

The hole cut inside the wooden seat is still much too big for a child and so Papa teaches Grete how to squat with her feet on either side of it and supports her by her armpits as she does her business. He always wipes her gently as well, despite Grete insisting she knows how to do it herself, and reminds her that girls should always wipe from front to back because they're built differently than boys and have little holes where boys have little tails. Grete knows that much—she's changed her brothers enough times—but listens compliantly nevertheless, because that's what children ought to do. Listen to their parents. Because parents know best.

Grete grows to loathe the outhouse. She holds it in for as long as she can and tries not to drink too much water even on the hottest days, so as not to make frequent trips to the dreaded place.

When *Mutti*'s parents arrive from the city to work on the farm in exchange for food, it's *Oma* Anna who notices Grete squatting with her heel pressed against her buttocks one day.

"What are you doing, *Maus*?"

"I have to poo."

"Do you want me to take you?"

"No. I'm afraid of it."

"What are you afraid of? The dark?"

A pause. Eventually, "Spiders."

Grandmother Anna nods her understanding and points to a bush next to which she's been weeding. "Go right here and tell me when you're done. It could use some fertilizer."

It's such a strange relief to be going alone and in the open, away from darkness, creepy-crawly critters, and her father's hot hands.

Oma Anna buries it later without a word and resumes her weeding, and Grete climbs up into the hayloft and wonders what an easy solution was there the entire time. She also wonders why her father never came up with it.

FIFTEEN

NOW

Refugees pour in from the east now that there's not enough manpower to contain the Soviet offensive. These are ethnic Germans, from westerns parts of Poland and Sudetenland—women mostly, tugging carts filled with whatever possessions they can carry and children or the elderly sitting on top. Original warhorses, dating back to prehistoric times. Maggie watches their funereal procession and wonders how it is that it's men who always start the wars but it's women who always pay the price. She snaps pictures of them as they trudge forward, much too exhausted and weighed down with their troubles and entire moveable households to pay the foreign correspondent any heed.

Snap. A shoe held together by a string, a detached sole slapping through sleet.

Snap. A child's pram abandoned on the side of the road due to a broken wheel.

Snap. An old woman picking her way along the rubble with the help of a makeshift walking stick.

Maggie steals a few glances around and, after ensuring there are no GIs in the immediate proximity, approaches the group of refugee women and points at her C patch with a soft smile. They scoff at the healthy-looking American and her fancy camera and wonder out loud if they—American women, that is—are truly so bored as to travel overseas just to feel something. Should have lived through what they lived through. Then, they'd think twice, spoiled little adventure-seekers.

"I'm not here for the thrill of it," Maggie interrupts them suddenly in German. "I'm here to hear your stories. So, please, tell me."

They stop and stare at her with a mixture of mistrust and surprise.

"Your German may be excellent, but *you're* not German," one of them states eventually after looking Maggie's uniform up and down.

"I'm a journalist. I'm here to report things, that's all. Does it matter what I am?"

"It does," another woman chimes in, more resigned than spoiling for a fight. "Everyone knows that the victor writes history."

Maggie has nothing to say to that—the woman is right—but she doesn't want to let the group go either. She senses something about them, and not just as a journalist hounding for a story. They carry their sorrows around them like mourning veils. Maggie sees in their eyes the reflection of her own grief which they so thoroughly try to hide.

"All right, no interviews," she says, making a step to prevent them from leaving. "Woman to woman," she lowers her voice further, "do you need any feminine supplies? The US Army sent me here with more stuff than I could use in a year and my family keep sending me parcels with feminine products. I'll gladly share if you need them."

The women stand there in somewhat stunned silence, either from Maggie's directness or the offer itself, but then, suddenly, the one in the blue kerchief holding her hair in place bursts into tears.

Unsure if she offended the German lady, or if it is something unrelated to her entirely, Maggie produces a handkerchief and hands it to the woman in the only gesture of comfort she can think of at the moment.

The woman takes it, hides her face in it, and soon squats next to the building's wall, resting her back against it as she sobs.

"Now why would you have to go and mention that for?" Their leader, the tall brunette who accused Maggie of not belonging to the German race, turns to face the journalist once again.

Her companion, the one in the green coat who correctly stated her opinion on the writers of history, shushes her quickly. "Don't be rude, Frieda. She's trying to help."

"We were doing just fine without her help."

The woman in the green coat waves the sentiment off with an impatient gesture, takes Maggie by the elbow, and leads her a few steps away from the group. "Don't be cross with my friend, please. She's been through an ordeal... well, we all have. That young girl, the one who's crying, that's her sister. She's very protective of her."

Maggie nods fiercely. She understands it all too well. She would kill for her own sister in the blink of an eye.

"You stay there and I'll walk with her to get the goods," the woman in the green coat tells the others. "You'll thank me later, when you come to your senses." She gestures for Maggie to lead the way and continues in a confidential tone: "My name's Angela—Geli. We're from Sudetenland. As soon as our troops pulled out, the Soviets poured in. Frankly, we didn't have the time to pack anything. One day our boys are gone and, in a few hours, the Ivans are there, kicking the doors in and helping themselves to everything that's there for the taking. Made themselves right at home whenever they wanted, ordered us around to make them food and bring out whatever alcohol we had. We did—what else were we to do? They ate and drank and broke whatever they could loot first and then got to raping. For several days it was going on as the new troops replaced the old ones that moved on with their offensive. Imagine sweaty, filthy troops marching through your town, through your home, helping themselves to your body one by one when your own husband is locked in the bedroom."

Maggie throws a glance in the direction of the group over her shoulder, but Geli's chuckle stops her question in its tracks.

"No, there isn't anything wrong with your eyes. You haven't missed him. When I began packing and telling him we better leave because I couldn't take it much longer there, he announced that I should head off myself and he was staying put *until this all blows over*." A sardonic smirk twists the woman's lips. "Didn't have to spell it out, but the feeling was there. I was dirtied by the Ivans. He would never touch me again for as long as he lived."

Some ancient, righteous anger surges in Maggie and boils her very blood. "So let me get this straight: judging by his racial stance, he likely voted for the NSDAP. He most likely supported the occupation of the Sudetenland by the German troops. He likely supported the entire idea of the war, but now that the tide has turned, he is suddenly disgusted that the consequences caught up—not even with him—but with you? And it's all somehow your fault?"

"You don't have to reason with me," Geli chuckles bitterly. "That's why I haven't looked back since I left. I'll be reminded of that week for the rest of my life by my own brain. I don't need verbal reminders from my own husband on a daily basis, thank you very much."

They walk into a former boarding house, where Maggie and several officers presently quarter, and ascend the stairs to the second floor, where Maggie's room is. Once inside, Maggie pulls

a backpack from under her bed and dumps its contents on top
of the bed cover. "Same happened with Frieda's sister?" she
asks, collecting feminine hygiene packets that have amassed at
the bottom of the backpack but now lie covering the rest of the
backpack's contents.

"Same, but worse. She thinks she's with child. That's why
she began crying when you mentioned the stuff," she says with
a nod toward the discreetly packaged women's pads.

Maggie freezes for a moment with about two dozen of the
pads in her hands before regaining control of her emotions and
gesturing toward Geli's bag. "Has she seen a doctor yet?"

The woman shakes her head and opens her bag for Maggie
to dump the pads inside. "We've been walking without stopping
this entire time. Crossed the whole country, figuring this ought
to be far enough from the Ivans. We'll try to find someone for
her later, as soon as we settle."

"It may be too late then. From her reaction, I gather she
doesn't intend on keeping it?"

"Pfft. What woman in her right mind would? If it's too late,
she'll just leave it somewhere, I suppose, once she has it."

"I can ask one of our doctors to help." The words leave Maggie's
lips before she even considers what she's offering and just how will
she go about it. Her very feminine essence issues them instead of
the brain hardwired for logic. It's just something a woman will do
for another, out of solidarity, because if we haven't been there yet,
we will be, and if not us, then our sisters or mothers or daughters or
friends. Every woman knows a woman who has been through
things she hates talking about. Not every woman wants to listen.
Certainly not every woman chooses to help, but Maggie does.
Because that's what sisters do. "If you wait for me here, I'll be back
in a few. Medical quarters are only ten minutes away."

Geli nods.

When Maggie returns in less than half an hour, she finds

Geli still standing in the exact same spot. The woman's face is a hopeful question mark.

Maggie is both beaming and trembling with her entire body, as if there's suddenly not enough oxygen in the room. "Let's go get the girl. Our doctor, he'll help her. He'll have to do it here though, not in the hospital. Better for her though, because she'll need to rest for a while after he's done. No more marching, at least not for the next couple of days."

They're running down the stairs, both out of breath, and burst outside at the same time, in a rush to announce the news to Frieda and her sister.

The young woman blinks uncomprehendingly from one woman to another, crushing Maggie's handkerchief in her bloodless fist. "Right now?" she whispers finally, her eyes opening wider as the lines of agony gradually smooth over her pale, pretty face. "He can do it right now?"

"Yes, but it has to be only you and your sister in the room," Maggie says, not minding in the slightest the fact that Frieda's hand is clutching her forearm with a force the young woman likely doesn't realize. "You can stay there with me too for the next couple of days, but after that, I'll be leaving, together with our vanguard. I'm sure the lady who owns the boarding house will let you stay longer after the troops leave."

"We have gold hidden on us," Frieda says readily. "We'll be able to pay, it's no trouble at all."

When they enter Maggie's room, the US Army field medic is already there. He works fast and clean and is finished in no time.

"That's all?" Frieda asks for her sister, who lies back on the pillows, white as a sheet from the pain but smiling faintly all the same. Not a sound escaped her lips even when the medic's tools dug into her tender flesh without any anesthesia—it was Maggie's profound conviction she would have tolerated her limb being sawn off without a peep as long as it meant she could be rid of the last remnants of her violation.

Maggie translates the question and the answer that follows. "She wasn't too far along, so yes. Just had to scrape some tissue off and she's done. She'll bleed for a couple of days, nothing more than an ordinary period. If she suddenly starts hemorrhaging more, call me right that instant. If I'm already gone, find another doctor, but if you mention my name, I'll deny everything."

"Oh no, we would never!"

They're still thanking him as he leaves, with Maggie on his heels.

The walk back to the field hospital where he has an office is silent. Neither of them speaks even when they're inside and the door is closed and locked and the field doctor is undoing his uniform trousers. Maggie undoes hers as well and bends over his desk with patient charts neatly stacked on one side and forms on the other. It's over in only a few minutes and the doctor is gentleman enough to offer Maggie a sterile napkin to clean herself with behind a screen, despite using prophylactics.

"If you report any of this, I'll report you as a spy," he drops casually as he disposes of the evidence.

Maggie pushes the screen away and tosses the napkin in the same trash basket, on top of his napkin ball. "Why would I report any of this?"

"Initially, I refused to even listen to you."

"I know."

"It's you who refused to leave off and insisted on showing me 'all your gratitude' in exchange for my medical services, which I didn't want to perform in the first place."

"I know."

"All to aid German women."

"Yes."

"Very suspicious."

Maggie says nothing.

"You also concealed the fact that you speak German from your superiors yet you speak it fluently."

"I forgot to mention it." Maggie sighs and, for a split second, wonders if it was worth it, trading her body for another woman's chance to regain control of hers, but feels that yes, it was. It feels right, there in the pit of her stomach. Disgusting, but so very right at the same time.

No, wrong terminology. She's not disgusting, she's *disgusted*.

With her head held high, she unlocks the door, pushes it open, and grins at the field medic. "Thank you for your help, doc. Be well."

"You too."

"While I'm here, got any Luminal or Benzedrine?" He squeezed what he could out of her; might as well squeeze what she can out of him, self-loathing be damned.

"A junkie, to top it all off." The field medic regards her with disgust but digs in his well-stocked shelves all the same. He throws a couple of familiar cardboard packs into Maggie's awaiting hands and refuses to spare her another glance as he takes his seat at his desk. "Close the door after yourself."

Maggie blows him a sarcastic kiss and leaves it purposely open.

Later that week, when she sends the story on widespread rapes to the *Times* Paris headquarters, she receives a short telegram back:

Soviets are allies. Report Nazi crimes only. Next assignment— Zipper is GIs' best friend: ways new fashion invention saves lives.

She still stares at it later in her bed, stares for a very long time, until Luminal dissolved in whiskey blurs the words into senseless nothing.

SIXTEEN

THEN

Mutti is asking Papa where the money has gone. She has just been paid and there was enough to see them through the next two weeks even after they paid Frau Götz for their rooms. Papa throws an empty bottle of brandy at her, which narrowly misses *Mutti*'s head and smashes into the wall behind her. That's for questioning his authority. Big-mouthed bitch.

From the corner in which she's hiding, Grete sees *Mutti* stand her ground despite the danger that emanates from Papa in almost physical waves of heated, poisonous rage. Why does he get to keep the money that she makes? It's not like she takes it for herself, she needs it for their children. To feed them and clothe them; she doesn't even buy them toys, she makes them out of whatever materials she can to salvage the money. And he goes and drinks it all—

Papa's suddenly on his feet, a fist balled, ready to strike.

Grete lurches to her feet as well and positions herself between her parents, bawling her little eyes out, hugging her *Mutti* by her legs, protecting her from Papa's rage with her three-year-old body.

He notices her, mellows suddenly as if by some dark magic.

He's all smiles as he lowers to his haunches in front of the little girl. "No, no, don't cry, Gretchen, *Maus*. It's your old Papa. You don't have to be afraid of me. I love you more than anything." He's stroking her hair with infinite gentleness when all that Grete wants is for him to disappear from their lives once and for all. She's not afraid that he's going to hurt her, she's afraid he'll hurt her *Mutti* and then who's going to fend for her? "All right, all right. Papa will go for a walk and you go to sleep. When you wake up in the morning, it'll all be a dream. Yes?"

Grete nods, because agreeing means he'll leave and that's all she wants.

Leave. Go away, scary monster. Leave us alone.

SEVENTEEN

NOW

Maggie waits together with the rest of the troop in front of the mail truck. By the time it's caught up with her and their fast-moving vanguard, there are four parcels in it for her and a whole bunch of letters. Mommy, Daddy, and Norma write to her every few days.

Next to her, another Maggie shifts impatiently from one foot to another. Maggie knew of her from Lee but only met the young blonde for the first time here in Germany. Back in London, when the small female correspondent troop celebrated their reunion and Christmas, Maggie Higgins lived with her husband. Now, it appears, Lee's prediction has come true, like most of them have: no ring on Higgins' finger. Only a camera at the ready and questions pouring from her curious tongue as soon as they exchanged handshakes.

"Spill it out, namesake. What's your secret?"

"What secret?"

"Whose bed did you have to jump in to be allowed on the frontline the entire time the rest of us had to report on Pétain's bowel movements and share a room with Hemingway's girl-friends in Paris?"

Maggie smirked at the smart mouth which sounded just like her articles—curt, to the point, and taking no prisoners. Higgins looked just like her portrait too: blonde, pretty, and deceivingly innocent. "Whoever happened to be at the frontline," she countered, deadpan.

Higgins must have appreciated the response. "Your article about the Malmedy massacre deserves a Pulitzer."

Maggie detected no flattery in her voice, only the honest opinion of a fellow wordsmith. "I thought the same about your front page on the women liberators of Paris."

"Thank you, but no one much cares about women's stories. That's why it was printed in *Mademoiselle* instead of *Stars and Stripes* or my very own *Tribune*."

Maggie Sullivan recognized a kindred spirit in Maggie Higgins. It was anyone's guess how much time they would spend working and lodging together, but for now, it was "two Maggies for the price of one" as the local GIs joked whenever they saw the two women walking together side by side.

Higgins is still waiting by the mail truck, but Maggie backs away from the vehicle so as to allow others to claim their little pieces of home. No one has the patience to venture far. They pour into the nearest taverns and houses and sit cross-legged right on the floor as they tear into the parcel paper and envelopes. Maggie wants to do the same, but, instead, she picks up her Kodak dangling from her neck and snaps photos of the GIs' animated faces. They smile differently when they produce photos out of the envelopes and show each other wives, brides, or other family members. There's impossibly touching, somewhat childish, warmth to them, caught on camera in those intimate moments. These are the photos Maggie loves taking the best. If only all of humanity could finally get it into their heads that this is what all of them truly need—to love and be loved, to co-exist in peace, instead of blowing each other to pieces.

In Maggie's own parcel are snippets of the Brooklyn life she left behind. Mommy managed to stuff Mr. Vaccaro's, their beloved butcher's, smoked sausages inside, along with cookies from Macy's—the fancy, Christmas kind in bright red boxes tied with golden ribbons. There are warm socks Mommy knitted herself, which will come in very handy since Maggie's toes have long been poking through the old ones despite all the darning she's done in her free time. There's a new scarf and mittens and gloves, and even a small hat with a note attached to it: *I asked around and the GI mothers said this kind will fit just fine under a helmet. You are wearing it, aren't you? See that you do!*

There's a newly published book by Simone de Beauvoir, *She Came to Stay*, and Maggie's old favorites Daddy must have taken from her shelf: *A Room of One's Own*, *Three Guineas*, and *The Little Girl* by Katherine Mansfield. Maggie smiles as, sure enough, a note in his loopy cursive falls out of Virginia Woolf's *A Room of One's Own*:

> *I doubt you have any time to pass, but in case you need something familiar to keep under your pillow at night, here are your literary lady friends. Also, your mother told me to underline the fact that she doesn't approve of de Beauvoir, but knowing how much you admire her, she bought it for you as soon as she saw it in the bookstore.*

The familiar sound of a picture being taken startles Maggie back to reality. She blinks twice—the first time because she finds herself on the other end of the camera, and the second because it's Orso who's smiling at her from behind it instead of Higgins, who is prone to such tomfooleries. Orso, her fellow Brooklynite, the war crimes investigator whom she left behind what feels like ages ago.

Overwhelmed with unexpected emotion, Maggie cries out his name and throws herself onto his neck, books scattered around as she clutches him in a bear hug.

"You were fast, but I caught up at long last," he says, laughing into her hair. He smells like home and feels like it.

"Look what my parents sent me!" After releasing him, Maggie holds up the sausage and cookies for him to see.

Orso narrows his eyes at the sausage, then takes a deep smell and prods its wrapped end with his fingers. "If you tell me they got it from a local Irish butcher, I'll call a lie. That's an Italian product if ever I saw one."

"Could be Polish," Maggie taunts him with a serious face.

Orso shakes his head, as certain as a sunrise. "Italian."

Maggie finally gives up her game. "All right. You know your stuff."

"Don't forget, I'm an investigator." He arches a playful brow.

"Which brings me to a question: what are you doing here? And with a camera around your neck, no less?"

Orso's beaming smile dims a notch. He pauses for a few moments, just enough for Maggie to suspect the gravity of the situation.

"We can discuss it now or we can enjoy this fine Italian sausage and some nice French Brie I happen to have, together with some delectable Beaujolais, and leave it for later."

"Now that you mention it, I smelled some fine, real coffee in one of my parcels as well," Maggie concedes with an ease that surprises even herself. "How about I make us some of that first, we'll dip our cookies in it, and only then we'll get to your wine?"

"That's all backward."

"True, but bad news goes down easier with good wine. And something tells me it is bad."

"Not bad per se..."

"But not festive cookies and coffee-type news."

"No. Definitely not."

Orso helps her carry her parcels to the room he's staying in —quite an improvement from the quarters he had to share with

Harlow when Maggie had just met him. His German landlady doesn't wish to hear of her "guests" brewing the coffee themselves and insists on "the children" going back upstairs—she'll brew, pour, slice, arrange, and bring everything up herself.

"It'll be hard to go back to New York," Orso says as soon as they're upstairs. "I'm getting used to this hospitality."

Maggie's smile is somewhat crooked in response. "They're going out of their way because we're Americans. And they heard from the eastern refugees what the Soviet troops do when they come through their parts."

"I heard about that, too." Orso lowers his eyes.

"Widespread rape, starting with children as young as seven years old and ending with grandmothers as old as their nineties."

Orso shakes his head. "Detestable business."

"On which I'm not allowed to report." Maggie smirks cuttingly.

"We aren't investigating it either," Orso responds quietly. "Not even allowed to mention it once we meet with our Soviet allies."

"When do you think we'll meet?"

"Judging by how fast both fronts are moving, I'd say another month or so."

"Sometime in April?"

"I would guess."

They fall silent as they sit side by side, staring into worlds of their own. Not even a year here, in Europe, and both have already seen enough to last a lifetime.

"Do you know if the troops caught up with that Panzer army group?" Maggie asks, suddenly remembering what initially brought them together. "The one that slaughtered our GIs by Malmedy?"

"No, but we found out which Panzer group it was. Peiper, he's the man in charge of it. Himmler's former adjutant, I hear.

Harlow and I, we're currently gathering a dossier on him. If he served as Himmler's adjutant for as long as we think, he'll be witness to multiple crimes against humanity committed by his immediate boss."

Maggie steals a glance at him from under lowered lashes. "Do you think I can see it?"

The landlady enters, all smiles, a heavy wooden cutting board laden with cold cuts and coffee mugs in her hands.

Orso waits for her to deposit it and only asks once the door is closed after her: "Why, do you want to report on it?"

Maggie chooses the answer after a quick consideration. "If you let me, I gladly will, but frankly, I just wanted to see the names you may have there."

Orso's mug of steaming coffee freezes inches away from his lips. "Why?" he repeats, putting it down.

Maggie stares at the cold cuts instead of him. They have long lost all appeal to her, but it's simply easier to stare at them instead of meeting his inquisitive eye. "I will tell you. In time. Eventually," she proceeds carefully, "as I'm not even sure that those I'm looking for still exist. And I'm even less sure as to what I shall do if they do. My sister is in the sanitarium, you see. And I came here to— No, you know what? It won't even make sense to you with whatever minimal details I can tell you, but I'm just not ready to tell you the entire story, I just—physically —I can't."

"It's all right, you don't have to." Orso's hand finds hers and covers it and only then does Maggie feel it shake violently under his. Only then does she taste tears she didn't realize were streaming down her face. Everything inside her chest burns and she hasn't had a single drop of that French wine of his yet. It's the past that's churning old venom from the depths of her very soul. She's here, but Maggie still doesn't know if there's a way of purging it once and for all.

"I'm sorry," she says, wiping the wetness from her cheeks with the back of her hand.

"Don't apologize. There's no shame in crying."

"I know. It's just... I hate myself when I'm like this. I didn't cry when I was wounded."

"I imagine you didn't. One of your fellow reporters wrote a very nice article about your bravery under fire when your troop was fighting those *Hitlerjugend* kids."

Maggie cringes and laughs once again. "Please, don't remind me. He snapped a photo of me, too, when I was typing an article with a wounded arm. Much like you did, just this morning."

"You don't realize how well you come out in those pictures."

"I don't like being in pictures, I only like taking them."

"But people still take photos of you, whether you like it or not."

"My fellow correspondents—who also happen to wear skirts —and I were talking about it a month or so ago in London. You fellows are fascinated with us for some reason, and meanwhile, we're just doing our jobs. There's nothing remarkable about us whatsoever."

"But there is." Orso laughs, genuinely amazed by such a lack of self-awareness. "Not only do you look so very inspiring, whether you're typing with a wounded arm or reading letters from home on the frontline, you're also a female war correspondent. One of the very first."

"Lee Miller is a war correspondent. And so is Rita Vanderwert, Helen Kirkpatrick, Margaret Bourke-White, Ann Stringer, Martha Gellhorn—"

"I get your point, but there are *still* less of you than I can count on the fingers of my hands. You're a symbol, like it or not. You're paving the way for others. Like these writers I assume you enjoy?" He waves Woolf's book playfully in the air. "Do you know that my nieces are pinning your articles to their bedroom walls? My sister wrote to me when I mentioned that I met you. She asked for an autograph for the girls, but you jumped into some passing jeep and disappeared before I could ask you."

"Oh no, I'm so sorry!" Maggie moans, covering her face with her hands. "Now I feel like even more of a tool than before." Her voice comes out all muffled through her fingers.

"Don't you go crying on me again," he warns her smilingly.

"No, I won't. It's passed." Maggie inhales deeply, her brilliant eyes indeed dry once again.

Orso hands her a mug and a cookie and tells her to drink before the coffee gets cold. "And you don't owe me any explanations. I'll get you the dossier, read all you like."

He does, the same very day; drops it by Maggie's temporary quarters in a war widow's house and tells her it's hers, but just for the night. Harlow won't appreciate it if it's not in the office by the morning.

"Now is a good time to tell me why you're here, so close to the frontline," Maggie says softly, the dossier burning like hot coals through the skin of her open palms.

Orso pauses near the door. In the semi-darkness of the small bedroom she shares with Higgins, who is now thankfully gone somewhere, his expression is unreadable. "Have you seen any Soviet war correspondents' reports from their side?"

"We read most frontline papers in the morning, yes."

"You know about the multiple extermination camps they've already liberated then?"

"I do." Photos of Soviet journalists taken in Auschwitz-Birkenau are seared into her memory like a brand. Children, as young as five, bundled in everything they could find over their striped uniforms, rolling their sleeves to show numbers tattooed into their tiny forearms as if they were nothing more than cattle. Men with legs so thin, their kneecaps protrude grotesquely under shirts hanging on their emaciated bodies like rags. And, the worst of all, warehouses with mounds and mounds of artificial limbs, shoes, glasses, wedding rings, and the hair of all those who would never return from that human slaughterhouse.

She'll give her right limb to accompany the American troops to Buchenwald, which is getting closer by the moment and, hopefully, later—Dachau. Then, when she brings the photos she personally took back home, no Schenks will be able to say that this was all nothing but a Jewish fantasy.

Orso goes on: "One of the future indictment articles, Crimes Against Humanity, with which many Nazi perpetrators will be charged, sprang from those reports."

Maggie nods, all attention.

"They suggested we collaborate in investigating it together, so the Nazi criminals don't reject the charge solely because it stems from the Soviet side only. They have lots of bad blood between them. The Soviets had it the worst from the Nazis and now the Nazis are on the receiving end, and if the world wants a legitimate trial with acceptable results, it should come from all four sides: USSR, UK, France, and the US. After we liberate whatever we find on our, western, side, we'll join forces with them in investigating all of the extermination sites. I have already seen the photos they took. Imagine Malmedy and multiply it by thousands. Not even GIs, but civilians slaughtered in cold blood by the Nazi *Einsatzgruppen*—their SS execution squads. Piles of naked bodies everywhere, bones in crematoriums or open pits... I know, it's hard to believe—"

"No, not hard," Maggie says. "That's what's been going on in those camps all along. Our neighbors—they're Jewish—and the rest of the community who still had relatives in Europe, they've been saying it for a few years now. Scarce information, passed along through the grapevine from the rare survivors who managed to escape, or gentiles who risked all to tell the world in a smuggled note or letter. Certainly not enough for the naysayers to admit that 'tales' of Jewish ghettos and extermination camps were true. But now we're very close to Buchenwald." Maggie's hand reaches for her Kodak of its own volition, brushes its cold exterior. "And once I take the photos, then they'll see. And I *will* take them." No matter the cost.

She'll keep moving with the vanguard troops and sleep to the lullaby of the air-raid sirens and risk getting shot at so that finally, the world sees the ugly truth through the mirror of her lens. So they can no longer pretend, ignore or, worse still, deny it.

The saddest part, Maggie sees a familiar ugly mug in the midst of it. With sudden clarity, she realizes that this mass annihilation stems from one single thing, ancient as the world itself: one man's desire to dominate, to subjugate, to possess, and to control. Death to anyone who dares to stand in his path. Be whipped into submission or perish.

Chills travel down her arms and she rubs them vigorously, her mind already racing, caught in between the past, the present, and the future, over which her generation thankfully still has some control of. They can turn the tide in the right direction if they open their eyes to it. Now, if they would only let her write about it, put it in all the right words—

"I know you will." Orso's tone is soft as velvet and yet it still jostles Maggie out of herself like an electric shock. "And I'm sorry that I have upset you with this."

"You haven't upset me." She's all feverish and hunched over, holding herself together with her pale hands; it's no wonder he misinterpreted her state. "Thank you for the dossier."

"You're welcome." A gentle smile touches upon his lips as

his hand rests on the handle of the door. "Do you want me to stay here while you read it?"

"It's all right." Maggie throws the dossier onto the bed covers like a grenade at the enemy tank and then narrows her eyes slightly as something occurs to her. "Peiper, you say that SS tank commander's name is? What's his first name?"

"Joachim. 'Jochen.' Why? You heard of him before?" Orso hovers in the doorway, trying to read the clues on her face.

Maggie digs into her memory as if into a grave but comes up empty-handed. "No. He's the old guard, I assume?"

"Not at all," Orso replies with a smirk. "A young Nazi squirt, late twenties or thereabouts."

"Really?" Maggie's heart skips a bit. The age seems to fit, only not to the one she was thinking about. "Any unusual first names among his men?" She could ask for the last name directly, but it's too much of a risk. Orso is one of the good ones, for sure, but he'll still start digging and asking questions, and, God forbid, he uncovers Maggie's family's connection to all this mess. Best keep it to herself, track them down on her own.

"Unusual first names?" Orso blinks. "Like what?"

"Something Nordic, like Ragnar?" How alien it sounds even to her, the name long entombed and undisturbed for ages. Can't be the father, but could be one of the sons her mother never mentions. And if her assumptions are correct concerning all three, that's precisely where boys their age would have ended up: the SS. The father would kill them before he would let them be anything else.

"I can't recall off the top of my head, but keep in mind that many first names in the dossier are abbreviated and sometimes altogether incorrect. Don't forget, the information at this stage is supplied by the captured SS personnel and many of them either clam up entirely or are sly as snails and feed us misinformation on purpose. Why? Is there some lead you're pursuing?"

"Officially, I'm pursuing zippers," Maggie mutters, her mind still much too far away, and opens the file before he can ask anything else.

From the corner of her eye, she sees Orso pull the door closed after himself as silently as possible.

EIGHTEEN

THEN

It's Grete's fourth birthday and when *Mutti* brings her home from the park where she rode the carousel and ate candy apples and ice cream—a rare treat in itself, just like *Mutti*'s day off on a Saturday—Papa surprises her by crawling out of the bedroom with a huge stuffed tiger on his back. He's making roaring noises and Grete is squealing with delight at both the size of the toy and the fact that for once Papa doesn't smell of brandy. He's sober and has a present for her birthday, and for a few hours, Grete hopes that everything will be all right from now on.

But the next day, *Mutti* is putting her makeup on—it's Sunday and they'll be going to the circus that has traveled all the way here from Romania—and Papa goes to hug her from behind, and she gets mascara in her eye and runs to the communal bathroom to wash it off, and here it is, the screaming, alerting the entire tenement that the Bullers are at it again.

"You always do this, Wald!"

"Apologies for trying to show affection for my own wife! Won't happen again. Nasty bitch!"

"There are chemicals in mascara! Do you want me blind?"

"Well then, why are you putting it on your face in the first place?"

"Trying to look pretty for you!"

He grumbles something under his breath. Grete hears the familiar sound of the bottle clinking. It's not a secret any more she needs to keep from *Mutti*. He drinks out in the open now and to hell with what his wife has to say about it.

She stands in the middle of the hallway, torn between the two biggest parts of her entire world, alone and miserable in her birthday dress, white bows in her hair.

Awakened by their parents' screams, the twins begin to wail, adding to the cacophony of sounds around her. Holding her ears covered, Grete escapes to the staircase and, from there, to the street, to wait it all out.

None of the girls with whom she usually plays are out and so she waits by herself on a bench in the shadow of a dead tree which used to scare her as a child, but now that she's turned four, she doesn't feel like a child any longer. She's seen too much, felt too much, and long ago learned that monsters don't come out of trees or crawl from under the bed: they wear human skin instead.

She picks up a piece of limestone from the ground and begins to draw a cat she so wants *Mutti* to allow her to have. All of a sudden, a pair of hands lift her in the air. Her godparents are here—Papa's comrade from the war, *Onkel* Sander, and his wife, Lina. Lina kisses Grete with her bright red lips and smooths the lipstick prints with her thumbs over Grete's cheeks.

"Doesn't blush look good on her, Sander?"

"Sure does. She'll turn heads when she grows up."

Lina laughs and shows Grete a toy tea set she's got her for her birthday. Grete's eyes grow big with wonder and disbelief— a real toy set, not handmade but bought in a department store. Could this be the best birthday ever? But Lina takes it away before Grete has a chance to hold it even for a second. "I'll leave it inside with your *Mutti*. No sense taking it with us to the circus, right?"

Lina disappears inside and Grete is squirming in *Onkel* Sander's arms, hoping to be put down so she can run after Lina and study her present some more, but he's holding her fast. He asks her what she's most excited to see in the circus. Grete thinks about it for some time. She's never been to a circus before but has seen multiple posters advertising it.

"Lions," she finally responds.

"Why?"

"Because they're the biggest cats and in Africa, everyone's afraid of them."

"Not when they're put in a cage and a ringmaster whips them," *Onkel* Sander laughs. He wears the same paramilitary uniform Papa put on that morning. It's rough against Grete's tender skin.

"When they get angry enough, they still kill people," she insists. "I know. It was in the newspapers, Papa told me."

"But then they get shot themselves."

Grete doesn't say anything to that. Death is a vague notion to her still—she isn't sure how to feel about it.

"They are fascinating animals, I'll give you that," *Onkel* Sander says in reconciliation, finally setting Grete down on the bench, to her relief. "The only big cats that have fur tufts at the tip of their tails. Did you know that?"

Grete nods. She saw lions in the moving pictures, she knows what their tails look like.

"Does your tail have a fur tuft?" *Onkel* Sander asks and, before Grete can even give him a look to see if he's stupid to ask such questions, for humans don't have tails, he suddenly shoves his hand under her skirt and inside her new white panties.

Acting on sheer impulse, Grete twists like a snake stung by a scorpion and sinks her small baby teeth into her godfather's wrist, hard.

He yanks his hand back and jumps away, shaking it in stunned surprise just as Grete's parents come out of the doors with Lina in tow, laughing about some joke they've shared inside.

"What's the matter with your hand, comrade?" Papa asks *Onkel* Sander, smiling as if he wasn't screaming at his wife just minutes ago.

"She bit me," he replies, incredulous. "Grete, she actually bit me."

Grete feels heat rising in her cheeks as all four adults turn to look at her. For some reason, she can't tell them why she bit her godfather. She isn't even sure if she should have. Girls ought to be nice at all times, *Mutti* says. They ought to sit with their legs closed and be polite to everyone. Good girls certainly don't bite.

But he tried to put his hand where he wasn't supposed to, to her private parts Grete knows no one is supposed to touch. But what if it was only a joke and she overreacted and it was her fault all along, because she wasn't a good girl like others, she was damaged somehow? That's why Papa made her run around naked and always bathed her himself and wiped her privates even if she told him so many times that she knew how to do it herself. What if she brought it all on herself somehow?

On the verge of tears, she forces the words out of herself, "I was only pretending to be a lion."

If only she was one, all claws and muscle and razor-sharp teeth. No one would touch her then.

Thankfully, Papa bursts into laughter. "She's obsessed with jungle cats of late. I got her a tiger just yesterday and I swear, she slept with the damned thing! Oh, stop shaking your delicate little wrist! Did she really inflict so much damage, this little fawn?"

Onkel Sander mumbles something about "a fawn being a spawn is more like it," but Papa jests about mentioning the incident at the next Party meeting and *Onkel* Sander clams up for the rest of the day.

Grete watches lions jump through hoops later, inside the red circus tent, and feels sorry for them. If it were her, she'd bite the ringmaster's head off. And then, shoot her if you want. She'll die with a satisfied smile on her face.

NINETEEN

NOW

Inside the room she shares with Higgins—no electricity, no running water—Maggie opens Joachim Peiper's file. There's a full profile on him in the first two pages, along with photographs of a handsome, polished young man nearly always behind Himmler's shoulder. Maggie flips through those pages—it isn't Peiper who she's interested in. She only stops when she comes across a list of possible connections, associations, fellow servicemen, and superiors.

Peiper has had an eventful service, even prior to enlisting in the Waffen-SS Panzer division. They are plenty of names in that list. They aren't in alphabetical order and most have numbers with cross-reference file numbers next to them.

Through the thin wall, she hears the nurses lodging in the adjoining room making themselves dinner on the kerosene-fueled stovetop and wonders where Maggie is. She never rests, her namesake. If she's not chasing a story, she's learning German by playing educational records instead of the music ones the nurses prefer, or forging friendships with local pilots who may just give her a lift whenever a hot tip comes through. She's young and hungry and has the grip of a pitbull and

Maggie can't help but think that this is what she could have been if it weren't for—

Her heart grows cold when her eyes suddenly catch the name she's been trying to unearth and erase in equal measure: Sturmbannführer Buller. Next to it, no first name but a written word instead: *Buchenwald*, and a question mark beside it. Under it, in a space left by the typewriter, ~~Totenkopf~~ crossed out and *Waffen-SS, Battle Group Peiper, newly enlisted* added in red pencil. Even the rank is right, likely proudly carried by a former shock troop officer from the First World War into the Second.

"Battle Group Peiper," Maggie whispers as if to taste the name of the troop named after its ruthless commander and snorts with all the derision she feels pulsing through her veins. He belongs with Himmler's former adjutant, all right. What a perfect unit for him and what a fitting end to such a "glorious" career, shooting unarmed GIs in open fields along with his new comrades.

She and Norma wondered many times, between pulls on a shared cigarette, about the life Buller may have led. Norma's guess was a new marriage, but to someone with money this time.

"She has to be young, too," Norma would say, squinting through the rings of tobacco smoke hovering languidly between the sisters. "Younger ones, they're easier to impress with tales of old battlefield glory. Gotta be a nationalist as well—he won't go near anyone liberal or communist or women's emancipation types—so she's already buying all that 'serve your husband and procreate in the name of the Fatherland' crap. He won't risk a second mom."

"I don't think he'd remarry at all," Maggie would counter, teeth tearing into the skin near the nail already bleeding. "Must be in the SA now, purging the streets of Berlin of the remainder of the Reds and Jews. Now that Hitler's in power and he can legally assault people like a good, law-abiding, swastika-bearing citizen, that must occupy him full-time."

That was back in the 1930s. In the 1940s, when the war was burning a hole through the world map, they weren't so sure anymore. The man drank a lot, even in his youth. He could have been dead, for all they knew. Still, Maggie set off to find him as though she felt something on an instinctual level—and find him she has.

Now what?

Maggie rubs the grit from her eyes, thinks of popping to the nurses' room and inviting herself in for a drink in exchange for Macy's cookies, but finds that she can't make her limbs move. They're heavy as lead, and yet, her thoughts are even heavier.

Nose around the command post and find out where Peiper Group presently is? Screw some pilot in exchange for an airlift? And then what? Duck behind the tanks, ankle-deep in mud, and hope not to get her head torn off by the cannon before she can—what? Hope that Peiper Group surrenders and ask to interview one of its members? That won't be suspicious at all. Maggie tosses her head with a sardonic smirk at such a plan.

"Plan. There's no fucking plan," she mutters and throws another desperate glance at the wall through which singing and laughter are flowing freely. They have alcohol, the nurses. They always do. And she doesn't feel the effects of Orso's Beaujolais any longer and she just can't be sober right now. Maggie wipes her palms down her face with a moan, her mind spinning like a rodent in a wheel, faster and faster and faster.

And even in the miraculous case of her surviving the pursuit and being granted the interview, just what precisely will she do then? Ask Buller in front of the MPs how could he do what he did to his own daughter? Put a bullet through his skull without preamble—offender deceased, case closed?

But then what of Buchenwald and her promise to herself and to her neighbors' family to bring them closure? What of her mission to open the world's eyes to the horrors committed by Hitler's regime? Buller is only one criminal, who only destroyed one family, one woman's and one little girl's life. What has happened in the camps has been orchestrated and performed by multiple Bullers, against hundreds of thousands of people, authorized and encouraged by the regime they thrived in.

To go or to stay?

To remain personal or impartial?

A woman or a journalist?

The choice is far too much for her poor head, already pounding with a growing migraine, and so, Maggie shoves the dossier in her backpack and heads out. Running, once again, and to hell with it.

A journalist. Yes. It's much more important.

Delaying the inevitable, are we? another inner voice chimes in. *Hoping he'll croak in the meantime?*

Maggie ignores it.

There's a curfew in effect, an MP reminds her half-heartedly at one of the checkpoints, but Maggie taps her correspondent insignia and disarms him with a smile. Reporters get tips at all hours and breaking news doesn't wait. He waves her through with a grumble of disapproval.

Of course, Orso doesn't sleep either. Maggie finds him in his room, in the middle of the floor, surrounded by photos and reports and candles in mugs of all shapes and colors as if some ancient warlock summoning a demon at midnight. Seeing that it's her who has appeared in his humble abode, Maggie wonders, in a bout of morbid humor, what it makes her. A lost soul haunting something until her unfinished business is complete.

"That was fast," Orso says by means of hello.

"Perk of the profession. We're used to scanning through documents quickly when searching for information." Maggie picks her way carefully among the papers and sits across from him, legs crossed. "Here, so Harlow doesn't miss it in the morning."

Orso takes the dossier from her and throws it on top of the bed covers. "I don't mean to pry, but I will be able to help better if you tell me what it is that you're after. You don't have to say why."

Instead of meeting his eyes, Maggie casts her gaze around the maze of paperwork surrounding her. Now that she has found the name but decided against going after the man, she feels a relief of sorts, a temporary one, the same kind experienced by a patient when a dentist has to cancel an appointment. The pain is still there and the impacted gum is still festering, but at least the torture of opening the infected tissue, of pulling the rotten tooth is delayed. And there's that small, pitiful hope: what if it stops by itself?

Maggie recalls exactly what happened to her in the very real situation that gave birth to the metaphorical one just now. She, too, hoped to wait the wisdom tooth out, instead of extracting it. She was a new wife, much too busy cleaning the house, cooking, washing, and making appointments for her husband to have any time left for herself. After weeks of sleepless nights and far too many pain pills popped, the unbearable throbbing did go away, leaving only a faint echo of itself in its wake. But, only a couple of weeks later, Maggie suddenly woke in the middle of the night burning with fever, the sheets wet with her sweat, half of her face swollen to grotesque proportions, and her head banging as if someone was hammering red-hot nails inside her very brain.

"You could have died, you know," the emergency-room physician told her casually that night, after she came to after urgent surgery. "The poison, it doesn't stay put. It has to go somewhere. If not outside, then inside. Through the soft tissue, through the blood vessels, square into your brain. Sepsis. Blood poisoning. Death."

Death...

Norma is hiding from it presently, by means of voluntary confinement at the Bellevue Hospital. That's what festering wounds do to a person, both physical and mental.

Maggie shifts her pose. She'll have to face those demons sooner or later.

But not tonight. God, please, not tonight. Not just yet.

"Did you develop that photo you took of me?" she asks instead.

"Sure did."

"Give it here. I'll sign it for your nieces while I'm still here. You never know what to expect of me next—I like to bolt."

"That, you do."

He rises to his feet and winces slightly at the sound of his cracking knees. Maggie watches him sympathetically, knowingly. It's happened to her so many times—losing herself in work until her limbs go all pins and needles and working blood back into them turns into medieval torture. And sleeping in bedrolls in the middle of winter and riding in open jeeps, snow covering one's lap and all, doesn't quite do wonders for one's joint health. It'll catch up with them later yet, if they make it to ripe old age, that is.

"Here," Orso says, handing Maggie two identical photos printed on matte, grainy paper. It lasts much better than regular paper and will withstand long-distance travel. It's meant to be kept. Wherever he unearthed the paper from is anyone's guess, but it couldn't have been easy. Maggie suddenly feels very warm inside, as if a litter of soft rabbits nestle in the pit of her stomach. "Their names are Barbie and Jeannie— No, wait! Should we make it out to Barbara and Jean instead? I've been gone so long, I'm not even sure what they like to be called nowadays."

The imaginary bunnies' tiny paws are tickling Maggie's very soul at the sentiment—so very small, and yet, so impossibly telling. She's met fathers who have struggled to recall their children's names and ages. An uncle who is concerned with getting his nieces' names just right so as not to offend their ever-changing feelings at that delicate age is the stuff of fairy tales. "How old are they?"

"Just turned fifteen and sixteen, both in winter."

"Ah, teenagers. Now I understand the implications of using the wrong name. But wait. Fifteen and sixteen? You aren't old enough to have such big nieces. You must be my age. How old are you? Twenty-eight? Twenty-nine?"

In the shifting candlelight, Orso's teeth are white like ivory. Dark stubble is already covering the lower part of his face. His eyes are bloodshot from looking at the paperwork in such a dim light but are smiling all the same. "I'm thirty-four."

"Damn you and your Italian genes! That sausage we shared this morning? Mr. Vaccaro, who owns the butcher store it came from, he's in his seventies and yet doesn't look a day older than fifty. Just remarried, Mommy wrote it in her letter."

"When I grow up, I want to be just like him."

Maggie play-swats him and they share a laugh inside walls that haven't heard anything other than the whistling of bombs raining down from the sky and cries of horror for the past few months. A nice way to change the narrative, it occurs to Maggie.

She makes the photos out to Barbara and Jean. That way, they won't be embarrassed in the future to share the memento with friends or lovers or, who knows, maybe their children. Maggie hides a smile and thinks that a girl can certainly dream.

"Only see the world through your own two eyes," Orso reads the message she wrote for the girls and places both photos almost reverently face down, to let the ink dry. "Thank you. They'll appreciate it. And even more so as they grow up. The world is a bitch," he suddenly declares with a bitterness Maggie didn't expect from his always good-natured, level self.

She straightens up a little, visibly, but shuts her mouth

just before her reporter self blurts out the question already sitting at the tip of her tongue. Orso gave her the courtesy of not prying into her past, the least she can do is return the favor.

But, it appears, even if Maggie is not in the mood for sharing, her fellow Brooklynite is. "It's because of their mother that I got on the force," he says, digging in his breast pocket for his small notebook. In between its pages is a photo of a stunning woman any Hollywood film studio would be fortunate to put on their silver screen. Her eyebrows are fashionably plucked into two thin lines and lustrous locks crown her delicate face, but the familial resemblance between the siblings is undeniable. "Gabriella."

The pause that follows is much too long and Maggie feels something dark creeping into her thoughts.

Orso reads her like a book and shakes his head with a faint smile. "No, no, she's alive and well. I was just... remembering."

"Don't you hate it when that happens?" Maggie offers him her own brand of dark humor, which, just like alcohol and pills, numbs everything to the point where it's tolerable.

"They say lobotomies help." He shoots back a just-as-morbid reply that instantly turns him from an acquaintance to a fellow traveler. A fellow sufferer. Someone who has waded through enough cow dung flung his way by life to understand. "She was gorgeous, as you can see. The whole of Bensonhurst was in love with her. Wealthy men offered my father insane dowries for her, but he didn't bring his family to New York from Sicily to be following old village laws, despite marrying my own mother when she was only fourteen and he was sixteen, which was very much the norm then." A brisk smile. "No, he wanted for his little Gabi to finish school—something that he never did —and decide for herself what she wanted to do with her life and who she wanted to marry."

He pauses and his words hang in the air like storm clouds

heavy with rain. The room is so silent, Maggie can hear herself breathing.

"But fate has an odd sense of humor," Orso continues at length. "It followed my father across the ocean and claimed his daughter all the same. Out of all the men she could choose from, she fell in love with a gangster. He was a handsome devil, I can't deny that, but he was cold-blooded, like a snake. Which, naturally, one doesn't know right away. He courted her so beautifully, too. Rivers of flowers and brand-new cars, back when no one saw any cars where we lived, and truffles from the city and cuts of silk of all colors and patterns—we were drowning in declarations of his love. My father knew of his affiliations and didn't approve, but Gabi had fallen for him and she was turning eighteen and had finished school just like he had intended. She was an adult, there wasn't much he could do. She married the guy."

Maggie listens to him and tries not to breathe too loudly... and not to wince when he finally gets to the part that will slice like a knife—she already knows it will. Why are all of their stories so goddamn similar? And when will the vicious cycle finally be broken? And by whom? The men in their lives or the women themselves? By mothers raising their sons differently from their fathers, or by brothers putting themselves between their sisters and the wolves in sheep's clothing?

"They were very happy at first. Honeymoon in Italy, a new house he let her decorate to her taste. Barbie and Jeannie showered with gifts as soon as they were born. I don't know what the hell he was doing for the Mafia, but whatever it was, they were about to give him a button, to make him a made man—you know what I mean?"

"A promotion, yes." Everyone in New York is familiar with the Mafia and their lingo. No explanation is needed for Maggie, Irish or not.

"Well, someone from his own gang got insulted by that since he was older, did more 'work,' and deserved seniority and proximity to the boss much more than some young upstart. So, he went and spread a rumor that my brother-in-law wasn't that much of a man and couldn't even satisfy his own wife and he, someone with experience, had to visit her and show her a good time. And then he added that he wouldn't be surprised if after his visits a son would finally be born—something that my brother-in-law didn't have the balls to conceive. Gabi was pregnant then."

Another deep sigh, heavier than a headstone.

"My brother-in-law flew into such rage, he drove home, took a razor he always carried with him, slashed my sister's face, and stabbed her in the stomach."

Maggie's nail is bitten to blood, but she doesn't taste it. Neither does she feel the physical pain, the emotional is much stronger.

"She's a smart girl, my Gabi. She stopped resisting him and pretended to be dead, and, as soon as he went to the bathroom to wash up or take a piss—whatever—she called my father on the newly installed line, paid, ironically, by my brother-in-law. Only, he wasn't at home—I was. I also knew where our father kept his gun, because, as I said, even when one wants to leave Sicily, Sicily doesn't always want to leave you, and he knew that, somewhere deep in his soul, my old man." Another fond grin.

Somewhere in the house, an old cuckoo clock strikes twelve. In the distance, very mute, bombs are exploding. They hear the sounds, but they don't quite register. Both are back in Brooklyn, far away from Germany.

"My brother-in-law didn't expect to see me when I showed up on his doorstep, gun in hand. His surprise didn't last long though. He soon started laughing because, you see, he was a killer and I was a sixteen-year-old pup who only began shaving a year ago. I must have looked hilarious indeed. But I had already seen my sister lying there in the pool of blood, in the middle of her perfectly clean, white marble kitchen. I put all the bullets I had in him before he could utter a word and then took his car and drove Gabi to the hospital. They saved her, but not the baby. The doctors said it was a boy—his, of course. Gabi never so much as looked at another man, let alone cheated on her husband. She worshiped the ground on which he walked and he nearly murdered her for one idiotic rumor."

Orso picks up the photo once again. His gaze caresses the features of the woman he killed for, and rightly so.

"They could never reconstruct her face, though. The gashes were so deep, they damaged some nerves. Whenever she talks or smiles or yawns or cries, it's all mismatched and pulled in all the wrong directions." Orso waves the words off as if they aren't worthy of his sister. She's so much more than superficial beauty to him—Maggie can see it clearly in the tears he keeps stoically confined to his eyes. Not a single one spills. "We were just happy that she was alive. Well, my father was happy that both of us were alive as the police thought to arrest me and certain gangsters wanted to chop me up and bury me in different parts of the state, but their boss put a quick end to such discussions. Touching a woman or a child is against the rules. In his opinion, my brother-in-law deserved the vendetta and I had the full right to exercise it. As for the police, they closed the case quickly enough. From their perspective, I took a gangster off the streets while rightfully defending my sister and, who knows, maybe nieces from death. When I applied to join them right after school, they gladly took me. But I digress... As I said, we were all just happy that she was alive, but Gabi didn't know how to live with that new face of hers. In the end, she did decide to live for her daughters, but at first, she tried to kill herself more times than I care to remember."

And then, as if the dam has burst, it all pours out of Maggie in a flood of tears and words contained for much too long.

"So did my sister. And so did I."

TWENTY

THEN

Mutti is with child again and Papa is drinking even more than usual. The twins have long grown out of their makeshift crib in the bottom drawer of the dresser and have to sleep in bed with *Mutti* and Papa. Papa wasn't happy with such an arrangement to begin with—there was too little space, too many hot bodies in one narrow space—but once one of the boys wet himself in his sleep, the deal was sealed, as far as Papa was concerned. He will sleep with Grete from now on, in her cot by the window, and Grete's mother can have the pissing brats to herself.

    Mutti is too exhausted to protest. Or, perhaps, relieved even —or so Grete suspects. Despite her tender age, Grete has grown very attuned to people's emotions, in a household where reading faces can avert a catastrophe, tell her when to run and hide so she doesn't have to witness yet another fight that will leave *Mutti* with bruises on her arms and face and Grete trembling like a fawn for the rest of the day or night. Whereas other children play without a care in the world just outside her window, Grete is always vigilant, like a little soldier, always on guard, always listening, watching for the smallest signs of a brewing storm.

Still, Grete resents her mother for not putting up a fight for her little girl. *Mutti* may forget herself in dead sleep, but Grete has to lie still as a board for hours, pretending to sleep and not notice as her father's hands creep all over her body like giant spiders, up and down her legs, her bare arms, hair, and neck, her tightly closed thighs. Grete pretends to swat at them in her dreams, but they always return, robbing her of her sleep, and leaving her silent and subdued the following day.

In the mornings, Papa is always in a wonderful mood and sometimes even pats his wife's behind affectionately as she cooks him and their children breakfast. And since he's in a good mood, so too is *Mutti*. She sings as she serves their breakfast and kisses the tops of her children's heads as the neighbors who share the communal kitchen with them look on and comment on what a good-looking, sweet family the Bullers are.

Grete smiles too, even if at this point the smile is an artificial mask. She's learned by now that this is what women do if they want to keep the peace: be silent, smile, and submit. And everything will be all right.

TWENTY-ONE

NOW

Knuckles between her teeth, Maggie still thinks of how to begin her story, when there is a sudden rush of steps along the corridor. In an instant, the door is thrown open. Harlow stands in the shadows dancing along the walls chaotically cast by beams of flashlights. His torch pauses on Maggie, momentarily blinding her. Yet, he ignores her, addressing only Orso.

"Pack up. We're leaving in thirty."

"Leaving?"

Orso's surprise is more than justified. It's the middle of the night—the clock struck one not that long ago. There were plenty of times when such middle-of-the-night calls used to catch them unawares last summer, after D-Day, but as winter set in and the Battle of the Bulge ran out of steam, such occasions grew rarer and rarer. The reporters could still expect to be roused by a hot tip delivered by one of the carefully cultivated connections, but certainly not the investigators.

"Where to?" Orso calls to Harlow, who has already made the motion to leave.

"General Patton's forces are planning to liberate Buchenwald early in the morning."

"I thought it was scheduled for April 15." Orso stares at his colleague in apparent confusion.

"Purposeful disinformation, so that the SS wouldn't bother pulling out until then. After what the Soviets reported from the eastern side, General wants to catch the SS with their pants down." Harlow's jaw moves as if chewing on something before he adds, "That's my thinking, at least. At any rate, he wants us there to properly document everything."

He's gone and in the wake of a draft from an opened door, the candles go out one by one, as though extinguished by some cold, spectral breath. Maggie hears Orso scrambling for the flashlight in the dark and is both grateful and disappointed that her story came to such an abrupt end, without even starting properly. And then another thought occurs to her, somewhere on the periphery of the circles left swimming before her eyes, thanks to Harlow's bright torch.

Buchenwald. There it is, her chance.

Maggie lurches to her feet while Orso's still hunting for the flashlight in the depths of his backpack. "Thirty minutes he said? Wait for me, I'll be here in fifteen."

"What? Maggie, no!"

But Maggie is already out of the door, cutting straight into a current of personnel running to and fro, weighed down with gear and bedrolls. So, they aren't expecting to come back. What-ever else does Patton have in store for them?

Outside, there's just as much commotion as drivers start up their jeeps. Curses and laugher mix together in a heady cocktail of an army on victorious march.

Blood pulsing wildly in her temples, Maggie runs as fast as she can back to her own quarters and begins to shove freshly laundered underthings into her backpack. They're still wet—there's no heat in the radiators to dry them overnight—but this isn't the first time she'll have to dry something on herself after pulling it out of her knapsack. Taking her Kodak from under the pillow, Maggie puts it around her neck and is glad at the familiar weight of something oddly grounding and reassuring. With her own flashlight, she begins to scan the room to ensure that she hasn't forgotten anything, when suddenly a beam of light cuts her namesake's figure out of the night.

"Where you off to, Sullivan?"

Recovering herself from the start Higgins gave her—Maggie hadn't noticed her tiny sleeping form under the covers—Maggie motions the flashlight toward the window, to the east where the army shall soon move. "Following the investigators' unit to Buchenwald."

Instead of questions as to why now and whose orders and what of the original date, Higgins drops a single *wait for me* and throws off the blankets, scrambling for her journalist gear. Like most of them in these unheated quarters, she sleeps in full uniform to keep warm.

"Catch up, I'll try to stall them!" Maggie cries and bolts out of the door.

Impressively, Higgins does catch up with Maggie within minutes. Slung over her shoulder is a backpack stuffed with equipment that weighs almost as much as she does. "Sullivan, wait up! I have an AP fellow here who can give us a ride," she says, out of breath, jogging next to Maggie, who is picking her way between the army vehicles ready to take off.

Maggie tosses her head at the proposition. "We'll go with the investigators. If Patton wanted investigators there, he most likely sent word to Gallagher as well to round up all the correspondents in the area. If we go with one of them, we'll just get booted out of the jeep as soon as he sees that we're women."

"Who's this Gallagher and why does he care what we do?"

"He's the head of AP operations in Germany, which means he's our superior as long as we're here, on his territory. And on his territory, in his opinion, women belong not on the front but in some backwater office writing columns on cooking in wartime and how to fashion a spring jacket out of an old overcoat."

"Screw him and his opinion!"

"While I share the sentiment, he still has the authority to recall our travel orders and send us home. So, if you want to make it to Buchenwald together with the troops, it's best to avoid him."

"Why do we have to jump through such hoops? Why does anyone care if we're on the frontline? We made this choice. We want to be here. If we get injured and die, so be it. I don't see how it's anyone's business but ours."

That's how it should be in an ideal world, but the world they live in is anything but, and so Maggie says nothing in response.

By the time they reach the investigators' billet, Orso is already sitting inside the army jeep, checking his wristwatch every five seconds. His expression brightens as soon as he sees Maggie, but he does a double take at the sight of her companion.

"This is Maggie Higgins," Maggie introduces her colleague as she hurls her load into the back of the jeep. "She wants to come too."

"Maggie, there's only enough space for one person," Orso tries to protest, but Maggie pats her knees after helping Higgins lift her equipment into the truck.

"It's all right. She's small, she'll squeeze right in."

"I'm so tiny, you won't even notice me," Higgins promises as well, settling in her namesake's lap.

The driver mutters something about such arrangements being against regulations, but Orso tells him to mind his business and drive.

Harlow, who's riding shotgun, ignores the entire exchange completely as if pretending they don't exist.

As they set off, so too do warplanes above their heads, ferrying troops and ammunition to support the ground assault.

Somewhere in the distance, a lone anti-aircraft gun's shells trace the night sky in graceful arches, but it's silenced almost instantly, obliterated together with the roof on which it stood and the building and, if Maggie would wage a bet, the entire street.

The sky is full of Allied fliers. They carpet-bomb everything with the relish of an army that has more bombs than it knows what to do with. Soon, the horizon is lit up with infernal orange fires that engulf everything in their path. General Patton's army bulldozes its way forward, meeting little, if any, German resistance. From the column of the GIs traveling directly in front, cheers rise each time a particularly fearsome fireball paints the sky blood-red—now to their left as they curve around the burning cities. Despite the distance, Maggie feels the heat on her face and in the metal of her helmet.

Her namesake in her lap must feel it too. Higgins is working the straps to pull her helmet off, but Maggie catches her hands and lowers them down onto the *Tribune* correspondent's lap.

"Shrapnel," Maggie explains to the younger woman's inquisitive glance over the shoulder. "There are munitions factories in and around these towns. If a bomb hits them, the shrapnel from exploding shells can travel as far as several miles. Plenty enough to take one's head off."

Higgins doesn't argue with someone who has more experience with frontline reporting than she does. Instead, she half-turns to Maggie, as far as their unorthodox seating arrangements allow, and asks if she truly believes all those rumors about Buchenwald.

"What do you mean?" Maggie asks back.

"The rumors and all those Soviet reports that it's not just a labor camp but one of the extermination camps where all sorts of horrors are going on. As in, whatever Jewish population they transferred there from occupied territories, they're supposedly murdering them in those camps systematically."

"Yes, I did hear that." The image of their neighbor, Mrs. Goldblatt, appears before Maggie's eyes.

When Maggie was small, it was always she who would go to the Goldblatts' house and switch their lights on and off on Sabbath and big holidays. Once she moved out into her own apartment in the Village, Daddy took on the duty. It was he who took it the hardest when Mrs. Goldblatt asked him naively if he could find out what happened to her parents who still lived in Germany and suddenly stopped writing a few months ago. He was the police, the authority she knew and trusted. Daddy tried to explain it to her that the New York police were nothing like the Gestapo that knew everything about everyone, but she only blinked at him with her big trusting eyes and kept her hopes up.

That was in 1942. By early 1944, when the rumors began swelling of the mass deportations and outright annihilation of the European Jewish population, Mrs. Goldblatt stopped asking, only sat on the stoop and stared into nothing, much like Norma sometimes did.

"But do you believe it?" Higgins insists, calling Maggie back to the present.

"I do," she responds without a shadow of a doubt.

Higgins gives a shrug. "See, I don't know. I have always thought that it was just something made up to rile our troops. I mean, it just sounds like something taking place in the Middle Ages, but it's Germany we're talking about. They're much too civilized for that sort of thing. I do believe that they're operating labor camps where they're exploiting slave labor, but gassing people and burning them in ovens? It just sounds too macabre to be true, don't you think?"

Maggie still hears her namesake's voice but feels her eyes glazing over, her entire being dissociating from reality while remaining in it at the same time. She thinks thoughts so dark, they are unutterable, too charged with the pain of the past to fit into one simple answer. It takes all her effort to return to the present moment and say something just for the sake of saying it, so that Higgins will leave off with the interrogation that is stirring things in her she wants to remain dormant.

"The civilized Germans you're talking about murdered our boys in cold blood near Malmedy, and they were Americans. So, yes, it's a nation that's certainly capable of gassing and burning those they deem undesirable."

"But being capable and actually going through with it, those are two entirely different things, don't you think?"

Maggie leaves this question without response and, oddly, this time Higgins doesn't pry further. Instead, she surveys the burning city they're passing and remarks in a voice that is controlled and yet underlined with an awestruck wistfulness Maggie can fully relate to: "When we're done with the coverage of Buchenwald, I'd like to return here to report on the results of the firebombing." She goes silent and then adds so quietly, only Maggie can hear her, "If there are any civilians left to interview."

"The Army must have dropped the leaflets warning the population of the bombing." Maggie suggests, something she, herself, doesn't fully believe. If Patton decided to attack earlier than planned, she doubts he went to the trouble of warning the local population.

"Why should you care at any rate?" Harlow suddenly swings round in his seat to face the two women. "This innocent population you're referring to? These civilians? These are the same Germans who supported their murderous regime. These are the Nazi supporters who legally elected their genocidal, warmongering leader. They didn't mind at all when their *Feldmarschälle* obliterated half of Europe and the Soviet Union. They didn't bat an eyelid when their SS began rounding up and exterminating their Jewish population. And now that they find themselves facing the business end of a metaphorical gun, they shall whine about the unfairness of it all? And you shall write a report on it, saying, 'poor German civilians, they didn't deserve it. Poor innocents, paying for the mistakes of their government. Bad American government, destroying historical cities together with the people inside.' This is why no one wants you here, ladies. You show compassion to the very people who would have killed you, given half a chance. I should know. I have enough files on the Gestapo members who strung your reporter lot on piano wires in their Gestapo cellars. But you won't report on that."

He swings back around, visibly disgusted, but Maggie isn't in the mood to let him have the last word.

"I'd love to report on that," she counters sharply. "I'd love to report on a lot of things, but you won't share your findings."

"I thought Inspector Orso shared plenty of information with you. Isn't that why you're sticking to him like a leech?"

"Inspector Harlow, I don't care if you're my senior. You shall apologize right this instant to both Miss Sullivan and Miss Higgins." Orso doesn't raise his voice, but there's such a lethal steel in his tone, Maggie suddenly regrets having said anything at all.

"Gentlemen, please, it's unnecessary," she tries to defuse the situation that is growing progressively more charged. "We're not offended, and it's not the time nor place for any internal squabbles, let's just get there and do our work. Inspector Harlow, we do appreciate the ride and we promise we'll stay out of your way."

This time it's the driver who, in an effort to garner favor with his superior, mutters something about women on the front and the trouble they cause and their quarrelsome nature, and how it would be better for everyone if they just kept their mouths shut and minded their business.

At this, Orso snaps and grabs the front seat very close to the scruff of the driver's neck. "These ladies *were* minding their business. They were talking among themselves, discussing their job that has nothing to do with you or Inspector Harlow. Now, follow your own advice and mind your own driving-the-damned-jeep business and shut your trap before I shut it for you!"

Maggie has to press her lips together to conceal the chuckle that is ready to slip past them. One can take the investigator out of Brooklyn, but one can't take Brooklyn out of the investigator. From behind the polished façade of his Manhattan English, Orso's Italian Brooklyn drawl reappeared as if summoned by magic, and all at once, Maggie feels oddly at home in the midst of burning Germany.

TWENTY-TWO

THEN

Both of Grete's closest girlfriends, Ursula (Uschi) and Irma, envy her. Her papa is the neatest papa. Their fathers want little to do with them, but Grete's papa likes spending time with them. Instead of leading them, he follows their lead; instead of prohibiting, he allows everything. He buys them lollipops, shows them how to shoot a gun, and takes them to abandoned tenements and lets them throw bottles against the brick walls. He explores derelict construction sites with them and tells them scary stories in the dark of the cellars. And those are not some childish fairy tales from the Brothers Grimm books. His are something else entirely, about medieval times and the Spanish Inquisition and the tortures they inflicted on the heretics. The girls hold their breaths in fear-laden excitement as he recounts the exploits of cannibals and witch covens operating in the back door of the French monarchy in the seventeenth century. He details human sacrifices and the worshiping of the Black Goat and copulation with the animal embodying the devil the witches revered.

Wide-eyed and emboldened by his openness, the girls venture further and further in their questions and he answers them all, without admonishing or reservations. Their parents would smack their mouths silly simply for asking about copulation, let alone with a goat, but Grete's papa explains the process in great detail and with such knowledge, they can't help but admire his bookish smarts and the fact that he treats them as equals. They trust him with all their might and swear not to tell anyone about their little cellar gatherings.

And they don't.

"We have such a neat thing going," Irma proclaims, her brilliant blue eyes shining with excitement. "Why ruin it?"

If Ursula has her doubts, she doesn't voice them. Her father drinks as well, but he's a mean drunk—she has fresh belt welts on her upper thighs to prove it. Now, Grete's papa, he's funny and generous and kind. He never says no when Uschi asks him to give her a boost so all three can climb the tree together and share more dark, forbidden stories away from prying eyes.

Sometimes, Uschi says she wishes she had a papa just like Grete's.

Sometimes, Grete wishes she had no papa at all.

TWENTY-THREE

NOW

The first thing that hits them when they reach the gates of Buchenwald is the stench. The unbearable, revolting stench of decomposition, sickness, and rot that sends even the most battle-hardened men gagging and quickly fashioning face masks out of anything available just to avoid breathing this poisoned air. Both women too scramble for cloth masks. They fasten them to the straps of their helmets and only then do they set foot in front of the wrought-iron gates with the words, *Jedem Das Seine*—to each their own—crowning them in the culmination of mockery of human suffering.

Both snap photos of these gates but then wander in opposite directions—Maggie Higgins following the GIs and Maggie Sullivan, the investigators.

"Good Lord," Maggie hears Orso whisper and turns just in time to see him cross himself as he stares at something in the distance, white as a sheet.

She regards the stack of firewood next to one of the barracks that his gaze is fixated on and feels her own stomach spasm painfully as soon as her eyes recognize what her brain refused to process at first. It's not firewood but bodies—naked, skeletal human bodies that are stacked with German meticulousness atop one other in plain view.

Tasting bile in her mouth, Maggie makes her gradual approach toward the ghastly pile, one step at a time as her legs are suddenly all cotton and don't listen to her very well. It's not just her, either: all around, GIs spit bile and openly vomit and wipe wetness from their faces, then curse at the tops of their lungs until all of this emotion swells into a crescendo of a communal outcry.

A stern mask barely concealing his true infuriated state, General Patton directs the investigators and the camera crew that must have been traveling along with him to document the horrors in real time. "Film it," he commands in a voice shaking with outrage. "This one, with the bashed head. Film it up close, as close as you can get. Briggs, send your men to Weimar and bring every single civilian you can find here, so they can see what their glorious leader did to their fellow humans."

"Women too?"

Patton swings to him, murderous. "Men, women, children, elderly, I don't give a fuck! They're all complicit! Bring them and shove their fucking noses into all this!"

With a shaking hand, Maggie writes down his words in shorthand and snaps a quick photo of him among the sea of human corpses.

There's so much death around, one's brain refuses to admit to the reality of it. Maggie struggles with this nightmarish dawn, wades through the remnants of the morning fog as she walks further and further inside this purgatory. Her hands shake so badly, she has to retake some of the photos. Even then she's unsure if anything clear will come out of them.

From time to time, her ear picks up snippets of Orso's voice as he narrates what he sees to the stenographer.

"A man seemingly in his thirties, severely malnourished, with injuries old and fresh consistent with something akin to a horsewhip on his back and buttocks, likely died by multiple blunt-force traumas to the head. Pieces of the skull are missing from the left temple and the top of the head. The brain is also visibly damaged; the brain matter is recognizable and in close proximity to the victim's head."

Maggie photographs it all—the bashed-in skull, the eyes forever frozen in agony, the teeth bared by lips pulled back in a grimace of horrid, unmerciful death—and straightens, suddenly remembering her editor's words. This is not what people want to see. They want uplifting stories of the triumph of the human spirit, of victories, of smiling GIs and relieved civilians in front of white sheets celebrating surrender. The censors won't allow them to publish any such pictures. Let the investigators collect them and use them in their prosecution cases and remain forever locked in their filing rooms, collecting dust, while humanity dives head-first into yet another conflict.

Though, maybe this time it's different. If Patton himself wanted the press here, the rules of the game must have changed. Perhaps, they'll let her break the story after all—the darkest one yet, for the entire world to see. Because, sometimes, people need to come face to face with mounds of emaciated corpses to be reminded of what happens when a nationalist dictator is allowed to do as he pleases with human lives. In the name of protecting his precious folk and preserving that folk's way of life, he'll issue laws that will stop all progress in its tracks, strangle all opposition, and then incarcerate and slaughter the undesirables. Glad are the Germans who proudly fly his blood-red flags from their porches: no more "perverts" to put up with, no more Jews to rip them off, no more intelligentsia to muddy the government waters and worry about the world's opinion. No more conflicting opinions in the government-owned press. Women are pregnant or mothering, staying home where they belong. Men are in their uniforms, imposing their authority on anyone willing and unwilling, as men should. And if everyone who doesn't fit into this picture is getting gassed or shot or burned, well, that's too bad. Should have left when there was still a chance to do so.

Maggie snaps shot after shot and hopes for vengeance in the name of every single soul these "glad Germans" annihilated.

"Told you Sullivan would be here first."

Swinging on her heel at the familiar voice, Maggie breaks into a smile at the sight of her war sisters, Lee Miller and Ann Stringer. Their faces are also obscured by cloths, but their eyes wrinkle in the corners all the same, in spite of the ghastly scene surrounding them.

Maggie opens her arms to them and buries her face in Ann's hair. It's grown even longer and smells like pine and not the rotten flesh and ashes she's been breathing for the past hour.

"You all right?" Lee asks, searching her face despite a deep scowl creasing her own brow under the edge of her helmet.

Maggie gestures vaguely around—how can one ever be all right after seeing this?—and wipes her eyes with the back of her hand. This is a morbid reunion, not at all what they had in mind when they planned it. Back in London, they parted ways, promising each other to take a group photo in front of the fallen Reichstag in Berlin. Instead, they find themselves among mounds of corpses and scattered groups of survivors who are almost dead.

"Where did you come from?" Maggie asks, just to force some sense of normality into the air around them.

"We were working near the Rhine for the past few weeks," Lee starts and glares at her lover, who is snapping photos of the three women from a distance. "David, not the time nor the place! I'm not the story here."

"Oh, leave him," Ann whispers to her. "It's his job, to photograph you doing yours."

"Again, not the time nor the place," Lee repeats, this time to Ann, and points David to one of the barracks that stands gaping with its doors thrown open. "Go inside and photograph the liberated inmates, much better use of the film."

Maggie doesn't know David closely and tenses, expecting an argument to break out, but he simply nods with an apologetic smile and heads into the barrack, camera at the ready. Frank, Maggie's ex-husband, would definitely pick a fight over this. Ordering him around, challenging his authority in front of other men. And it doesn't matter if she's right, what matters is his ego and his ego only. He would start pointing his finger in her face right in front of these people who are literally dying at their feet just because, in Frank's mind, he was the main character and everything was about him. All else was just a setting.

"Working?" Maggie forces her attention back to her colleagues. "You had full monopoly on the Rhine region. They dubbed you the Rhine maidens for good reason."

"Rhine maidens, my foot," Lee grumbles but not without pleasure. "It was like pulling teeth, trying to get assigned to a good story. Gallagher and his idiotic regulations. It's only thanks to Patton that we're here—he wanted all hands on deck for the liberation, every single reporter he could summon." Her eyes veil over as she scans her surroundings. "Now we see why."

Ann says nothing at all, just pulls a notepad out of her pocket with a stub of a pencil attached to it by a string and gestures to the barrack next to the one into which David has disappeared.

"Call if you need an interpreter," Lee shouts after her and pulls her own camera from her neck. "Well, duty calls."

"It was good to see you," Maggie says during their parting hug.

"Next stop, Dachau?" Lee asks, walking away backward.

Maggie nods. "And after that, the Reichstag."

She's already heading in the opposite direction when Lee's voice reaches her once again. "Hey, Mags?"

"Yes?" She pauses next to a field ambulance. A GI Jesus—

the platoon's chaplain—is praying over a mound of corpses nearby.

"Have you found what you've been after yet?"

Once again, a reminder of a duty she's been trying to avoid for so long, as if providence itself prods her forward. And she's so very tired of the past chasing her, snapping at her heels just as soon as she dares to slow down, for years on end. It's in the eyes of the women fleeing their homes never to return. It's in the voice of Frank whenever he raised it. It's in the stories she wrote using names other than her own, and in the very soil she walks on to finally confront it.

"Not yet," she lies because it's easier than trying to explain the truth. "But I will."

"Let me know if you need help."

Maggie nods but already knows that this is something she'll never do. She is the one who always helps and never the one who asks for it. Somehow, it is much easier to carry it all on her own shoulders than put her trust in someone else.

Suddenly homesick, Maggie bites her tongue and pushes herself toward a small group of liberated prisoners surrounding American medics and GIs—to do the work she signed up for. Few of the former inmates can stand, but those who can cling to their liberators for dear life and touch their faces as if assuring themselves of the reality of all this. Those who can only crawl, crawl out of their barracks and into the gray April morning, reach with their bony limbs to the GIs' uniforms, and kiss the trousers and even the boots of their saviors—whatever they can reach— despite the soldiers' tearful protests.

Maggie photographs it all and changes the film in her camera just in time for the first civilians from nearby Weimar to walk through the camp's gates. There's plenty of press here now, lots of familiar faces hounding the well-dressed women in their fancy hats and suited men with startled eyes as they are pushed into a narrow line formed between the mountains of human corpses.

An interpreter delivers General Patton's words with perfect pitch: "Don't you dare look away. Don't cover your eyes, lady. Take a good look, a good long look, at what your dear leaders did. What *you* did. Every single death is on your conscience. No running! Walk, and walk slowly. I want you to memorize every single face of every single person you see today. This was someone's father, mother, daughter, brother, child. And your leaders bashed their skulls in when they pulled out last night, cowardly bastards. Take a damn good look!"

With the sun come the flies, black, fat swarms of them. They crawl all over glazed-over eyes, disappear inside mouths opened wide as though in their final, agonized scream. After changing yet another roll of film, Maggie photographs all this as well, just as she does the open sores, the broken limbs, the shaved skulls still crawling with lice, and the bulging bellies of those who must have perished days before Patton's army overran the camp.

"Exactly how long have they been left here?" she asks a group of liberated inmates, who are busy slurping soup the American medics are presently distributing among the surviving population.

"Those?" Quite a few of them speak English, at least to some degree. "A week or two. Ovens didn't have space, SS didn't have men. No time to burn the dead. So, they stay here."

"Ovens?" She swears she can smell ash and burned flesh even through the cloth covering her face. "Where are the ovens?"

They point and Maggie runs off, her camera swinging. By the squat building, the GIs are smoking and staring into space with faces hard as granite. Maggie slips past them without any acknowledgment and finds herself in a concrete chamber with piles of clothes lying about in disarray. Out of nowhere, several inmates materialize. In somewhat better shape than the others, they grab hold of her and urge her in their broken English to follow them somewhere else.

Only when one of them pulls the heavy door open and reveals a chamber with corpses all but spilling out does she dig her heels in and refuse to take another step forward. But the inmates' hands are stopping her from retreating. They nudge her in the back and plead with her in a variety of languages to commit the atrocity to the memory of humanity once and for all so that nothing like this will ever happen again to the world.

"Take photo. Please! Take photo. Gas room. Take photo, please!"

Her head is swimming, but Maggie lifts the camera which feels as though it weighs a ton and takes photos of a heap of bodies that shall haunt her memory for as long as she lives. But at least now they will have their proof—the Schenks, the other Germans feigning ignorance, the American white supremacists siding with them, who, just a few years back, marched with swastika flags along the streets of New York. She'll shove the photos in their faces and ask them kindly to explain to Mrs. Goldblatt the reason why they thought it was OK to gas her parents in these chambers together with countless others. Explain to Mrs. Goldblatt's children why they shall never know their grandfather and grandmother.

She'll shove the photos in the face of anyone who will ask her neighbors why they don't patronize German businesses or buy German cars or boycott those who profited from this murderous regime, from this slave labor employed for big-name companies so familiar to every American.

Because such generational traumas don't just erase themselves from humanity's genetic blueprint. Because decades will pass and it will still hurt—entire families, not just those who suffered directly. Maggie knows this much, from her own life.

She swallows hard, collects herself a bit, and this time asks before she's prompted: "Where are the ovens?"

They lead the way and she follows, tasting ash long before entering the crematorium itself. The SS must have indeed pulled out in haste, for the gurneys sticking out of the opened ovens still bear their ghastly load. Skulls, singed but easily recognizable as human, stare back at her with their empty sockets as Maggie aims her camera at them, feeling not like a reporter, but a witness to the apocalypse itself. It has arrived on their doorstep without announcement and engulfed the entire world in its madness, and now she's left to pick up what's left of the old world order.

Only, how to do it if she can't seem to pick up what's left of herself?

Thanking the inmates, Maggie stumbles out of the building and automatically takes the cigarette one of the GIs standing guard offers her.

"They said in the last few days the SS didn't even bother with gas," he says, holding the light inside Maggie's cupped, shaking hands. "Burned them there alive. Imagine? Alive."

Maggie nods even though she doesn't want to imagine, doesn't want to hear any of that anymore, but she stills herself for one last effort. "Go get the investigators so that they can document it. They're by the medical block, names are Orso and Harlow."

Let them deal with that. She can't. Not just now.

TWENTY-FOUR

Pulling on her cigarette, Maggie wanders aimlessly until she stumbles across an administrative building, long abandoned and standing with its doors thrown open. It's eerily quiet inside as she enters and pulls the door closed after her to mute the world around her at least for a few minutes. Unaccompanied and glad of her solitude, she drifts through the offices and snaps photos of smoldering cigarettes sitting in ashtrays, cups with unfinished coffee serving as makeshift paperweights for the documents no one had time to get rid of.

Maggie doesn't touch them, leaving the evidence for Orso and his team. Instead, she makes her way into the dim room lined with shelves, each heaving with files the SS must have had to abandon without destroying. After opening one of them and discovering a photo of an inmate with his full intake information, Maggie inhales sharply, the musty air clawing at her throat.

Inmate records, largely untouched.

She's not supposed to; she knows she's not, but what if she can finally bring peace to Mrs. Goldblatt?

After a swift glance over her shoulder, Maggie begins her search with a focused determination, sifting through files with lists of names. Only the earliest ones, dating back to the late 1930s, have full information for each inmate. The others, starting with 1941, are mere summaries filed under each month and corresponding year. The numbers were so great, the SS simply didn't have the time to process them all.

She pauses at a random file marked "July 1943," her fingers trembling slightly as she opens it. There are easily hundreds, if not thousands, of names typed onto the official paper with the Buchenwald KZ letterhead and signed by an indifferent hand. No alphabetical order, no rhyme or reason, no dates of birth or gender even. Just last names, initials, and corresponding numbers attached to them upon arrival. Maggie finds too many Goldblatts, just in July alone. Human lives, reduced to mere memories buried beneath bureaucratic coldness. It's inconceivable to even imagine the number of people who perished in the unspeakable horrors of just this one camp.

Maggie closes the file, nauseated and lightheaded from the ghastly discovery, and begins to leaf through other camp documentation just to occupy her hands with something until she recovers herself. These have been shoved here as if in a rush, likely during the last few days as the SS were preparing for the orders for evacuation from their higher-ups. Some are lists of foodstuffs allocated to the SS canteen, others are much more interesting and even newsworthy, she realizes as she comes across a dossier on the former Kommandant Koch. Her German is good enough to understand the contents. Apparently, *Herr Kommandant* was helping himself to the jewelry and money stripped from the inmates upon arrival and must have gotten greedy and refused to share the loot. Either way, an inspection came into the camp and must have discovered so much that even the SS bigwigs were appalled. Into the same camp *Herr*

Kommandant went, where he was later executed by firing squad.

But, suddenly, the slight satisfaction Maggie felt at the thought of Koch meeting a very befitting end is snuffed out. With all her attention on the former *Kommandant*, she missed the name of the SS man in charge of the inspection. But now it's staring her right in the face, with a signature faded and smudged: "SS Sturmbannführer, W. Buller."

The paper slips from her hand, Maggie's entire world tilting on its axis.

Waldemar Buller.

She got it all wrong. Waldemar Buller was never the one with the Peiper Group. It must have been one of the twins. The revelation hits her like a physical blow. She stumbles back, a storm of emotions surging within her. She's not ready for this; it's still much too soon, no matter what she has promised Norma.

Her mind races, piecing together fragments of her past. The name that was banished from the household, the language Maggie's mother refused to speak, the unspoken void of the nameless man's fate until Norma's split-open veins summoned him back to life—all now paint a chilling picture.

Maggie sinks to the floor, the files scattered around her like fallen leaves. She's trapped in a vortex of her own history, the line between right and wrong blurred by blood ties.

A sister.

A daughter.

A woman.

A journalist, the seeker of the truth.

"Still alive then, eh?" She kicks the paper with her army boot, leaving a muddy print on the bottom of it. "I was hoping you'd kicked the bucket by now, but I guess you never liked making it easy on people. All right then." Holding onto the filing cabinet, Maggie pulls herself back to her feet and dusts off her hands. "Let's get this over with. I assume your other son is also somewhere nearby."

The truth, no matter how painful, cannot remain buried. She has to confront the past. With one last glance at the file bearing Buller's name, she steps out into the hallway and heads back to the door she ignored before. It's at the very end of the corridor, painted green and bearing the sign "Personnel and Staff Records," and thankfully, unlocked. Maggie pauses in front of it, but then pushes the door open with sudden resolution. Here, abandoning her camera in the middle of a clerk's desk, she begins pulling out drawers one by one.

With her teeth clenched hard, Maggie finds the letter B and feels a cold sweat breaking all over her body as she pulls the drawer out and slams it hard atop the desk. There, without any regard for evidence handling, she begins removing one file after another, checking for photos and names and ages, all of which are wrong. She's about to lose hope, when, suddenly, Hansjörg Buller stares back at her from a black and white photo. Maggie doesn't need to check his date of birth to know exactly who she's looking at.

The file still in her hands, she drops into the chair, feeling as though the ground suddenly goes from under her, and remains in this position for who knows how long. In the perfect silence, all she hears is the measured ticking of her service wristwatch and the sound of her own heavy breathing. The past, which half existed, and half didn't, like Schrödinger's cat, up until now, slams into her and knocks the wind out of her lungs. Raised in a good family, by a father who actually had morals, Hansjörg could have grown into someone who resisted the regime, who could have easily been among the inmates here, but on the right side of history at least. But instead—

A sound interferes with her chain of thoughts, like a mouse

scratching behind one of the tall lockers lining the back wall. Instantly on her feet, she eyes the lockers. Expecting to see exactly that—a rodent of some sort—Maggie pulls the door open and starts at the sight of an SS man cowering on his haunches inside the narrow cabinet.

Acting on instinct, she takes a leap back and fumbles for the service weapon on her hip. But it appears that the SS man is more scared of her than she of him. Throwing his arms up and squeezing his eyes as if expecting a shot in the head at any moment, he begins to plead with her in a mixture of English and German.

Having recovered herself and having assessed the situation, Maggie yanks the German out of his hiding place and shoves her gun into his ribs, nudging him toward the desk. "Sit in that chair and put your hands on the desk, palms down, so I can see them."

He obliges first and only then realizes that the strange GI addressed him in his native language. "Are you German?" he half-whispers hopefully.

"I'm asking the questions here," Maggie says, ice-cold, and takes a position on the opposite side of the desk. She got lucky catching him unawares, but what if it comes into his head to wrestle the gun out of her hands and go out of this life as a damned hero, shooting an American soldier first and himself right after? Best to put some space and obstacle between them, she reasons. "What's your name, rank, and what the hell were you doing hiding there?"

"I'm only a private, just a lowly private," he begins, raising his hands in surrender once again as if to drive the point home. "Name is Fuchs. When the administration fled, they left a few of us in charge of destroying the paperwork. Well, at first we did, but then we realized that it was only us versus the inmates that no one was guarding anymore and decided to make a break for it as well. Well, the others did, but I stayed here, figuring I'd just wait until your forces entered and then I'd come out, surrender myself."

"You were afraid of the inmates?" Maggie arches her brow even though he likely can't see her skeptical expression behind the combination of the helmet and makeshift face mask. "They can barely crawl, thanks to you and your comrades."

"No, no, not the general population." Fuchs shakes his head vehemently. "The *Sonderkommando*. The ones who worked in the crematoriums. They had much better rations than the others, they're very strong. In Auschwitz, they even staged a revolt last autumn. I wanted very much to surrender to the American Army, but I didn't want them to get me."

Maggie considers it for a moment and thinks the sentiment makes some sort of sense. The crematorium inmates indeed seemed much healthier than the regular population. They also had more than enough reasons for revenge.

"Those men, they're savage," Fuchs doubles down on his previous explanation, hoping perhaps to either gain sympathy or flatter his way into freedom.

Either way, it has the opposite effect on Maggie. "Perhaps it's because they saw your comrades burning their friends or family members alive in those ovens—who knows?"

Under the harsh light of the overhead lamp, the German begins to sweat bullets. His face is round and perfectly childish, without any lines or even a hint of facial hair. His uniform is wrinkled and unkempt, and smells of stale sweat and wet wool. "No, no, not me! I was only conscripted and sent for service here a few weeks ago. I'm just a guard, I swear! I had nothing to do with any of that—"

Maggie swats at his excuses and instead pushes the file she was perusing under his nose with the tip of her gun. "I couldn't care less for your circumstances. Now, do you know this man? Yes or no?"

Fuchs studies the photo in front of him, longer than Maggie

hopes he would. "No," he offers his verdict at last. "Never saw him."

"Wouldn't it be strange for the camp administration to have a file on him if he supposedly was never in the camp?"

Fuchs swallows. "I'm not saying he was never here. Maybe he was. But so many of the personnel were called to the front in the recent few months, he may have been transferred before I was sent here. I'm only saying that I never saw him personally, though..."

"Though what?" Maggie feels herself tense.

"The name sounds familiar."

"From where?"

Fuchs stares uneasily at the barrel of the gun instead of Maggie, as if afraid it might go off by itself. "Heard it from other guards, right before the troop pullout. They were drinking a lot those last few days... They were telling us to grab whatever we wanted—gold, money, whatever—because Buller had other, more important business to attend to instead of coming here for inspections."

Maggie narrows her gaze on the file. Can't be Hansjörg he's talking about. And if this Fuchs never saw him, it must have been Hansjörg who was transferred from Buchenwald, from SS-Totenkopf—concentration camps guard division, to the armed SS—the Waffen-SS—and namely the Peiper Group, according to Orso's files. Which can only mean one thing: Waldemar Buller has had a much more prosperous career under Hitler's regime than Maggie and Norma originally thought.

Just to prove herself right, she fixes the guard with her steely gaze once again. "Did you hear the first name of that Buller they talked about?"

A toss of the head.

"A rank? Anything?"

"No. Just Buller. Maybe it wasn't even Buller... Maybe it was Muller and I misheard..."

Maggie is about to pistol-whip him on his stupid face in earnest when a sound makes her freeze.

"Sullivan! What is this?"

Once again, the world stands still.

TWENTY-FIVE

THEN

Grete doesn't want to remember. Doesn't want to relive it all again, but the memory is like a splinter that'll only keep festering until addressed. Her mother is fast asleep, but Grete is wide awake despite the late hour, nestled against *Mutti's* growing belly and wondering if it was all her fault, if she had invited it all on herself, if she was to blame for what happened.

It all began with Bruno, the neighbors' son's cousin, arriving to visit from Munich while his parents were away on the fields, working as hired hands to help local farmers with the harvest. Whatever invited his unwanted attention, Grete couldn't possibly tell; she was minding her own business in the communal courtyard, immersed in her Brothers Grimm tales. There were no other books for her to read, but even if there were, something about the darkness of the stories resonated deeply within her. Here, girls locked up in towers were threatened with violent death if they didn't do the king's bidding. Here, monsters lurked in the woods and mothers were invariably dead, and daughters had to fend for themselves and even princes couldn't be relied on to save them from imminent danger. With her brothers playing with wooden blocks on their blanket in front of her, Grete swallowed one page after another and wondered if Rumpelstiltskin was real and if he would agree to spin her and her *Mutti* gold in exchange for two boys. Gold was money and "good" money, unlike paper money—that much she knew without knowing the reason for it—and "good" money could pay for her and her *Mutti*'s ticket to Australia, which was so far away, no one would find them there.

And then, suddenly, the book was yanked from her hands by a tall boy she'd never seen in their tenement before. Grete saw that he wasn't an adult yet, but certainly not a boy her age. He still wore shorts despite his height and had a sheen to his badly pimpled face and an oily lock of dark hair falling over one eye.

Grete stared at him incomprehensively as he waved the book in the air with a wicked grin. "Well? Don't you want it back?"

She nodded and outstretched her hand, only to be slapped on it, hard.

"What's the magic word?"

"Please." Her eyes were riveted to the book he was handling so roughly. It was the only one she had, her personal treasure that allowed her to escape reality whenever she wanted—a magic portal to a world where she, for once, was in control. Grete always took great care of the book the boy was now dangling in the air like a gutted fish.

"My name is Bruno." He smirked tauntingly.

"Please, Bruno." Grete felt her chin beginning to quiver. There was something dangerous about the boy. The very air around him was charged with tension, the same way it was with her father. He could hurt things, destroy them—she could see it plainly in his eyes.

"Nah, you're going to have to do better than that. Beg me. Get down on your knees, fold your hands together in front of your chest, and beg me. Or I'll tear the whole thing apart."

Her heart sinking, Grete scrambled to her knees and folded her ice-cold hands just as he told her to. "Please, Bruno, I beg you, give it back." She hated the humiliation, the whiny pitch to her voice already giving way to tears, the very fact that she was so small, so defenseless against him and his threats. But, most of all, that very second Grete hated being born a girl. Boys got into fights all the time, but where they took a punch, they could always give one back and particularly if they had their gang behind them. Girls didn't have gangs. That's why they chose to play in dark cellars of abandoned buildings—the streets belonged to the boys.

Bruno feigned hesitation, his eyes gleaming mean at her tears. He was reveling in having that power over her, of being able to submit another human being to his wishes and in front of an audience, no less.

"Your sister is a crybaby," Bruno told the twins, who forgot their blocks and were now staring at the boy with their fingers in their mouths. "Watch me and you'll know just how to handle her when you grow up. She'll do anything, too, you just wait and see."

Grete was crying in earnest now. She kept scanning the windows with desperate, tear-filled eyes, but no adults were coming to her rescue, and running inside to get one wasn't an option either. The boy would tear the book up in an instant, given half a chance. There was nothing else for it but to plead with him to give it back.

"Show me and I will," Bruno finally said with a sneer that was universal to boys of his kind.

And to the men they grew into.

Grete blinked the tears away, confused.

"Don't pretend you don't know what I'm talking about. Show me," he demanded again, growing impatient.

There was some restless excitement about him. Grete wanted to shrink away from it, disappear entirely, just stop existing altogether so as not to be faced with it. But this was no fairy tale and the monster was real: she had to deal with him, one way or the other.

"I don't know what you want."

"Yes, you do." He was suddenly on his knees too, very close to her now. His breath was stale and revolting. "Lift up your skirt, drop your undies, and show me."

The realization finally dawning on her, Grete tried to scramble to her feet, all her instincts screaming at her to run as fast and as far away as she could, but Bruno grasped the book by its spine and pulled at the pages hard enough for her to hear the binding beginning to rip.

"No, please, don't!"

"Then stop being a prude and do it."

Grete didn't know what "prude" meant, but it couldn't have been good. Either way, there was no escaping it. If she let the boy tear her only book, her only means of escape from this nightmarish world into the one where anything was possible, *Mutti* would get so upset and likely yell at her for not handling the book with more care, and if Grete told her what the boy asked her to do, she would only get madder still. Or not believe her at all. One thing Grete was sure of, *Mutti* wouldn't simply replace it with a new one. As for Papa, she didn't even want to think of asking for anything. With him, everything came at a price.

No one would help her, she knew. It was just her and the boy, alone, in the entire wide world, and the fate of her book hanging in the balance.

With her ice-cold, shaking hands, Grete pulled her skirt up and, struggling with the elastic for a moment, pulled her underpants down, looking anywhere but at the boy's face, stiff as a statue, frozen in the moment that felt like eternity.

"Gross!" the boy cried in delight and, hurling the book in Grete's face, jumped to his feet. "Dirty whore! Dirty whore!"

He disappeared inside the tenement and Grete, her face burning with shame, collected the twins' toys without a single word and, having wrapped them and the precious, saved book into the blanket, tied its ends with a knot to carry it inside. The twins crawled after her like obedient puppies, but Grete hated them more than anything just then—for being unwitting witnesses to her humiliation, for being born after her instead of before, and for not protecting her as they should have and, lastly, for not being the object of Bruno's fancy. Just as with their father, they were of no interest to him. Only Grete was—the prude, the dirty whore.

It got worse still when Papa entered their room later that night, his eyes dark as thunderous clouds, and asked Grete about the rumors that the new boy, Bruno, was spreading all around the neighborhood, saying that she was showing anyone her "little kitty." Grete burst into tears and told him the truth, expecting the spanking of her life, even if Papa had never laid a hand on her before.

Her father listened without interrupting, his expression unreadable but chest heaving visibly.

"Did he touch it?"

"No."

"Are you sure?"

"Yes."

"Let me see it."

More tears flowed; Grete felt she was drowning in them with nothing to hold onto. Why did she have to show it again? She only wanted for everyone to leave her alone—was that too much to ask?

"Margarete, I am your father. Let me see, so I can make sure he didn't hurt you."

What happened after is shrouded in darkness, like the rest of Grete's life that is to follow. Something broke in her that day, and even the ghastly sight of Bruno's face, which her father had beat into a bloodied mess, didn't elicit any emotion from her.

It's been months now and not a day without Papa touching her—for her own protection, he claims—whenever *Mutti*'s not there. But even when she is, Grete doesn't know how to tell her without upsetting her and so, like now, she nestles against her pregnant belly and stares into the darkness, only four and a half and already dead inside.

TWENTY-SIX

NOW

Maggie turns around and sees Harlow and another fellow from the investigators' team whom she doesn't know the name of. There's a silence that falls over the room and it's thick enough to be cut with a knife. Harlow stares and Maggie stares back, two gunslingers from the Wild West, each awaiting the other to make the first move. To complete the picture, both have their service weapons drawn—Maggie's pointing at the newcomers and Harlow's, at Maggie's stomach.

Seeing how it can be misinterpreted, Maggie slowly lowers her gun all the way to the floor and rises back up with both hands in the air, showing that it was for the German only, that she means no harm. Harlow's weapon though remains on her.

"Who's the Nazi fellow and what were you discussing so passionately before we interrupted you?" Harlow's tone is conversational, but the words bite hard.

"Just a guard who was hiding in one of the lockers here. He didn't want the inmates to get to him and wanted to surrender to the US army instead."

Harlow's expression remains dispassionate and he

approaches the desk and glances at the disarray of files, one particular folder lying on top of them all. "What's that?"

Maggie tries to swallow, but her throat is entirely dry. To win some time, she slowly unbuckles her helmet and removes it, together with the makeshift mask.

The SS guard makes a surprised noise, likely realizing he's been talking to a woman the entire time.

"Just files I found."

But Harlow is an investigator for a good reason. He doesn't buy it. "What were you doing here in the first place?"

"Looking for material to print."

"Not enough of it in there?" A nod toward the camp outside the building's walls.

Maggie stares back at him, stubbornly silent.

"Miss Sullivan, give me one reason I shouldn't call the MPs and place you under arrest for espionage."

"Espionage? For what?" The situation does look bad, Maggie won't deny it, but bringing her up on espionage charges is taking it too far.

"All I know is that some fellows from the special camp commando came to see me and told me that the reporter called for my team to document the gas chambers and the crematorium. But when I asked where the reporter was, he pointed me in this direction. And here I am, finding you in the middle of a conversation with an SS man we had no idea was still in the camp, going over other SS men's files in rather perfect German." Harlow suddenly turns to the guard and asks him in his own very good German, "Do you know this woman?"

"No, I didn't even know she was a woman," the SS man begins to stammer, all helpfulness and innocence mixed in one. "I was in one of the stalls, waiting for someone from the army to come in, but when I heard the noise and someone going through the filing cabinets, I decided to wait for a bit to make sure it was an American soldier and not one of the inmates. There are slots on the sides I could see through, but they're very narrow, so I had to wait till she got close enough to one of them, so I could make out the uniform. Then I scratched at the door and she let me out."

"And then what?"

The guard shrugs. "She began interrogating me about this Buller fellow in the personnel file. I thought she was one of ours, to be frank, one of the werewolves. There were cases when they wore US uniform to confuse the enemy—"

"Why did you think that?"

"She speaks German like a native, not like you. I can tell you're an American, even though your German is very good. But she speaks it as though she was born here."

"Does she now?"

Maggie doesn't lower her eyes at the very long hard look Harlow gives her, only presses her mouth into a thin, hard line. "I assure you, I am no spy."

"Who's Buller?"

Maggie stares directly at the photo in the file Harlow holds up for her but says nothing.

"Why are you looking for him?"

"Personal reasons."

"You'll have to give me more than that, Miss Sullivan."

"I'm sorry, but that's all you're getting."

Harlow draws himself up a bit. "This is no bargaining matter. You're either telling me the truth or I'm calling the military police to place you under arrest right this instant."

Maggie contemplates her options for a few moments. "I'll tell everything," she says at last, after wetting her lips, "but not to you. I'll speak to Orso only."

"Ha!" Harlow barks out a derisive chuckle. "The only one of our entire team who made the mistake of falling under your charms. How convenient."

"Do you not believe him to be an honest patriot enough to

give me up when he learns the truth? Do you truly think he'll cover up for me if I indeed turn out to be a Nazi spy?"

"No. But I do believe that he's the only person gullible enough to fall for whatever tales you spin for him, as I sincerely doubt you'll confess the truth."

"Suit yourself," Maggie says.

"No, Miss Sullivan. It's you who'll have to suit yourself."

In the span of thirty minutes, they put her in manacles and lead her through the camp's main thoroughfare, together with the SS man, under the stunned looks from Patton's men. By the gates, they are joined by more SS guards, all beaten within an inch of their lives, in their torn and dirty uniforms. A few GIs inspect their bloodied knuckles and spit at the pitiful column's feet. They do a double take when they discover Maggie in the Nazis' midst.

To make matters worse, her female colleagues are all here, staring at her with wide, uncomprehending eyes.

Lee calls her name and stares at Maggie in utter confusion, but Maggie only yells back, "Don't worry about me and go submit your report." She gestures to Maggie Higgins, also in the crowd, "Find Orso, please!"

That gets her a shove in the back from one of the MPs escorting them.

Before too long, they're in Weimar and, thankfully, Maggie is separated from the SS, but there's little rest for her in the tiny room they put her in. Almost in an instant, interrogators descend upon her like hawks and take turns coaxing and threatening her into a confession. She stares through them and repeats the only words they will ever hear from her: she will speak, but to Orso only.

They threaten her with court-martial that very evening, but she remains unmoved. They take her out to the prison courtyard, where one of the SS guards is strapped to a tall pole by his elbows and ankles, his uniform gone, only white undershirt and prisoner trousers remaining. He stares straight ahead when the firing squad takes aim and refuses the hood. Maggie also doesn't look away when multiple bullets tear into his chest and stomach and his body sags against its restrains.

The MPs shake their heads, now certain that she's one of them—the Nazis. How could a woman watch something so ghastly and remain so very cold? Only a German woman could —the werewolf whore. The dirty Jezebel who slept her way into their ranks to spy on them and spread her venom all around. Very convenient, too: that's why she was always at the frontline, moving together with the troops, knowing their next step before they took it, sending it in coded messages to her SS bosses via her articles. How impossibly, nefariously, disgustingly brilliant!

Only the Buller fellow question keeps stumping them. Is he her superior, to whom she was reporting? A lover?

"I'll tell who Buller is, but only to Inspector Orso."

That is all they get out of her.

Orso does arrive, when the night is already stealing across the dusty concrete floor of the interrogation room, but he isn't alone. Harlow follows him inside like some kind of demented shadow, his hawkish gaze on Maggie the entire time.

"Maggie, what is this all about?" Orso asks her, pulling up a chair still warm from her last interrogator. He's still here, his MP armband stark and white despite the shadows gathering in the corners. On the table, a dim kerosene lamp burns. There's no electricity in the entire town after the latest series of bomb raids.

"Get them all to leave and I'll tell you."

"Not an option, Miss Sullivan," the MP interrogator declares at once. "You either speak to all of us now or you're heading outside to the courtyard first thing in the morning. Even without your confession, there's plenty of evidence to convict you of your crime."

"I've told you already, I'm not a spy."

"From my experience, precisely the words any spy would say."

Maggie heaves a sigh and looks at Orso and he stares back at her, alarmed and confused but not accusing, and for that she is grateful. The courtyard and the execution squad don't frighten her. She has stared death in the face plenty enough times. Death is by no means the worst thing to happen to a person. In her frank opinion, living is much worse, existing in the limbo of nightmares and flashbacks and getting triggered by a single word, a single smell, a single sound. And now, this—having to turn her very soul inside out in front of these men, explain her motives and decisions... No. Thank you very much. She'll see herself out and put an end to this torture.

But then, what of Norma? Her sweet, innocent Norma, to whom she swore in blood to see this affair to the end. It was Norma's idea, to slice their palms and seal the sisterly promise in a handshake neither could back out of. Slicing was nothing new. Both bore enough scars on their wrists to prove it.

She thinks of asking them to stand behind her chair, against the back wall while she talks to Orso, but they'll refuse her of course—she already knows this much—and so, Maggie heaves a sigh and rubs her eyes, so very tired of this never-ending *bullshit*.

"I didn't plan on speaking about it in front of an audience," she begins. "Frankly, I was hoping to never speak about it. All I wanted was to forget. But it seems like it's not an option, so... Might as well get this over with."

She clasps her hands atop the table and squares her shoulders.

"The name I was born with is Margarete Buller. I was born

in Berlin, Germany, in 1918, to Alma and Waldemar Buller, the eldest of four children. The SS man in the photo is Hansjörg Buller, one of my brothers. He has a twin, Ragnar."

A long pause, entire years flashing in front of Maggie's glazed-over eyes. Her tongue feels as heavy as a boulder inside her mouth, but she has to turn it all the same to speak the unspeakable—for her sister's sake.

"Buller—" she spits out the hateful name, "my *birth* father— as I don't consider him my father by any means—he was a monster. Drinking, beating up my mother, making her work, and taking all of her money for himself, which would leave us starving on many occasions. My mother suffered, but she stayed for my sake, as Buller made it obvious that while he didn't care for his sons, he would rather kill us all before allowing her to leave with me. It was going on for over four years until..."

A quick gulp; eyes drawn to the ceiling. Rapid blinking. A hot flash of shame and nerves and all the poison that's been circling in her veins for decades now. It's more difficult than she imagined, speaking of it, no matter the circumstances, no matter the clinical terms.

"She was pregnant again, my mother. One day she told me that she was trying very hard to have a little sister for me, so I would have a playmate... I went into hysterics then and begged her not to. She must have felt that something was wrong and began asking me why, and I refused to tell her at first."

Maggie's hands are in fists, dripping sweat, but she doesn't realize it. All she hears is the wild beating of her own heart.

"He was doing things to me, Buller. Sexual things, which no father should ever do to his daughter. And not only him, but there were others, too... It was very widespread in those times, after the first war. Anyway... When my mother learned of it, as soon as she realized why I didn't want my sister to suffer the way I did, the way she did, she said that we were leaving as soon as it was possible. And she kept her word.

"One night, soon after that, when Buller left together with his fellow paramilitary thugs for some skirmish with the communists, she gathered me and whatever few things we had and took me to the train station. I don't remember the route itself, just trains and boats and men my mother likely slept with for money just to get us further and further away from Germany until we finally disembarked at Ellis Island as refugees. My brothers, she left at home. She couldn't travel with all three of us, pregnant herself, so she had to leave them with him, knowing that he wouldn't touch them the way he did me. They were boys, he wasn't interested in boys."

Suddenly, Orso's hand is on top of hers, squeezing fiercely, and all at once, the tears spill, huge and heavy as pearls. The room is so silent, Maggie hears them drop from under her chin, where they gather on the desk.

"James Sullivan, my father—my *real* father, the man who raised me, I mean—was a beat cop patrolling the streets where our new tenement was. He felt so sorry for my mother, whom he often saw waddling from one home to another with her huge belly—she was a cleaning woman—that he paid for the doctor to come and aid her birth when she went into labor and then paid our rent and groceries for the entire month while she was recovering and feeding Norma. She did have a little sister for me, after all," Maggie says with a wistful smile.

"He would bring groceries, toys, and teach us English as my mother didn't want to speak German. She hoped that I would forget the language together with the past. It couldn't have been easy for my dad. I barely spoke at all, I was mostly mute. But he wouldn't give up on me. Bought me a book with beautiful cut-out figures for illustrations, but I couldn't understand the story unless I spoke the language. So, little by little, he taught me. First, through the books, then through the movies. Asked me if it was all right with me if he married my mommy." Another smile, fond and fleeting. "I thought it was the most peculiar thing. They were very much a couple by then, but he still wanted to ask me for her hand. I said yes.

"We were a happy little family. And Norma was such a delight as a baby. I honestly believed that the worst was in the past. I honestly tried to forget it all, pretend that it never happened. Just a bad dream. I entirely erased my German identity from my own mind. I only spoke English and I was a Sullivan and my daddy was Irish and I was American. Except, the fact that I never spoke of it turned out to be the downfall of us all. My sister was so sheltered, growing up in a family that knew no violence, she followed some bastard into the neighboring building's cellar to see the kittens. He told her his cat just had a litter and she could choose one."

Maggie blinks through the film of the past and jolts slightly after finding herself in the room surrounded by all these strangers. She recovers herself quickly though; wipes her face with the sleeve of her uniform. Once again, it's dry and devoid of any emotion.

"Do I need to spell out what he did to her like I spelled out everything else?" She addresses the men in her perfectly dead voice. "He raped her and left her bleeding on the floor, like a discarded rag. She was only nine."

Harlow swallows uncomfortably. His eyes are on his shoes, but Maggie wants him to look up. He asked for this, after all, didn't he?

"From that point on, it was one hospital after another. She wouldn't sleep, wouldn't let anyone touch her even fleetingly, refused to eat. They had to force-feed her in the hospital, so she wouldn't die. Once released, she wouldn't talk. Wouldn't go outside. Certainly wouldn't resume school. It was only after I told her what had happened to me that she began coming out of her catatonic state, little by little. We developed a bond that kept us both afloat, but only just.

"Norma began to paint around that time, really dark,

disturbing stuff—the only way she could express her pain instead of cutting her skin or starving herself. When she was around thirteen, just as she returned from the hospital after an attempted suicide, she painted a picture that made me burst into tears, really ugly crying until my throat was raw. A dark, cold ocean during a storm and a piece of plywood getting hurled around, and on it, one girl pulling the other one out of the water, but, in the meantime, the second girl is dragging her down with her weight. The plywood will never support them both, it's already half-submerged, but the girl doesn't let go, even though it means that they'll both drown. That's how it was—still is— between us. Me, trying to drag her out of her own misery while drowning in my own."

Maggie draws herself up, an empty vessel with nothing else to give them.

"It's unsustainable, what's happening between us. That's why my marriage failed and that's why Norma is back in the psychiatric facility. We realized that we can't go on like this anymore. Something needs to be done. And that's the reason why I'm here: to look Waldemar Buller in the eye. If I finally get closure, maybe the plywood will turn into a boat and I'll have space in it for us both to reach the shore."

With his hand still covering Maggie's, Orso is staring at the two men with scarcely concealed cold fury but the sentiment is lost on them. Harlow and the MP investigator exchange looks and, after clearing their throats, begin their interrogation anew. Well, if this is indeed the God-honest truth, why did she not just say it at the beginning? Why the stubborn silence? Why almost choose a firing squad over just confessing it all?

The questions are so utterly idiotic, Maggie can't help but shake her head at the absurdity of the situation. "Do you think it's easy for a woman to talk about such things?" she asks them with a grim chuckle. "I haven't even told my father. I know it's not my fault, what Waldemar Buller did to me, just like it's not

Norma's fault for what that pathetic excuse of a man did to her. And yet, it's us who feel dirty, who feel shame, who think that there's something wrong with us instead of them. Do you think it's easy, sharing the memories I hate reliving myself with men— *men!*—I don't even know, just to be met with, 'Well, if this is indeed the God-honest truth'? And the funny part, I knew you would say that even before I began telling my story. Because you're men. You simply don't fucking understand." Her voice rises an octave, breath catching, as she stares them down with eyes gleaming with righteous fury. "You don't fucking under-stand that, yes, it *is* much easier to choose a firing squad over having to sit here, feeling like I'm stripping my skin and meat off my bones in front of you until nothing's left of me whatsoever, and even then, you'll say that I'm faking it. Fuck you and your questions and your opinion of me! I said what I had to say, only for Norma. If you still doubt me, go ahead and shoot me. I'm not uttering another word in front of you pigs."

Having said that, Maggie rises suddenly, turns her chair around and drops into it, her back to them, arms folded across her chest. Her ears are ringing and her head is covered with gooseflesh, but she clutches her own forearms tight until the feeling of fainting at any moment passes.

"If you have any decency left, get the hell out." Maggie hears Orso say.

In other circumstances, she would manage a faint smile—naturally, he knew that her very last tirade wasn't aimed at him, the first man on these continental shores she doesn't have to explain herself to—but she's too weak to feel any remnants of emotion just now. She's not faint any longer but still slightly nauseous and hurting all over as if after a beating. But it's the familiar pain: muscles screaming after being clenched for hours, carrying the burden of the past that would crush any of her interrogators if they lived even through a sliver of what she had lived through.

"Maggie." Orso's voice is infinitely soft as he calls to her once it's just the two of them in the room. "I'm so very sorry."

Maggie nods, but doesn't turn around. She can't face him yet—she doesn't even want to face herself.

"Shall I leave too?"

"No." She doesn't elaborate.

"Do you want me to talk or just shut up and be here with you?"

"Just shut up and be here with me."

Maggie hears the rustling of his uniform as he gets up from his chair. He approaches almost on tiptoe, lowers to the floor—next to her, not in front—and takes her hand as he crosses his legs. In perfect silence, their wristwatches measure time in unison.

TWENTY-SEVEN

A WEEK LATER

On the road once again, Maggie's leafing through the other reporters' writing. Higgins' article on the Buchenwald liberation—"Horror Comes Home"—got her a front page in the *Herald Tribune* and even a reprint in the *Stars and Stripes*. In her front pocket, several letters from her namesake sit. They only shared a room for a few nights and Higgins knew virtually nothing of Maggie, but she, along with her fellow war correspondent sisters, wrote and asked what the matter was and if Maggie needed her help.

"Just a misunderstanding," Maggie wrote back. "Nothing to worry about." She was already free and back to work.

Higgins dropped the subject without questions or judgment. Her next letter was about their shared Buchenwald experience:

> *I wish you interviewed those inmates instead of me. I was so proud of my journalistic skepticism, I turned from an interviewer into an interrogator, just when those poor people needed it the least. They tried telling me of things that happened and I demanded witnesses and cross-examinations. I'm so terribly*

ashamed! Shall I write an apology? I shall write an apology.
My behavior was inexcusable. Those crematoriums, my God!
Do you, too, have nightmares about them?

She would have, had it not been for the sleeping pills that
knock her out senseless and some local schnapps to chase them
down with. In an odd gesture of goodwill she never expected
from him, Harlow returned Maggie's confiscated pills to her and
even slipped her some morphine, wherever that came from.
Maggie thought of telling him that she had no need for it, that
the pain was in her mind, not her body, but then realized that it
was likely Harlow's own brand of apology and left it well alone.
He must have had his own Higgins moment of regret after
subjecting her to the third degree together with the MPs.
Maggie still shook his hand as they parted ways. She didn't hold
grudges. Only endless hatred for those who rightfully deserved
it.

Under Higgins' *Herald Tribune*, there's Lee's British *Vogue*.
No front page for the barely breathing Buchenwald inmates,
but Maggie discovers quite a spread on the liberation in the
middle of the issue. To her astonishment, they didn't censor any
of the images and instead published them—gore, death, and all
—right between a black and white photo of a model with a brilliant smile advertising a new brand of toothpaste and a color
photo of another bronze-shouldered girl in a swimsuit that will
be all the rage in the summer of '45. Maggie silently applauds
the editor-in-chief, both for the courage to publish them and for
the idea of putting Lee's photos exactly where they did. The
effect is both shocking and guilt-instilling—a rude awakening
for those who "chose neutrality." There can't be any neutrality
when violence is committed. One either fights it or serves as an
accomplice to it, and Lee has just shoved their faces right in it,
brilliant journalist that she is.

As their open jeep crawls to a stop, the driver taps Maggie

gently on her shoulder, calling her back to their surroundings. "Look, there's more of them, right there on the bench. Want to take a photo, boss?"

Maggie still fights a smile each time Patrick, the GI assigned to her as a driver, addresses her in such a play-deferential manner though the smile never stays on for long as she remembers how she got herself such an escort, not counting the other two jeeps following her progress at all times at the tail of the Twelfth Armored Division heading south from Weimar to Munich.

When Harlow returned to her holding cell later that night, he brought with him an entire mob of intelligence agents. It was such a delight for them to learn that Maggie Sullivan was in fact Waldemar Buller's daughter, their leader explained in a manner so tone-deaf, it might have been almost comical, if it wasn't so insulting. And if she was looking for him, they would help her do just that, as they were looking for him too. It seems that he rose through the ranks since Maggie saw him and traded his paramilitary uniform for an SA uniform, and later, an SS one. His name—together with the names of his two sons—was on the list of wanted criminals. Charge: crimes against humanity. Something to do with the administration of concentration and extermination camps. Maggie wasn't surprised to learn any of this.

Orso tried to protest that exploiting Buller's victim (he never, not once, called her Buller's daughter) in such a dastardly manner was the scummiest thing he'd ever heard of. But Maggie stopped him. She didn't care one way or the other if the Special Operations branch of the OSS—the recently established Office of Strategic Services—was using her to get to Buller. If it was easier to find him that way, she'd take it. She needed to look the bastard in the eye.

"And then what?" Orso asked, just her, very quietly, almost under his breath.

Maggie looked at him for a very long time, but in the end, she left the room without responding.

The truth was, she didn't know herself what she wanted from him. An explanation of what could possibly move him to such unspeakable acts? An apology? A plea for his life as she held a gun to his head? To watch him die?

They've been traveling south for a week now, in the direction of Munich, where Buller supposedly lives, and Maggie still doesn't have the answer. Only a fleeting feeling that she might be too late.

The OSS intelligence also mentioned that Buller resided there along with Frau Buller and Maggie can only feel sorry for the woman. Sorry and not sorry, at the same time. Maggie's mother married a soldier she waited to return from the trenches; this new Frau Buller married an SS officer, and a high-ranking one at that. Quite a big difference.

But, then again, who is Maggie to judge? Maybe the woman needed money or Buller's influence for whatever reason. A brother in a camp or sick parents needing treatment. Maggie has chosen to reserve her judgment until she's learned all the facts.

"You think they're related or just neighbors?" Patrick asks as Maggie aims her Kodak at the trio sharing a bench. A well-dressed man and next to him, two women, hair done, nails painted, and mouths open in the last soundless scream. "No gunshot wounds this time," he comments. "Cyanide?"

"Looks like it," Maggie says, snapping a photo.

They look like they're only napping, so serene are their poses. One of the women's ankles are crossed, her friend's (or sister's?) head resting on her shoulder. The man has lost his hat as his body must have stretched out in a quick convulsion and his hair is tangled by the wind, but otherwise they seem oddly at peace—a welcome change from some of the first violent scenes Maggie covered.

This time, her editor didn't reject photos of the first communal suicide Maggie took. That one was a massacre: the high-ranking Nazi didn't have the guts to kill his three children and wife with his gun and instead pulled the pin out of a hand grenade right at the dining table where they were sitting. The same gore her editor first objected to was not just acceptable but welcome now. This was Nazi gore. This was OK, dead children or not.

In a matter of only seven days, Maggie has seen more manners of suicide than she could imagine, and the further south they drove, the more bodies they uncovered. They were everywhere: in parks under the blossoming trees, at their homes, in the rivers and lakes, on the cobblestoned streets and in staff cars with Nazi pennants still attached to the hood. They slashed their wrists and jumped from roofs and shot themselves and their loved ones, and hurled themselves from bridges and into dark rivers, pockets full of rocks, and swallowed all the poison available at the first sounds of the approaching army.

Maggie's breath caught in her throat each time she approached yet another corpse in an SS uniform and only resumed when she saw that, no, it wasn't Waldemar Buller. If God indeed existed, He wouldn't let him take the easy way out, not after everything he'd put Maggie through.

"I can understand those Nazis." Patrick once again, all white teeth against black skin and the Harlem accent Maggie feels so at home with. They refused Orso's request to accompany her but unwittingly gave her someone just as good instead —someone who quickly became a friend, who, with his incessant chatter, made the trip somewhat tolerable. "What I don't understand is these ladies. Why do they kill themselves? They weren't in the army and no one is looking to charge them with any crimes."

"I heard from the refugees from the east that they were

killing themselves because the Soviet soldiers were raping them. And for women, rape is sometimes worse than death."

He listens to her with his head slightly cocked. "All right, fair point. But there are no Soviets here, we're US Army. We don't rape anyone."

Maggie wants to remind him of all the drunken orgies she witnessed in the newly liberated towns, when even she had to seek shelter at the officers' quarters from the inebriated GIs' advances, but then the realization dawns on her that she never, not once, saw a Black GI among those revelers. They were welcome to fight but not to share the same quarters, or the same bottle, and certainly not the same German woman with their white counterparts. Suddenly ashamed of her blindness to such an arrangement, she mentally marks it down, the title of a new article already forming in her mind when Patrick's words bring her attention back to the moment.

"If anything, German ladies always come say hello first. Even to me."

"Why wouldn't they say hello to you, you handsome devil?" Maggie nudges her driver playfully with her elbow.

"Oh, come now, Miss Maggie. You know how it is, even back home."

Yes, she knows exactly how it is, even back home. Even with the growing Black population in the neighboring Bed-Stuy, movie theaters in Williamsburg still have seats for whites and colored people, just like the diners, just like the schools and drinking fountains in public parks. Jim Crow is an American version of the German anti-Semitism, both ugly sides of the same coin.

"It's a white man's world," Patrick says and Maggie doesn't argue. "And white men don't like it when my kind socializes with white ladies, German or not. So, I let them say hello, share my gum or cigarettes, and get back to minding my own business."

"I don't imagine you ever minding your own business," Maggie grumbles in mock protest, alluding to his constant questions and observations, and receives another brilliant smile in return. "But, since you asked, I suppose these particular ladies, judging by their clothes and shoes and stockings, were either married to someone high up in the Nazi Party or related to them and now that the downfall was imminent, they chose to end it all instead of trying to rebuild their lives in a new Germany. Or they were simply fanatical Nazis themselves," she finishes with a shrug and jumps back into the idling jeep. "Either way, I'm glad I didn't grow up here. I would only have ended up the same way, killing myself—except, in my case, long before Hitler came to power."

Patrick knows her story. Once she'd shared it with the room full of indifferent MPs, Maggie found it easier to share it with someone she could trust, and besides, she needs someone to talk her options through before they reach Munich.

On the northern outskirts of the city, Helen Kirkpatrick jumps into Maggie's jeep and envelops her in a hug that is so warm and welcome, Maggie melts into it, eyes closed.

"Where have you been?" the *Chicago Daily News* foreign correspondent asks, searching Maggie with her bright eyes that are alert as ever, even if rimmed with black. "I haven't seen you since last summer!"

"I know! We keep missing each other." Maggie smiles and introduces Helen to Patrick.

"How did you get yourself a personal driver?" Helen gestures toward the direction from which she came. "I have to literally beg people to take me along."

"You don't want to know." Maggie cringes slightly with a glare at her OSS escort.

Helen narrows her eyes at them too. "I heard you got yourself into some magisterial shite at Buchenwald, Sullivan, but I thought they..." She doesn't finish, just looks at the agents of the Office of Strategic Services instead.

"I'm not in trouble of any kind," Maggie rushes to assure her. "But don't write about it, please."

Helen looks at her with exaggerated offense. "What am I, tabloid-employed yellow press? Besides, there are more interesting stories than you driving around with an intelligence service on your behind."

Maggie kicks her lightly on the shin and digs into her Kodak, still smiling. "You're a jerk, Kirkpatrick. But just because I was so happy to see your lovely face and also because I don't know if I'll have the time to submit it myself—here, take my last film. It's all Nazi suicides."

Helen studies Maggie for some time, the proffered film untouched between them. "Funny," she says at last. "Exactly what I've been working on."

"So, take it." Maggie nudges Helen's hand with it.

"Last time Bill Stringer offered his film to Ann to make sure that it got out safe, he got killed by a German tank," Helen says in an undertone. "What have you gotten yourself into really, Sullivan?"

"Nothing that involves tanks, I promise."

With great reluctance, Helen takes the film and puts it in her breast pocket. "Are you at least coming to Dachau? The Twelfth is barely meeting any resistance on the way there. Word has it, we'll overrun it soon."

Maggie steals a glance at her OSS minders and answers noncommittally, "If I can."

The over-the-shoulder glance doesn't escape Helen. "Do you need help? I can't offer much, but Lee has old friends in high circles—"

"No, no," Maggie grasps her hands with a quick smile. "I'm not in trouble, really." It starts to drizzle, a nasty, bothersome rain that doesn't drench one properly but contributes to the overall gray, depressive mood. "Don't just sit here, Kirkpatrick. Go. Do your job, for the both of us."

Helen climbs out of the jeep and pulls her jacket over her head—mostly to cover her camera from the rain rather than herself. "If you lied and you do die on me in the end," she says as she backs away from the vehicle, "I'll use that photo I took of you last June in London for your obituary. The one where you're sleeping in the tub, drunk as a pig, in that ugly red clown's wig."

"Deal." Maggie smiles and waves.

Patrick starts the motor.

"What do they want from you? The OSS?" Patrick asks as they get stuck in the column of refugees on the eastern outskirts of Munich they're circling round instead of driving through it.

The Twelfth Armored Division made a turn a few hours ago to proceed to Dachau, but Maggie's handlers quickly dampened her war correspondent's spirits. Buller wasn't in the camp, according to their intelligence. Nothing for her there. Maggie begged and pleaded for just a couple of hours, just a couple of photos, but all her words fell on deaf ears. Plenty of correspondents to report on the liberation without her there. Having one journo less won't make any difference.

Maggie's still sulking over it, not so much at the intelligence agents—they have a job to do, so she kind of, sort of, understands—but at Buller. So many years passed, and he still manages to rob her of something. First, of innocence, identity and name, and now, of the historic liberation of Dachau.

"They want me to talk Buller into surrendering instead of him offing himself. He could testify against the higher-ups they want to bring up on charges before facing trial himself."

"Do you think he would? Off himself, I mean?"

Maggie ponders her response for a while. "It's difficult to say. People like him, they're cowards, really. When in a position of power, they bully others relentlessly. But when the tables turn, they usually cling to their sorry lives until the end. Though, I might be mistaken. I could never understand what was going on in his head. That's why I want to talk to him now. Because it bugs me, still."

"I bet."

Patrick lays on the horn, but the river of refugees can only part so much, weighed down with the carts they pull themselves instead of horses doing so. Maggie wonders what they're running from, all of these people. The war is as good as over. Even the scattered Wehrmacht formations greet the US vehicles with white handkerchiefs and gladly deposit their weapons in the jeeps' backs. At first, she questioned why they always traveled in groups, those begrimed, haggard soldiers. But after she photographed the placard around the neck of the first Wehrmacht private hanging from the electric pole—"I surrendered to the Amis and deserve to die a shameful death" —it all made sense. It was more difficult for the last rabid SS military policemen to execute a small Wehrmacht unit for desertion instead of a lone youth in his *Hitlerjugend* uniform picking his way home through muddy roads full of bomb craters.

Though, today her OSS escort stops such a group of four and orders them to disrobe.

"What now?" Patrick groans, but not loudly enough for the men to hear.

"Bored, likely," Maggie quips but clambers out of the jeep all the same, camera at the ready. If they don't let her go into Dachau, she'll just have to photograph the OSS at work, which is only fair. They use her, she'll use them.

The Wehrmacht men exchange confused looks and mumble something as they point to one of their men who's looking a little worse for wear, but the American Intelligence squad shows little patience for negotiations.

"I said, everything off!" Lawrence, their leader, commands in German. "Undershirts as well. I don't give a damn about your comrade's pneumonia! Strip to your trousers and lift up your arms."

Maggie is about to take what she expected to be just an ordinary photo of soldiers being searched when the soldiers suddenly break out in different directions as she looks on, mouth agape. The couple that try to make it across the field are mowed down by the OSS men's machine-gun fire within seconds, but the other two dive into the moving column of refugees before the OSS can scramble for a response.

"Sneaky bastards!" Maggie hears Lawrence curse before he jumps into the bed of his truck and releases a round into the air. "Civilians, face down on the ground if you don't want to get shot!"

Women shriek in horror, but German citizens are well trained in war games by now. They drop into the mud in an instant, covering their heads with their hands.

Maggie's camera clicks away, capturing the attempted escape frame by frame. Exposed now, the first soldier throws his hands in the air and falls atop a man, sending his medic's bag flying. The other one gets only a few steps further before he, too, spins in the air and drops, first to his knees and then keels over entirely, evoking more screams from blood-splattered civilians that had the misfortune to be near the scene.

Maggie follows her OSS escort and watches through her lens as they produce their army knives and slice into the fabric of the soldier's sleeves.

"What's that?" she asks in puzzlement as one of the intelligence agents reveals a tattooed O near the soldier's armpit.

"Blood type," the agent explains, digging for the dead man's papers. "It's a new trick they recently adopted, the SS, to slip through our hands undetected. Only they—Hitler's beloved Aryan elite—were marked this way, so that field medics would know which blood type to use for transfusion even if the soldier is unconscious. The Wehrmacht didn't get such a privilege. They're conscripts, not ideological troops. Cannon fodder. Like this poor bastard was, whatever they did to him."

Maggie stares at the bloodied papers inside the stolen uniform. Indeed, the photo of the soldier inside has nothing in common with the dead SS man's face. "They're killing their own now?" she mutters, still digesting the events. "Just for the uniform?"

"They're the SS. Did you expect anything different?"

No, Maggie supposes, she didn't.

She watches the agent yank the dog tags off the dead man's neck and picks her way toward the second corpse, which another OSS man is perusing.

"Papers aren't his. Sullivan, take a look. Could it be one of the Buller brothers?"

"Your guess is as good as mine." Maggie shrugs, indifferent. "I only saw Hansjörg once, in his file photo. I've no idea what he looks like in real life, or Ragnar for that matter."

They're her blood brothers and yet to Maggie, they're about just as close as some stranger on a street. She digs into herself in search of, if not exactly an emption then at least an echo of it from her childhood days but comes up entirely empty. They were too small to develop any personality for her to remember and mourn. All Maggie recalls is their incessant cries and the spot in her mother's bed they stole from her. As for them, they likely don't remember her at all—the big sister who once kept them fed and dry, the mini-mother with a childhood stolen from her. All that is left in Maggie is resentment—for Buller, for robbing her of brothers who could have grown into good young men, and turning them into versions of himself instead.

"But do you think you'll recognize Waldemar? Almost a

quarter century has passed since you last saw him. And, unlike with your brothers, we won't be able to help you. He isn't Himmler or Göring. He isn't really known to the general public and neither do we have any recent photos of him."

"Don't worry about that." Maggie's eyes narrow as she gazes in the direction in which Munich lies. "I'll recognize him, all right."

TWENTY-EIGHT

"Bellevue, please," Maggie speaks into the receiver, covering her mouth with one hand. "Psychiatric unit."

The noise in the newly established SHAEF communications room on the outskirts of the city doesn't require such precautions, but Maggie still hides away from prying eyes, no matter how subtle they pretend to be. Rumors of her arrest and almost immediate release have been making the rounds in expeditionary forces circles and each new version obtained more and more incredible details that defied logic itself. Someone must have had a source within the intelligence unit: all of the accounts got her German origin correct, even if they disagreed on her ties with the Nazis and the reason for her going free. They don't say it to her face, but Maggie feels it all the same from them: the suspicion, the silent accusation, the mistrust.

Communications officers greet her with "how's it going?" but stare at her back as soon as she turns it on them. Maggie wishes at least one of her girls was here but Lee has gone from Dachau straight to Munich to photograph Hitler's apartment and Ann is likely still in Torgau, nursing the mother of all hangovers after covering the linking of Soviet and American troops on the river Elbe. The jubilation of the Allied troops all but poured out from the pictures Ann's photographer took, strategically placing Ann at the center of the celebration. Everyone's beaming, everyone's hugging, everyone's toasting and drinking and exchanging helmets and hats and addresses and promises to write—on that day, April 25, everything seemed possible.

"Good for you," Maggie whispered with sisterly pride as she saw the paper and swallowed a bitter lump that's been choking her for days on end now. Another victorious march. Another historic event that could rightfully get Ann the Pulitzer—another opportunity Waldemar Buller stole from Maggie. It hurt and enraged her, the fact that he still affected her life even in his absence. Instead of following the troops and documenting history as it unraveled before her very eyes, Maggie was stuck here, near Munich, with her useless Kodak, waiting for the OSS to pinpoint Buller's exact location.

Finally, they have but it's too late for Maggie-the-war-correspondent now. She missed it all.

She clenches at the phone as if to strangle it and only releases her grip a bit once Norma's voice reaches her from across the ocean.

"Hey, big sister."

"Hey, little one."

Maggie's chest is awash with infinite warmth that softens her eyes and touches upon the corners of her lips, albeit fleetingly.

"How are you?"

How is she? Maggie laughs hollowly into the mouthpiece. "Damned if I know."

"You found them." It's not a question. Norma picks up on the slightest intonation of Maggie's voice, just like Maggie knows exactly what Norma's feeling.

"The OSS just got a tip from the locals where Buller is." Maggie's teeth bite into her lip. Her escort urged her forward as soon as they got the intel, but Maggie refused to budge without this call to her sister. And now, here they are, talking, but it isn't easy in any way. She doesn't want to be here. She wants to be home, with Norma.

"Where are you?" Norma asks, suddenly all business.

"Near Munich. SHAEF headquarters."

"And he is?"

"In his summer villa, south of the city, closer to the mountains."

"You're not going there alone, are you?"

"What's he gonna do?" Maggie's Brooklyn drawl suddenly resurfaces in response to her sister's, making her more homesick than ever. "Kill me?"

Norma is silent for a while. Then, "I wish I was there with you."

"I wish you were too. But then I don't. I don't want you to ever meet him."

"You made sure of it, while I was still in Mommy's tummy."

"Fat lot of good it did."

"Mags, don't you dare! You hear me? Don't you dare blame what happened to me on yourself. You are the only reason I'm still alive."

"And you are the reason I am." Something breaks in her then. Maggie's chest begins to heave in spite of herself. All at once, she's a child again, defenseless and frightened, with the world a dark place and no one there to hold her hand. "It's not fair," she sobs into the phone and doesn't care any longer that anyone can hear her as a hush falls over the room. "It's just so unfair. Why us?"

"Oh, Mags, if I had a dollar every time I asked myself that!" Norma is cry-laughing, her sniffles mixing with a hushed *I'm-*

all-right, I'm-all-right likely aimed at her nurses. "Only, it's not just us. Most of the women here are like us, too. Most of the women Daddy's police department recovers from the Hudson, back alleys, and parks. And those are only the cases that get talked about, because there is a mutilated corpse and it ends up in the papers. But God knows how many women just go about their lives without anyone knowing. I know how much it hurts, but hey, Mags, we can roll over and die and let them win, or we can survive and thrive. If only out of spite."

"Spite." Maggie tries the word and discovers, to her great surprise, that she's actually laughing. "I like that."

"Too bad I can't claim it. It's our unit's new psychiatrist's take—I like her very much."

"She's a woman?"

"An Austrian lady, yes. She studied under Dr. Jung after being treated by him as a patient. Wanna guess why?"

"Some scum violated her?"

"You're no fun."

Maggie wipes her tears and smiles into the receiver. "You sound much better."

"You too, actually."

"I have been talking about it. First, quite literally under the gun, but then, just because I wanted to."

"So have I. We have a group, just us women, sharing our experiences. It helps so much. Also, Dr. Adler's invention."

"Can I check myself in once I'm finished here?"

"Join right in! You're one apple short of a fruitcake anyway."

Maggie laughs, but then remembers why she's here and feels the smile drop once again.

Norma picks right up on it and breathes into the phone, "Hey, big sister, I have you. Go slay your dragon. It's time."

Yes, Maggie nods to herself. *It is time.*

.   .   .

In the mountains, the snow still lies, but here in the valley, wet earth with the first sprouts of grass welcomes them. On Lawrence's direction, Patrick parks his jeep by one of the typical mountain huts that have dotted the region for centuries and will remain here for many more. The OSS men climb out, stretch their legs, greet the hut's inhabitants, who came out at the first sounds of the diesel engines rumbling to a stop. It's a couple in their fifties, faces weathered by the Alpine climate and decades of farm work. They invite the Americans in and the first thing Maggie notices is the telling absence of anything related to the events of the past ten years. No portraits of the *Führer* on the walls, no papers with the latest news from the front. Not even a photo of a son in a uniform, which is surreal on its own. It's almost as if they exist in their own time and reality, where the only changes that matter are the changes of the seasons and the years are measured by sowing and harvesting— just as nature intended.

The wife offers them freshly baked bread with butter Maggie has no doubt she churned herself and milk that came from the cow mooing mutely in the small adjacent barn. The husband thanks them for the crate of preserves and strong American tobacco and tells them that, yes, he knows the Buller family.

"There was a small farmhouse like ours there before," he says, motioning his hand toward the window overlooking the roof of the villa Maggie can't stop staring at. "But Buller bought it in the thirties. The inmates built this new one for him."

"Inmates from Dachau? The concentration camp?" Lawrence asks.

Only he and Maggie are listening closely. The rest of the group are busy tucking into the fresh produce as the farmer's wife looks on with a smile of approval.

"I don't know what they call it or where they came from, but they wore striped uniforms is all I know. Soldiers were minding them. The Bullers, they only lived there during the summer or came by occasionally 'round Christmastime to ski, sometimes with other families. That's when they'd send his driver or adjutant, or whatever the devil he was, to buy cheese, milk, and whatnot from us. The wife and the kiddies, they came here to stay permanently about three months ago."

"Two months," his wife corrects him. "That was when the soldiers tried to take our Poppy away to be butchered, but he spoke for us and they left her alone, praise the Lord."

"Poppy is our cow," the farmer explains. "Our last one. We used to have a whole herd, twenty heads, but now she's the only one left. They took them all away for the army, one by one. Anyway, he must have wanted his kiddies to have fresh milk every day, else, he would have let them take her."

Maggie's heart sinks as the farmer mentions the children. For some reason, the past stayed the past in her mind, with only she and her two brothers bearing the cursed Buller name. The new wife, she came to terms with. It's still a damned rotten business for the woman to share her name and bed with Buller, but at least she's an adult, much like Maggie's mother was when she escaped from him. This new Frau Buller can do the same if the occasion calls for it, but with the helpless children, it's an entirely different case. She reaches for a cigarette with a trembling hand and sends a silent prayer to the heavens for the "kiddies" to be boys.

"He, himself, didn't stay that time," the farmer continues. "Got here about three weeks ago, with his driver or adjutant—again, forgive an old fool, I can't say for sure. The young man is very polite, though. Comes down here every few days for foodstuffs."

"Could the young man be his son?" Maggie asks quietly. "He has two older sons, they would be in their mid-twenties now. Twins."

The farmer shrugs his wide shoulders. "I wouldn't know,

Fräulein. I only saw Buller himself once: when he came to speak for the cow. He wore a military cap, the driver always wears it—I can't say if they're related or not."

"The driver is still there now?" the OSS commander asks.

"He must be. The only passable road here is the one you took, and it goes past our house, so we see all the comings and goings. They're in the hamlet across the valley. On the other side of them are slopes and snow still as deep as a grown man's height. He couldn't have left through there, if that's what you're asking."

"This complicates things," Lawrence says in English with a glance at Maggie.

"No, it doesn't," she replies after another deep pull on her cigarette. The smoke burns her lungs pleasantly, leaving her head tingling. She knows he sees her shaking hands but doesn't try to hide them. "He's not going to start shooting with his wife and children there."

"He may put them in the cellar and decide to go out with a final bang. Or shoot them first—I wouldn't put it past him. I've seen plenty of them go out like goddamn Egyptian pharaohs, with the entire household as escort. And you did say he was violent toward your mother on multiple occasions and threatened to kill her if she tried to leave him."

"If she tried to leave him *with me*," Maggie corrects him.

She's in a strange state, oddly clear-headed, her entire body vibrating with some weird lightness about it—a feeling she's experienced only once in her life before. It was late June and Daddy took them all to Luna Park in Coney Island, where the new rollercoaster—the Cyclone—had just opened. Mommy looked petrified surveying the small wagons flying past as they carried screaming thrill-seekers. Over her dead body would he put her in that contraption, she declared. Norma was still much too small to ride it, but Maggie couldn't wait to try it out—why, she couldn't quite tell.

Perhaps to block out her memories of the other, Berlin Luna Park.

When their turn came, Daddy helped her climb into the seat and showed her how to hold onto a metal bar—the only barrier that was supposed to prevent her from flying out of the wagon. He'd hold her other hand, he promised. To Maggie, that was a much better assurance.

The climb was agonizingly slow. From her vantage point, people and booths were growing progressively smaller. In front, a wide indigo sky was replacing the madness of the Luna Park until its lights disappeared from Maggie's view completely. They paused at the very top, with only the yellow coin of the moon reflecting in the waters of the ocean, and for a few short instants Maggie felt suspended between the two worlds, between life and death itself, before finally plunging downward with neck-breaking speed.

Just like now; only this time, there is no one to hold her hand through it. This is something she has to see through herself—either to perish or emerge victorious and stronger than ever on the other side of the nightmare.

"You wait here," she says and stubs the cigarette in the stone ashtray. "I'll go there by myself."

"Sullivan, no—"

But Maggie interrupts Lawrence with her hand raised. "You said it yourself, he could shoot everyone there before turning on your squad. And yes, it's something I wouldn't put past him. But if I go alone, there's a chance you can get him alive. He *will* talk to me. Many things could have changed, but not one simple fact—I'm still his daughter. The only one he wanted."

Leaving her helmet, Maggie steps out of the hut and into the fresh April morning. The road that stretches ahead smells of wet earth and cow dung and, somehow, of the innocence of the childhood she was so cruelly robbed of. It's a long road and yet much too short at the same time. Maggie pushes forward and yet tries to slow her steps all the same, to delay the inevitable and yet to rip the Band-Aid off before she loses her courage. The two-story villa grows taller with each beat of her heart and soon, she can discern the intricate wood carvings framing the windows, the rocking chairs on the veranda stretching out the entire length of the second floor, the car parked near the entrance, facing east.

By the time she reaches her knuckles to rap on the door, Maggie's back is wet with sweat, despite her breath coming out in translucent clouds of vapor. She takes a deep breath, trembling with her entire body and flushed with heat at the same time. Finally, she knocks.

They must have seen her coming, for the door opens almost immediately. It's not Buller though, or his driver for that matter. A good-looking woman of about Maggie's own age holds a small child in her arms as another two look on from behind her. A girl and a boy, around nine and seven. Maggie's blood runs cold at the sight of the girl. She hoped for Buller not to produce any more offspring to abuse and corrupt, but here she stands, this young child with the eyes full of angst like those of a grown woman. It's best not to look at her else Maggie shall shoot Buller as soon as she sees him instead of delivering him to the OSS and their whole operation will go to the devil.

"*Guten Morgen*," Maggie greets the woman in a voice she doesn't recognize. "You must be Frau Buller."

"I am, yes," the blonde woman smiles, scanning Maggie's uniform with a mixture of interest and carefully hidden alarm. Her posture relaxes a bit when she notices the letter C on the armband circling Maggie's bicep. "And you are?"

"Margarete Sullivan, *New York Times*."

There's something vaguely familiar about this new Frau Buller, but Maggie just can't put her finger on it.

"I'm afraid we don't own a subscription." Frau Buller tries on a smile.

"We're new in town." Maggie smiles back. "May I come in?"

Frau Buller quickly glances over Maggie's shoulder.

"It's just me," Maggie assures her and can't help but glance at the girl, half-hidden in the shadows.

Unlike Maggie, she's blonde and blue-eyed and resembles her mother, whereas Maggie was the picture of Buller himself as a child. She used to hate her own reflection growing up, to such an extent she willed herself to grow into an entirely different-looking teenager and, later, adult. She ended up looking vaguely like her maternal grandmother Anna, which suited her just fine. Maggie wonders in passing what Norma's new psychiatrist would have to say about it.

"We're just a regular family." Frau Buller smiles again. "I'm afraid, if you're looking for a story, you won't find any here."

"I'm not here for a story," Maggie says evenly. "I need to talk to your husband."

"My husband?" Frau Buller blinks her big, beautiful eyes. "I'm afraid he's not here."

"Yes, he is."

"No, I assure you, he's—"

"Papa!" Maggie shouts into the house and can swear she hears the echo shout back at her, rolling down from as far as the mountains. "It's Grete. Come on out, say hello to your firstborn."

The child in startled Frau Buller's arms begins to wail. The small jolt of her half-sister's shoulders doesn't escape Maggie either. She used to flinch as well, each time the very word *Papa* was uttered. But it's Frau Buller's reaction that stuns Maggie when she thought she was way past being shocked by anything at all.

"Grete? Grete Buller?" she manages, the color slowly rising in her cheeks—a child caught red-handed at some mischief.

With the roar of a mudslide, it dawns on Maggie, the realization behind the familiarity of Frau Buller's face. It's Uschi, her friend Uschi from those half-starved, ice-cold Berlin days. Ursula, who longed for a papa just like Maggie's instead of her own, who whipped her with his leather belt at the slightest provocation. Ursula, who must have replaced Grete as soon as Grete was gone, hopefully, as a surrogate daughter only until she was of age. Though, with Buller, Maggie doubts that.

"No," she says in a voice that is half ice and half infinite pity. "Margarete Sullivan. Grete Buller is dead."

Ursula says nothing to that. Only reddens further and pats the child in her arms with growing desperation to silence its wails.

Before long, Maggie hears a door somewhere inside open. How very much like him, to send his wife to fend off the Amis while he himself is holed up somewhere safe, together with his driver. Maggie's lips twitch in a derisive grin. A quarter century may have passed, but he hasn't changed a bit. Not that she expected him to.

"Gretchen, is it really you, little mouse?"

Even his voice is the same, familiar to the point of pain in Maggie's clenched jaw.

The blood rushes to Maggie's head as the man she thought she had escaped comes face to face with her. He's unsure for a split second, but then sees something in Maggie's eyes that must call to the very blood in his veins and breaks into a tearful smile that would have been beautiful had it not been so grotesque.

Time hasn't been kind to him, Maggie observes with a certain satisfaction. Gone is the imperious military bearing of a dashing officer of the past, just like the dark mane he had always been so proud of. His formerly square shoulders slope visibly and the paunch is emphasized by the sweater he's dressed in. Even his face is like old wax, molten around the edges and hanging around the jowls and neck. His teeth are rotten stumps spaced widely apart, just as yellow as the whites of his eyes and just as revolting. Along his temples, sparse tufts of gray hair are brushed back in a vain and yet pitiful attempt to hide the skin still visible under them. He's somehow grown shorter, Maggie notices to her great surprise. Or is it she who has grown taller? Or is it because she only remembered him as a child, always so big and overpowering to her four-year-old self? Either way, she finds herself looking slightly down on him now, this monster who has been haunting her life to this day. It's an odd feeling. It throws her slightly off balance.

He moves his wife out of the way and goes to hug Maggie. She lets him, hard as a steel beam; her own arms straight down by her sides, she endures the hug. He goes for a kiss on her cheek, but this time she pulls back, dodging him.

"You're right," he concurs, unexpectedly pliant and respectful of her wishes. "Too much time has passed. It's too soon, isn't it?" When Maggie doesn't comment, he claps his hand and turns to his new wife. "Do you know who this is, Uschi? It's Grete, your friend from back in the day. Grete, this is Ursula, my wife. Surely, you remember her, don't you? I remarried, you see. In '32, ten years after your mother ran off with you. I was waiting and waiting and hoping that she would return, but..." He spreads his arms in a helpless gesture. "I hope you won't hold it against me."

Maggie's tongue is pressed hard against her teeth. She has a lot to say but doesn't want to cause a scene in front of the little ones, who are looking anxious as it is.

"So, America, eh?" he asks, after looking her uniform up and down. "This is where she took you. So far away. Did she have the baby?"

"She did." Maggie doesn't expand on this. The fiercely

protective big sister in her refuses to share even Norma's name with him—he doesn't deserve the knowledge.

Buller seems to sense this much. Still smiling, he nods and places his palm atop his little daughter's head. "We named her Grete, you know. After you."

Did he really marry her childhood friend, impregnate her, and name the daughter born out of such a perverted union after her? This is some new depth of depravity Maggie didn't even think possible for him to reach. She swallows and feels her hands close in fists. Her entire body is a tightly coiled spring, almost singing with a tension about to explode.

"Nice to meet you, Grete," Maggie says and holds her hand out. Her half-sister looks at her father and, after getting a nod of encouragement from him, puts her small, ice-cold palm in Maggie's. "My name's Maggie. Maggie Sullivan."

She notices Buller pull himself up ever so slightly at the name.

"Your mother, she remarried too?" he asks, still recovering from the surprise.

"Why wouldn't she? She's a beautiful, smart, hardworking woman any man would be fortunate to call his wife."

"Yes... yes, I suppose. It's just..." He stops himself, but Maggie knows exactly where he was going.

"It's just, generally men don't like other men's offspring?" She arches her brow, knowing full well she's hit the nail on the head. "Our daddy didn't mind in the slightest."

Buller tries to hide his wincing again, not just at the term of affection but at the warmth in her voice when she mentions this usurper father. His put-on smile falters, the steely gleam in his eyes turning his gaze to ice.

"Is he... a good stepfather to you?"

"He's a very good daddy, yes." Maggie rubs it in with a certain glee about her. "We all love him very much."

"That's good," Buller comments and chuckles—an old,

mocking sound that awakens an entire fleet of memories. Like ghost ships, they arise from the depths she'd buried them in and rush toward her, an armada of drunken violence and unspeakable grief.

But Maggie's ready for them now. She's ready for him.

"Can I speak with you?" she asks with intentional nonchalance. "In private?"

"Yes. Certainly." Buller gestures to the study, from which he emerged. "Uschi, make us all some coffee, will you?"

After watching Ursula depart with her children in tow, Maggie follows Buller across the hall. It's vast and rustic, with heavy beams under the ceiling and dead deer heads mounted on walls built by men who have all likely perished by now. After a quick scan of her surroundings, Maggie still can't see the driver.

Buller holds the door for her and pulls it closed after Maggie crosses the threshold. The study is bigger than their old apartment, it occurs to her, but just as oppressive. Beautifully paneled but so very gloomy; all dark, cumbersome wood and low armchairs of brown leather and thick rugs that swallow all sounds, as if one big, deep grave. It smells of smoke and brandy in here: Buller's smell.

True to himself, he's already digging inside the bar hidden in one of the wall panels—"looking for the good stuff," he claims.

"You're old enough to drink, aren't you?" he jests, producing a bottle and two glasses.

"I've always been old enough to do a lot of things," Maggie says in an even tone.

Buller laughs hollowly, feigning ignorance. "I'm pouring you one then. Here." As he hands her a glass, Maggie goes out of her way not to touch his fingers as she takes it. "*Prost*. To reunion!"

"Mhm." Cognac. Maggie swallows the drink she's detested

since childhood in two nauseating gulps. It burns on the way down, but, once inside, ignites the fire that's been only simmering so far.

Liquid courage. Is that why he always drank so much? Because he's a coward, first and foremost, and needed this fuel to act upon his most atrocious thoughts?

Maggie eyes Buller as he gestures toward one of the armchairs. He takes one as well, next to her, not across the desk. When he crosses his legs, the tip of his shoe almost touches Maggie's leg. She thinks of pulling away or leaving it where it is, but both options are equally in Buller's favor. Either he wins by making her retreat into her space or by forcing this contact on her. This has always been the dynamic between them, the adult and the child, the predator and the prey. Only, out of the two of them, she's the one who's carrying a gun today. Considering this, Maggie remains seated the way she was.

"You did well for yourself," she says after a look around. "Back in the day, they couldn't pay you anything at all. Mommy had to work."

He shrugs with insincere modesty. "I always told her that Party loyalty would eventually bear fruit. Unfortunately, she wasn't patient."

"Oh, she was patient plenty," Maggie says, regarding the glass. "Working six days a week, supporting three children and a husband who would drink the money she made and beat her up on the slightest of provocations. She had the patience of a saint. I was never as patient as a wife. The first time my then-husband tried to play the head of the household card—in the apartment that was rented in *my* name, with *my* money—I pulled a kitchen knife on him."

Buller laughs, as if expecting a punchline.

Maggie nods to herself several times, a dangerous smile slowly growing. "Yes, that's precisely what he did, too. Laughed," she says with a grin that is truly feral now. "Thought

I was bluffing. Tried to take it from me, thought I didn't have the guts to use it." She raises her eyes to Buller and smiles even wider when she recognizes uncertainty in them. "You should have seen him screaming after I slashed his hands and forearms. Was swearing up and down that he was bleeding to death, begging me to call him an ambulance. Don't lose your marbles over his sorry behind. He's very much alive. Alive enough to try to put me in jail, but Daddy's in the police, you see, and I was a damaged young girl with a sister in a psychiatric hospital. They called it self-defense, dismissed the case, and told him to stay as far away from me as possible if he knew what was good for him. So, I suppose, thanks are in order, Papa, dearest. A childhood like mine raised a tough little bitch."

She reaches out and clinks her glass against his, hard. Buller falters between a smile and a frown, visibly rattled. She isn't how he remembers her. He doesn't know what to do with this new version of her.

"How are Ragnar and Hansjörg?" Maggie switches subject, yanking another rug from under him just as he was ready to mount a response in his defense. Today, she's in control, on the offensive. Maggie can't help but revel in the feeling. She's hard as steel and invincible and powerful like a pagan goddess of old.

"They're good." Buller wets his lips and shifts his pose. His leg is no longer anywhere near Maggie. "Serving."

"SS as well? Camp administration also?" she asks, despite already knowing the answer.

The color drains from his face. His hand, with the glass in it, lies limp in his lap. "How do you know I work in—"

Maggie looks at him—*come now*. "I suppose, Hansjörg is in the Waffen-SS now instead of Totenkopf, isn't he? They transferred many guards to the front when it all went belly up for Germany?"

"You oughtn't talk this way, Grete," Buller says softly, rising to refill his glass. "Germany is still your fatherland. You were born here, whether you like it or not."

"Home is what you make it, not where you're born," Maggie counters. "I'm an American and a Sullivan whether *you* like it or not."

"Why such hostility, Grete?" Buller turns to her, suddenly tearful. "I know I wasn't an ideal father to you, or a husband to your mother, but times were tough. The entire nation was struggling after—"

"Don't talk to me about nation or struggles—your beloved *Führer* wrote a lengthy enough book on it that no one with half a brain wants to read. The only reason I'm here, the only reason I'm breathing the same air as you, no matter how disgusting it is to me, is to ask you one single question." She's on her feet as well, facing him and his constantly shifting eyes. "How could you do it to me? I was your daughter. How could you do what you did to me?"

He stares at her for a very long time, seemingly without comprehension. Then, he blinks as if awaken from a daze and chortles uncomfortably as he turns away to pour himself another drink.

"I don't know what you're talking about, Gretchen." The bottle in his hand clinks on the glass's rim loudly.

"Yes, you do."

"I assure you, I don't." He drinks his cognac, fast, away from her prying eyes. "I don't know what tales your mother put in your head after she kidnapped you—"

"Don't you dare talk about my mother." Maggie's voice is thunder. He shrinks away from her. "And don't you dare deny anything. You, disgusting, drunken pig, you began putting your filthy hands all over me while I was still in nappies—"

"Gretchen, no! Listen to me—"

"No, *you* listen to me! You don't get to wreck my life and backpedal out of the wreck. You don't get to live out your old age in peace and quiet, molesting a new daughter when the old one is no longer available. How old was she when you started with her? A year? That's how old I was. Did you bathe her like you did me? Do you still do so?"

"Gretchen, what has she done to you? What preposterous tales has she told you? I would never, sweetheart! I have always loved you; no, I adored you, I waited for you to return—"

"Well, now I'm here." Maggie holds her hand up and steadies her breath, eyes closed. She crossed an ocean and half of a continent to confront him and now he's trying to make her believe that this was all a product of her imagination? Brought on by her no-good mother who kidnapped her from his loving arms? That the nightmares she still lives with are nothing but flights of fancy? That her reality only arises from false accusations that Maggie's mother hurled his way? Talk about adding insult to injury.

Though, what else did she expect? An admission of guilt and an apology? An explanation of all things deviant and perverted in his rotten mind that moved him to become the monster that he is?

Maggie laughs at the ceiling, shaking her head in disbelief at her own naiveté. But she can't leave here without an answer. She needs to close this chapter, once and for all, no matter the cost. For herself. For Norma. For this new little Grete. Is she not her sister too?

"I expected at least an ounce of decency from you, but since you don't have any, we'll do this my way." She's enraged to the point of exploding inside, but Maggie's hand is perfectly steady as she pulls the gun from its holster and aims it at Buller's stomach. "You sit your old, saggy behind down and write a confession of everything you did to me and your new daughter, plus a detailed description of your service in the Totenkopf. You do that and you walk out of here alive to face the international tribunal and whatever local authorities for sexual deviance crimes committed against minors here in Germany. Or you keep being obtuse and I shoot you in the guts and go back home to live my life, satisfied with the knowledge that you will never ruin another little girl's or woman's life, ever again. To be frank with you, I'd prefer the second option, but my daddy raised me to be a fair person, so, to honor him and for that reason only, I'm offering you this choice."

Sickly white, Buller shifts his eyes from the gun to Maggie and back, as if testing the reality of the moment. He never experienced this—her, fighting back. He was the one always in control—a big, strong man with no one to challenge him. He isn't happy with this new dynamic—Maggie reads it clear as day in his darkening gaze.

Thrown into the past once again, she relives the day when she had to stand up for herself for the first time. She and Frank had just returned from France, having been married for only a few weeks. Frank was slightly homesick, but for France instead of his native Ohio, even though Maggie explained to him that New York's Village where she rented her apartment was close enough, teeming with writers, singers, and artists on every corner of its red-brick maze.

At first, Maggie didn't notice much of a difference. She'd been living alone for several years and had long grown used to taking care of herself. Now, it was two of them, but she was doing all the same things: the dishes, the laundry, the cleaning, the shopping—all the while delivering her assignments on time. In the meantime, Frank spent his days at Maggie's desk facing the window, gazing out of it for hours, sipping coffee Maggie bought, brewed, and poured. She didn't say anything.

She didn't say anything even when, on her days off, whenever she would curl up with a book on the window nook, Frank would suddenly need something from her: a sandwich, a fresh shirt, more paper, most of which ended in crushed balls in the waste paper basket by the desk.

When October came, Norma took a turn for the worse and at work there was suddenly an avalanche after not one but two photographers departed for Spain, where the Civil War had just broken out. Working nonstop for days on end while juggling a household and visiting Norma at the hospital, Maggie worked out a rigid schedule that slashed her days into hours and minutes, leaving a miserable five hours for sleep every night. She had just finished showering, ready to tackle another day, exhausted and functioning only on pep pills from Norma's extensive stash, when Frank intercepted her on her sprint to the closet. She had only ten minutes to get dressed and put her equipment into her work bag, and there he stood, handing her a list of literature.

He had just come up with a grand idea for a new book; the old one was garbage, he realized it now. He'll write about the Great War, like Hemingway, but since he wasn't actually at war —Maggie's eyes here shifted to the wall clock—he'll need to do some research. Can she stop at the library on the way to work and get him these books?

"Frankie, I can't. I literally don't have the time. You stay home every day doing nothing, can't you go there yourself?"

He stared at her as if she'd just slapped him. "I'm from Ohio," he said, underlining every word as though she were an idiot. "They won't give me the books because I don't live here, in the city I moved to because of you. And you won't even do this little thing for me."

It had been a long goddamn month, and this was the last straw. "Frank, I do everything for you as it is. I'm both a home-maker and a breadwinner. There's two of us living under this roof and yet I'm the one who does everything around here."

"Fine! One thing I asked you." He plopped back down into the chair behind the desk and threw his hands up, flustered like she'd never seen him before. "Go. Leave, if your work is more important than me. I'll never ask you for anything, ever again."

Maggie was about to swallow it, shelve the conversation for a later time when they had both cooled down a bit, but just as she began putting on her dress, she heard him mutter, "Nasty fucking bitch," from the other room.

The dress still around her chest, she walked into the living room. "Did you just call me a bitch?" Her voice, deceivingly even. *Apologize or deny it—it's all the same to me. You made a mistake and here's your only chance to correct it before I go off like a grenade with a pin pulled out.*

But the man turned out to be more foolish than she gave him credit for. Instead of taking it back, he decided to double down. "Don't take offense if you act like one."

Maggie's nostrils flared. Instead of Frank's, she saw her father's face. "Be mad if you like, but don't call me names. Have I ever called you names? No, so why are you insulting me then?"

"I'll call you whatever the fuck I want!" he suddenly roared.

"Oh no, you don't. Lower your voice. I won't be insulted in my own house."

"Watch how fast I'll kick you out of this house! *Nasty fucking bitch.* Go back into your room!"

"Don't tell me where to go and what to do in my own house. I pay the rent here."

"I don't care what you pay. I'm *the man* and you *will* respect me." He was suddenly on his feet, hand raised, preparing to get in her face.

"Like hell I will." Like a cat, she sidestepped him, leaped into the kitchen, and slid the biggest knife out of the block. She had seen how fast things escalated from shouting to slapping and outright punching in her childhood home. She'd sworn to herself that her mother's vicious cycle would break with her, and she'd be damned if she went back on her word to herself. "Get your things and get the fuck out of here!"

Frank laughed at her.

Then, he lunged.

Maggie slashed.

The rest is now history.

History that is ready to repeat itself.

"Go on," Maggie says to Buller, who appears to be contemplating the exact same tactic Frank mistakenly adopted. "Make a move, see what happens."

He does make a move. For his age and weight, he's surprisingly light on his feet as he goes for the gun. Only, the steel is always faster when one doesn't hesitate to use it. He doubles over as though punched in the gut before he has a chance to reach Maggie and yelps in a high voice in a mix of surprise and agony.

"You shot me!"

"You'll live." Maggie leaves him lying on the rug between the two armchairs with his hands holding onto his stomach and heads toward the door, her weapon at the ready.

Just as she'd expected, Buller's driver bursts through it, his gun also drawn. Maggie shoots at him several times—preemptive fire. She'll explain it to the OSS with no trouble.

Somewhere in the kitchen, Frau Buller is screaming and the baby's wailing. Maggie approaches the dead SS man and gathers his gun, just in case.

"This wasn't one of your sons, was it?" she asks Buller over her shoulder.

"You're a heartless fucking bitch," he spits out, all former goodwill gone and leaving no trace.

"Yeah, so they say." Moving without any rush now, Maggie holsters her gun and pockets the nameless SS man's weapon. Then, she takes the cover off her Kodak and approaches Buller once again. Her entire being is celestially light as she aims the lens at the bleeding man cowering before her with a grimace of helpless ire. "Say cheese!"

Maggie snaps a shot as he tries to spit at her, but misses.

"Thank you. This one will go on the wall. Pulitzer stuff, if I do say so myself. Well, ta-ta! The OSS will be here shortly to pick you up. Try not to bleed to death."

There's a spring in her step as she crosses the lobby without a single glance back.

"You may come out, I have no quarrel with you," Maggie throws in the direction of the kitchen, where Ursula is still hiding with her children, and pushes the front door open. In front of her, spread like an Alpine valley with countless possibilities, an entire new life is beginning.

TWENTY-NINE

"You're Margarete Sullivan?" The MP looks up from the black-and-white photo to Maggie's face and back.

"The one and only. Inspector General Harlow is expecting me."

She was hoping to spend fall at home, with Norma, but here she is instead, presenting her passport to the MP standing guard at the gates of the Palace of Justice. The building, which has miraculously survived the bombing of Nuremberg, is imposing and resolute, its stone façade bearing the weight of what is to come.

They really went all out with the security here, Maggie observes as the MP studies her closely. She doesn't look like the uniformed woman in the photo. Her hair has grown out and is lying around her shoulders in soft waves, instead of the shock of wild curls she sported in wartime. The uniform is also gone, replaced by a smart tweed suit and sensible heels. But surely she is still recognizable?

"You used to be in the Army?"

"Yes, as a war correspondent. They discharged most of us after the German Instrument of Surrender was signed."

"Do you have your discharge papers with you?"

"Yes, sir." Maggie produces them from her valise. It's been months and she still can't get used to how lightweight it is compared to the cumbersome affair she lugged everywhere for nearly a year.

The MP notes the honorable discharge and only then puts her name into a thick ledger and motions her through the gates.

Another MP searches her valise at the entrance and also marks down her name. In the distance, a reporter is taking a photo of MPs walking the perimeter atop the roof and Maggie rubs at her chest wistfully, soothing the pain of her Kodak missing like a phantom limb. She was hoping she would be documenting the ultimate justice served. Instead, she will be confined to a witness stand, probed and prodded by both defense and prosecution in front of countless spectators. In the hotel where she's staying, they sell tickets to the auditorium. Maggie isn't sure how she feels about the whole business.

"Where can I find Mr. Harlow? He's with the American prosecution team."

"They're on the first floor, past the Grand Courtroom."

Inside, the air is filled with a sense of historical urgency. Allied prosecutors and military personnel move with purpose, transforming the Palace of Justice into the stage for an unprecedented trial. The most prominent Nazi leaders the Allies were fortunate to capture alive will be tried here. The opening arguments are scheduled for the following few weeks. In the meantime, the last preparations are made.

Maggie walks along corridors that are alive with the echo of hurried footsteps and the murmur of multilingual conversations. On her way to Harlow, she pauses by the Grand Courtroom and steals a quick glance inside. The carpenters are still working on it, slathering plaster along the cracks, likely sustained during last spring's aerial raids, but the high ceilings and imposing woodwork have survived just fine and will look good in the photos, she concludes after scanning the room with her trained eye. Rows of wooden benches and tables are arranged, and electricians work diligently to string wires and set up microphones, ensuring every word will resonate across the globe.

The scent of fresh paint and varnish hangs in the air, a reminder of the building's recent renovations. Outside, military trucks arrive with the last crates of evidence—each one a silent witness to the crimes to be addressed. The MPs carry them past Maggie and into the vast room occupied by the US Prosecution team. Once inside, she can't help but wonder how exactly the jurists will begin to sort their way through this mess. The boxes, folders, and crates rise around desks equally stacked with paperwork, turning the room into a maze of human suffering committed to paper.

Maggie stops one of the secretaries and asks for Harlow, for it is obvious now that she will never find him here on her own.

"Are you one of the victims?" The young woman is the picture of efficiency, reminding Maggie of her younger self. "Where from? Dachau? Buchenwald? Ravensbrück? Auschwitz?"

"Oh, no, I'm not... that kind of victim." Maggie smiles, feeling guilty for some reason. "I'm a witness for the prosecution for the Buller case." Seeing no recognition in the secretary's eyes, she clarifies, "He'll be testifying as a witness for the prosecution himself, for Kaltenbrunner and Göring, I believe."

"Ah, he was with the inspectorate of the concentration camps," the secretary quickly catches on. What admirable memories they must have, Maggie marvels to herself as the young woman leads her through the labyrinth of desks, toward the back of the room. Here, kneeling on the floor, Harlow is going through a box of files, so deep in concentration, he fails to notice the women until the secretary calls his name. "Mr. Harlow, here's your witness for the Buller case."

Harlow looks up, his forehead creasing in annoyance at being interrupted. Then, to Maggie's astonishment, he smiles at her once the recognition sets in. "Miss Sullivan."

Stiffly, as he has clearly spent quite some time on his knees, he rises to his full height and offers Maggie his hand before thinking better of it. His entire palm is smudged with black ink from handling mounds of paperwork, just like the tip of his nose, which he must have scratched at one point. For some reason, he looks much more approachable now. Not as hostile as Maggie remembers him.

"Thank you for coming to testify, Miss Sullivan."

Maggie gives a small shrug. "Not going to lie, I would have rather watched the trials from the press bench and not a witness stand."

"I understand." Contrary to the old Harlow, this new one lowers his eyes, almost apologetic.

"I still don't see what my personal history with Buller has to do with his indictment."

Harlow nods, somewhat pensive; opens his mouth to say something, but then gestures for Maggie to follow him out of the room instead. "Let's talk someplace more private, it's much too noisy here."

He takes her to the courtyard, where the air is crisp and isn't tainted with the hints of varnish and plaster and the only company they share is that of the MPs patrolling the vicinity from their high perches atop the unscalable walls.

"Here's where they have their daily exercise," Harlow says and Maggie knows he means the big twenty-four. Hitler, Himmler, and Goebbels—the biggest perpetrators, the ones the Allies wanted to face the music the most—chose a bullet or a cyanide capsule instead, but at least Göring is here, along with

Hess and a couple of *Feldmarschälle*. "I was surprised you didn't stay to document their surrender."

"My photos of Göring surrendering his gem-encrusted marshal's baton and a golden service pistol would stand no chance next to Miller's," Maggie says, but only half in jest, and goes on to explain, her eyes focused on nothing in particular in the distance. "I needed to get away for some time. To process everything that's happened."

"I understand."

"No, you don't."

"No, I don't," he agrees surprisingly easily.

Maggie looks at him askance, but he's anything but sarcastic.

"They are all already bargaining," Harlow begins as they set out on the path trodden by the perpetrators of the biggest genocide of the twentieth century. He fixes his glasses and clasps his ink-stained hands behind his back. *"I'll give you this testimony in exchange for dropping this charge.* All guilty as sin but thinking that they may just come off as innocent if they pile enough dirt on their former counterparts. Your father is no different."

"Don't call him that."

"I apologize. *Buller* is no different. He and his lawyer are painting this picture of him as a heartbroken father who, after mourning his wife abandoning him and kidnapping his daughter, turned to the Nazi Party as a pro-family instrument that would ensure that such a thing would never happen to any other father in Germany. His lawyer has already promised that Buller will testify to anything we bring up against anyone complicit in the Crimes Against Humanity charge, but only if we agree to a short prison term of no longer than five years for his own participation. Now, many of my colleagues, who are after bigger fish like Göring, Kaltenbrunner and Hans Frank, they don't mind agreeing to it."

He pauses, suddenly looks up sharply.

"But I'm not. And neither is Orso—though we differ in our opinions concerning your role in all this. He thinks we have a good enough chance for a death sentence without your testimony. I don't. And that's why I wanted you to testify in front of the court, so they would see that he's not some poor parent suffering the loss of a wife and a child but a vile human being who ought to be hanged, both for his crimes against minors and for his crimes against all those poor wretches his office worked to death in extermination camps."

Maggie draws a breath in through clenched teeth. Orso's unwillingness to call her to testify has nothing to do with the prosecution's chances. He simply doesn't want to put her through this. It's not just Maggie's wild guess either. Orso himself spelled it out, clear as day, in the letter that reached her before Harlow's summons: *I tried my best, but he insists on summoning you. I just want you to know that you have all the right to refuse him. You don't have to come back.*

She didn't, but she did. Because there is her half-sister, little Grete Buller, to be considered and Maggie simply won't be able to live with herself if Buller is released back into society after a slap-on-the-wrist sentence. Back to Grete, back to the other little girls he finds.

"Should've shot him dead," Maggie mutters under her breath.

"You took a good chunk of his already-abused liver. He's on a strict no-drinking regimen according to his physician. Thought that would cheer you up."

"Not enough to do cartwheels about it."

Harlow halts abruptly and turns to face her. Behind his lenses, his eyes are a mirror image of the gray skies overhead. "I was wrong about you from the very beginning, Miss Sullivan. And for that, I'm deeply sorry. I mistook your desire for justice for personal ambition and judged you accordingly. Like you have all the right to judge me now. But I still hope that you will see that I'm also here to set the record straight—and not out of a desire for promotion. I'm fifty-three, I'm too old for such ambitions. I'm planning to retire after the trials are over and to teach law, instead of practicing it, back in Massachusetts—"

"I'm not the judges, Mr. Harlow. It's them you'll need to persuade. As for our past, it's all water under the bridge. I'm not holding anything against you. I will work with you. I will testify. But the sooner it all ends, the better."

Harlow nods, his face etched with determination. "I'll do my best, Miss Sullivan. You have my word."

THIRTY

They have no chance to exchange anything other than a handshake and a couple of hellos during Maggie's second visit to the prosecutors' quarters in preparation for her testimony, but the evening immediately after, a concierge knocks on her door and tells her that a gentleman caller is in the bar downstairs to see her.

"A certain Riccardo Orso." He delivers the card with his gloved hand and Maggie feels her breath hitch as she takes it.

The concierge is adamant, but Maggie insists on his taking the tip—"Don't be daft, it's American currency—" before heading downstairs.

She spots him right away, effortlessly elegant in his suit and tie, hands clasped around a glass with something clear in it atop the polished bar countertop. *Riccardo Orso*. It's suddenly both amusing and somewhat sad, the fact that she has only just learned his first name, and from a German concierge here in Nuremberg, no less.

"I went to both Randazzo's and Gargiulo's," Maggie says by way of greeting as she slides onto the stool next to him. "You were right. The presence of white napkins around waiters' arms does make oysters taste better."

He beams at her, a brilliant smile against his still-tanned face. Maggie, herself, has long lost all her color, even after spending nearly the entire summer on Coney Island with Norma in tow. "Told you so."

"What's that you're drinking?" Maggie thrusts her chin at his glass.

"This?" Orso lifts the glass up. It's strange to see his hands so clean, framed with immaculate white cuffs, instead of begrimed army fatigues. "Club soda."

Maggie arches her brow.

"They have plenty of hard stuff, but no decent wine, and I'm more of a wine drinker," Orso explains.

"Snob."

"Why, thank you." He mock-bows in response.

When the bartender swipes the bar in front of her, Maggie orders a vodka coke.

It's an international hotel in the US zone of occupation. The local provisional government stocked the bar well with all the familiar goods.

"Don't judge," she tells Orso when the bartender places the drink in front of her. "I've had a hell of a day. Club soda just won't cut it for me."

"Frankly, after the cross-examination Harlow subjected you to, I'm surprised you aren't drunk already." He raises his glass and toasts her.

"Norma and I have a new rule: we don't drink alone anymore."

"How is she doing?" Orso asks after they take their respective sips.

"She was out of the hospital the entire summer. We went to the beach a lot. How was your summer?"

They haven't been in contact ever since the events at

Buchenwald. After slaying her dragon, Maggie needed time for herself—to heal before she could even consider getting involved in a relationship. She didn't want to repeat the mistakes of the past, such as choosing the wrong man, as had happened with Frank. But first and foremost, she needed to sit alone with herself, sober and clear-headed, and find out who Maggie Sullivan really is—the one who isn't determined by her past.

"I haven't been able to go back to the States yet—too much work here. But Gabi was very grateful for your autographs I mailed her for my nieces. They are all dying to meet you one day."

"Soon, hopefully."

"Yes." He pauses and studies her so closely, Maggie can't help but feel warmth creeping under her skin. "Brooklyn did you good," Orso finally says. "You look very... *healthy*."

Maggie's cheeks glow and she can't quite tell if it's because of the alcohol or his observation. He's right, though. She feels healthy. Both in body and mind.

Gone are the days when she would cut into her inner thigh with her father's disposable razor because only the physical pain could distract her from the emotional one. Gone are the days of putting herself in the line of danger because death seemed like a much better option than to exist in this recurring nightmare. Gone are the days of falling asleep without washing her face or without showering or forgoing entire meals because it took too much work for her long-suffering brain, which kept fighting its battles every single day just to keep her alive.

On Dr. Adler's advice, Maggie and Norma made a point of treating themselves to full, nutritious meals, to new sundresses, to lying prone in the sun for days on end simply because it felt good to do so. Also, on their shared psychiatrist's advice, the sisters only spoke about themselves in positive terms and corrected one another whenever one of them uttered a self-deprecating joke. It was hard to unlearn old habits, but together, they were doing the work.

"I hoped you would stay home," Orso says abruptly and Maggie feels her teeth catch the thick rim of the glass. "Not because I didn't want to see you," he offers quickly, realizing how his first statement could have been misinterpreted, "but because I hate to see you being dragged into all this again."

Maggie touches his hand fleetingly—no need to explain, she understands—and draws herself up, squares her shoulders. "It's all right. It was my decision, to testify. I'll get through it."

Orso's look says it all: *I'm sure you will, but at what price?*

"These lawyers, whoever picks up these Nazis' cases," he begins at length, "they are quite nasty customers themselves. They're in it for publicity, to make a name for themselves. They don't expect to win, all they want is headlines. I expect them to play dirty. It could get ugly. Are you sure you need this right now?"

Maggie considers her answer, despite already knowing it deep in her very bones. "If I don't testify, will Buller walk free?"

"I can't say with all certainty, but the talk is that the prosecutor general doesn't mind taking his plea deal and letting him walk away with a five-year sentence. Same as Schellenberg, the fellow who worked at the RSHA, the Reich Security Main Office, under Heydrich and Kaltenbrunner."

"Yes, I know who he is." She's silent a beat, turning her glass in her hand this way and that. The pleasant warmth is gone from her chest. No vodka in the world will ever be enough to dull the pain of knowing that Buller is still breathing the same air as she does. "I could have killed him that day. I didn't, because I wanted him to face his day in court. I wanted the world to know what kind of man he was, because he isn't the only one. He isn't an anomaly. There are far too many of them out there, preying on those who are weaker than them because power is the only thing that gets them off. So, the answer to your question is no, I don't need this any more now than I needed it back when I was a child, but I do need to see this through. I can't let him walk away from it in exchange for his testimony."

Maggie tries to smile bravely over the rim of the nearly-empty glass, but it comes out like a grimace.

Orso's own face changes in an instant in response to her pain. He gathers her free, frigid hand in his and presses it tightly. "You are one of the bravest women I've known and I just want you to know, you won't be going through this alone. I'll be right there with you, every step of the way. You have my number, both the office and the apartment I'm staying at. Day or night, no matter the hour, call me. I'll always answer."

Maggie knows he will. He came through once already, for his sister. Having an ally with Orso's track record in her corner is certainly comforting, and especially if that ally asks for nothing in exchange. She has grown to expect such things, these payments for friendship or career advancements or whatever favors women are conditioned to produce. That's how her mother bought their passage to the new world. That's how her fellow women correspondents got airlifts to the hottest spots to report on the stories that would otherwise go to their male colleagues. That's how some women in the concentration camps survived—she has just learned it from their own testimonies, in the same Palace of Justice. Sex in exchange for a piece of stale bread or a few days in the sick bay to get some respite from the back-breaking work. And now German women are doing the same; one can distinguish them by a single look at them. Their bodies are healthy and supple, their hair is curled and lustrous; their dresses are of the latest fashion and they smoke Chesterfield or Camel next to their GI beaus. It's the oldest barter in the world, normalized to the point where even questioning it seems radical.

And yet, that's precisely what Dr. Adler, the Austrian expat who studied psychiatry under Dr. Jung, has done and, as a result, has turned her patients' worlds upside down.

"Imagine that your house has been broken into. Will you not take care of it anymore or burn it down altogether afterwards?"

"No, of course not," the women in her group replied, chuckling at the absurdity of it.

"But this is precisely what you're doing whenever you're cutting yourself or drinking or swallowing pills or going for a night swim where rip currents are known to be or driving along highways at night with your headlights off. Or simply neglecting yourself. It isn't any different from giving up on a perfectly good house because someone broke into it. I'm not minimizing the pain of it in the slightest. I know precisely how it feels, seeing these metaphorical muddy footprints all over the pristine living room you took such pride in. I wanted to burn it down myself, multiple times. But then I got mad. Why should I burn it down? I'd rather go and burn down that thief's house instead. And if you don't know who the thief is, the entire damned neighborhood until I smoke him, and the likes of him, out."

Maggie had never felt more alive than during that session. The group were angry, but not at themselves anymore. And it was good anger. The kind that leads to revolutions, the echoes of which will reverberate over centuries.

After that session and the summer she shared with Norma, toes digging into hot sand, waves lapping at their ankles, ketchup dripping from Nathan's hotdogs onto their bare legs, she gradually learned to see her body differently. It was no longer some separate entity from her being, no longer something she could offer to a lover just to prove to herself that it belonged to her and not Buller and that he didn't really break her and that she could do whatever she pleased to it, with whomever she pleased. Neither was it something to treat almost like hard, cold currency, trading it for medical services a fellow sister in need wouldn't survive without.

It is her house now and even if she doesn't mind inviting this particular guest over, it's neither the time nor the place for such visits, and thankfully, he doesn't even think to insist.

As if to confirm that very last thought of hers, Orso releases her hand after one parting, warm squeeze. "I won't keep you any longer. You've had a long day. Go back upstairs, take a hot bath, and try to go to sleep if you can."

"I have sleeping pills. They knock me out cold."

"Should you be mixing them with alcohol?"

"I told you I've quit drinking alone. Now you're coming for my pills? One step at a time, mister."

Orso's all smiles as he raises his hands in mock surrender and Maggie carries that image of him back upstairs—her own tiny sliver of Brooklyn in a hostile land she could never call home.

THIRTY-ONE

When Maggie wakes up the following day with the shrill of the alarm clock, the chill of fall is seeping through the window of her hotel room. The heavy drapes do little to soften the morning light, casting long shadows across the room. Asking for breakfast to be delivered to her room will cost extra, but she can't imagine throwing off the comfort of the warm blankets just yet. The sleeping gown she brought from home is much too thin to handle such nippy mornings.

The air is frigid on her bare arm as she calls downstairs for her order and whatever papers they have today. She snatches it back under as soon as the concierge assures her that it should all be delivered in fifteen minutes.

The hotel staff member knocks on her door precisely at 9:15.

"Come in!" she calls, then sits up and greets the bellhop with a smile, half-concealed by the blanket pulled all the way up to her chin. "Just leave the tray right here, in front of me. Thank you. And if you could just grab me my sweater; it's right over there, on the chair by the window."

She digs in her purse for a tip and thanks the bellhop once

again as he backs out of the room with small bows of appreciation. Once the door closes after him, Maggie pulls the sweater over her head and only then dives into her eggs and toast. The papers are underneath the steaming coffee cup. She scans the headlines after putting the cup aside, but her very blood runs cold once her eyes catch the photo next to one of the articles. Her father's face stares back at her, his expression is that of a professional mourner. There is a quote in italics just under his pleading, clasped hands: *"One good thing came out of my ex-wife stealing my young daughter and filling her impressionable mind with lies: I got to see my Grete one last time, even if she returned just to shoot me."*

She doesn't want to read any further, this op-ed penned by Buller's lawyer, Oskar Henning, but she does nevertheless, the distorted tale he's concocted twisting in her stomach.

A delusional, brainwashed American, kidnapped at a young age from her loving father's arms... A woman (twice!) driven to attempted murder by her mentally unstable mother and a stepfather who have spent decades setting her against her biological father... But indoctrinating one child wasn't enough for them. They did the same with their second daughter, Norma, who ended up in a mental institution due to their systematic abuse... Girls, taught to hate men from an early age... the evidence is ample... Margarete Sullivan's knife attack on her husband after a simple request to bring him some library books for research...

The room feels smaller as she reads, each sentence tightening around her chest. Her father's lawyer dismisses the abuse as pure fantasy, a fabrication of an American woman poisoned against her own blood, her own heritage. The article is a cruel attempt to discredit her, to twist the truth of her suffering into a narrative of betrayal against a Germany that she hates, that all Americans hate, hence these kangaroo trials, this mockery of justice.

Maggie closes her eyes for a moment when the words

become too much to bear. They get under her skin like hot needles, reopening the wounds which she's worked so very hard to turn into old, faded scars.

Orso was right. What is she doing here? She doesn't need to put herself through this. She can just gather her things and go back to her family, to Norma, to Brooklyn, and forget it all, like the nightmare it is—

Only the newspaper is a New York one. If they read it here, they have certainly already read it over there. Anonymity is no longer an option. Neither is running. And why would she? She's the one in the right here. She has nothing to be ashamed of, Maggie reminds herself, forcing her eyes open. The trial is her chance to speak, to be heard, to confront the man who stole her childhood.

"Fuck you, Oskar Henning," she says out loud, and for some reason, the profanity feels just right, fueling her with the same anger Dr. Adler first opened her eyes to. The good kind. The righteous kind. "Fuck you, Waldemar Buller, and fuck your little story. See you in court."

She stands, shaking off the remnants of doubt, and throws the drapes open. Outside, the sun is shining brightly.

"Long time no see, colleague."

Maggie swings round, the key she was about to leave with the concierge dangling from her finger. A familiar man is grinning at her, even though she can't seem to recall his name.

"Am I so unmemorable?" He pretends to be wounded by placing his hand to his chest. In the other, he's holding his hat. His suit under the unfastened trench coat is visibly wrinkled. "December 1944, the what's-its-name castle?"

"Ah. Jack Knightley, the *London Times*." Maggie finally nods and puts on a suitable smile, even if she cares little for reminiscing about the night on which they parted. Last thing she remembers is the flask of brandy being forced under her nose and his stale breath much too close to her face. "Good to see you, colleague."

"Same, same." He nods and motions for the bar, just visible from the hotel lobby. "Got a couple of minutes?"

"Not really." Maggie makes a point of leaving the key with the concierge and gathering her valise. "I'm just on my way to the Palace of Justice. I'm working with the prosecutors' team."

"It's all right. I can walk with you."

Maggie clenches her teeth inwardly but shrugs at the self-invitation. *Suit yourself.*

"When do you give your testimony? End of the week?"

"This Friday, yes."

"They made you come so early," Knightley says as they exit the hotel. "Must have a lot riding on your testimony."

Maggie stops abruptly to face him. A gleeful grin is sitting on his face. He hasn't run into her by accident. Neither is he here to make small talk or gossip about old times.

"What do you want?" she asks, her shoe tapping the ground impatiently.

Knightley feigns innocence, but only for a moment. "Well, I figured you owe me a little something."

"I owe you?" Maggie nearly breaks into amused chuckles. "Whatever for?"

"For that night you got me drunk just to run off with that lieutenant and take the very first border crossing photo. It could've been mine."

"Maybe think about that the next time you decide to get drunk on the job," Maggie offers with a sweet smile and sets off on her way.

Only, Knightley doesn't leave off. "Why such hostility? I'm doing you a favor here. People have been asking about you, and since I know you personally, I could give them the story they want. But I'm a decent fellow, I don't do sneaky."

He's needling her about that night and that border-crossing damned article Maggie doesn't give a toss about, but she refuses to take the bait. Only when he says, "I figured, I'd give you a chance to speak for yourself, in your own words," does she slow her steps.

"You know how it is," he continues, lighting a cigarette with feigned nonchalance. "The story will be printed either way. You decide if you want to tell it or not."

Maggie gives him a look—the last one he'll ever get from her —and smiles through the thinly veiled threat hanging between them. "Do what you have to do."

THIRTY-TWO

"It's worse than we thought."

Harlow greets her in his office, an array of papers scattered atop his table. Maggie purposely hasn't read them these past two days. Maybe she should have. At least she would have been informed.

Orso, who's been smoking by the window, stubs his cigarette in the empty coffee cup and tries on a smile as he moves to offer Maggie a chair.

"Worse than Henning's story? Is that even possible?" She tries to joke but is met with silence.

So, it is worse then.

All eyes on her, Maggie slowly sits down. "All right, enough with the suspense. What is it now?"

Harlow and Orso exchange looks. Their colleagues look anywhere but at her.

At last, Orso clears his throat. "Someone spoke to your editor from the *Times*. He said you wrote certain articles, anonymously, on—"

"On violence against women," Maggie nods impatiently. "Yes, I did. I would have written them under my own name if my opinion weighed as much as the 'concerned male citizen' I claimed to be. What's wrong with that?"

"Nothing wrong," Harlow says. "As a matter of fact, your editor is planning on suing for libel after the reporter twisted his words. Your editor only brought up these articles to explain why women's issues were so close to you personally and how you've always championed the change in laws, or even the manner in which we view such violence. Only, the reporter made you out to be a mentally ill feminist and a dangerous misandrist who wrote conniving articles under a fake name and gender, and something to the extent that if you made that up, what else would you make up?"

"He framed it all as mere questions that ought to be asked before they let you testify," Orso supplies with a disgusted glare at the paper stack on Harlow's table.

"Is that all?" Maggie asks quietly.

There's silence in the room and it's louder than the beating of her own heart.

"No," Orso says with a sigh. "Another reporter found your ex-husband and interviewed him."

"I imagine that must have gone well." Maggie feels her hands beginning to shake and clasps them over her knee. "Let me see."

Orso hesitates but finally fishes out the newspaper in question and hands it to her.

She scans the interview quickly:

"I knew, deep inside, that there was something very wrong with her, but when you're so deeply in love, you only want to see the goodness in people. And I tried to be the husband she wanted me to be. I abandoned everything I knew in Ohio and followed her to New York because she would never consider moving out of state, supposedly because of her sick sister... I didn't want to point out that she lived in France when we met—everything

with Maggie led to an argument, and all I wanted was peace. A simple life we could share and, hopefully, children one day. But she was very against children. Didn't want to have them. Claimed she didn't have it in her, to be a good mother, and I suppose it's true. Maybe it was a blessing in disguise."

"You still stayed with her, even when you learned that she had no desire for motherhood?"

"Yes, I stayed with her. I hoped she would change her mind one day."

"But instead she tried to kill you."

"She did... I'm sorry. It's still hard to talk about it."

"I can imagine. Can you tell me what led to the attack?"

"I asked her to stop by the library on the way from work. She worked as a freelance photographer those days; she could come and go as she pleased, so I figured, she has plenty of time on her hands for a quick stop. I was writing a novel, you see. I was trying to finish it as soon as possible so that I could sell it and have my own money, as this was the main point of our arguments—the money. She claimed, since I didn't bring anything into the household, I had no rights to anything. Every day she reminded me that I only lived there because she kindly allowed me to. I thought, if I finally sell my novel, it'll bring balance back to our relationship. That's why I asked her for that one small favor. I would have gone there myself, but they wouldn't give me the books since I was still legally an Ohio resident, not a New Yorker. I made the mistake of trying to explain it to her, but it only enraged her. She went to the kitchen, grabbed the biggest knife, and attacked me with it."

Maggie bursts out laughing—a hollow, cold laugher that echoes around the room. In her lap, the newspaper lies crumpled. "What complete and utter bullshit! We never argued about money. He asked me for it and I provided, no questions asked. Children, we never even spoke of. We were hardly married for two months! And as for that day, it was he who charged at me. I simply defended myself because I saw what happened to my mother when she didn't. Do I regret it? Hell, no. And yet, I'm the villain here."

"You're not a villain, you're a victim," Orso says quietly but firmly and throws the paper in the trash, where it belongs.

In the following days, they keep coming, the opinion pieces in which both Maggie's name and past are dragged through the mud with relish. Yellow press mostly, as her colleagues from the more reputable papers refuse to touch the subject with a ten-foot pole, but the damage is done. She is no longer Maggie Sullivan, a child valiantly saved by her mother from a violent father and his abuse. She's an unstable, damaged, mentally-ill product of her equally mad mother who planted such disturbing fantasies into her two daughters' minds, it's no wonder one ended up in a mental institution and the other turned into a cold-blooded killer. Margarete Sullivan is a threat to society, a dangerous individual who should not just be banned from testifying and working in the press lest she spreads her madness onto her fellow female readers, but ought to be institutionalized.

"Shall I say something?" Maggie suddenly feels unwanted in the prosecution team's room. In the past couple of days, she's heard enough suggestions for her testimony to be dropped altogether and to just take Buller's plea deal and to hell with him, he's not that big of a fish anyway. Orso and Harlow both shot such ideas down with vehemence, but there were only two of them on her side. And what feels like the entire world on the other.

"Save it for your testimony," Harlow says with a pointed glare directed at the room. "Which will take place, as scheduled, this Friday."

THIRTY-THREE

Orso walks Maggie back to the hotel Thursday evening. Some of the reporters have been staking her out at the hotel lobby, purposely provoking her in the hope of an outburst of any sort they could feed to the printing press later. Even though Maggie has been an example of self-control, Orso still volunteers as her escort. Men, for some reason, lose all desire to fight if another man is present.

"Do you want me to stay for dinner?" he asks as they pass a line of locals queuing for the US Army-stocked grocery, their food coupons at the ready. "We can eat in your room if you don't want an audience."

Maggie thinks of rejecting the idea—her stomach has been in knots the entire past week and the very idea of food is nauseating. But then she remembers Dr. Adler and the mantras she drilled into her patients' heads with the fierce love of a mother and conjures up a stiff nod. "I think I can manage some soup."

"Nervous?"

"What do you think?"

"I'm sorry."

"For what? I came here myself."

"I wish you didn't have to."

From one of the GI billets they pass, cheery music is pouring through open windows. Local girls' laughter mixes with the tunes. Against the backdrop of it, Orso's next remark goes straight to Maggie's hurting heart.

"I wish you had a very unremarkable, purely statistical childhood."

Maggie swallows and pulls her light overcoat closer around her neck. "And I wish your sister had a very unremarkable, purely statistical marriage," she says into the shadows of the gathering night. "But neither of us did, but then we're both still alive and kicking and that's already something, wouldn't you say? Don't look at me like that."

"Like what?"

"With pity. It's the worst."

They walk for some time, staring straight ahead. Through the new glass windows of the stores they pass, their reflections glide, hands almost touching.

"I've been dreaming of him lately," Maggie says eventually, grateful for the time Orso has given her to put herself in order, for not arguing when all she needed from him was just to walk next to her and listen. "Of Buller. Strange dreams. Last night, for instance, I dreamed he came to see me with a bag of running shoes. He said it was a gift for my birthday and left. And before that, I dreamed of our old apartment. And the funny thing, he's always sober in my dreams. Always sober and always so sad, so full of remorse." Falling silent, she gazes at the cobblestones under her feet. "But they're all just dreams; I wake up and realize that and it's the worst part."

"Do you want me to guide you through your testimony tomorrow?" Orso offers. "Instead of Harlow?"

The tenderness radiating from him is almost physical. Maggie feels the warmth of it through the sleeve of her coat.

"No," she says at length. "It's better if it's Harlow. You'll be too good to me and won't ask me certain things because it'll be too revolting for you to ask, but he will, and I need to answer all those questions. I need to finally pull that splinter out tomorrow, pus and all."

Orso nods and offers her the crook of his arm. "We're almost there. Hold onto me."

Maggie does, and together, they pass through the doors and the small pack of vultures gathered there in the hope of a piece of pecked flesh. Tonight, they don't descend upon her though; only follow the couple with their small, evil eyes until the elevator door hides them from view.

"Thank you for walking me back tonight," Maggie tells his reflection in the Art-Deco door with the rays of sun radiating from the center.

"I'll come get you tomorrow morning as well. You won't be going through this alone."

Their steps are silent as they walk through the carpeted hallway, the only sounds accompanying them the staccato echoes of typewriters issuing from behind several doors they pass. The lawyers, writers, and interpreters sharing the floor with Maggie are hard at work before the big day.

"Did they make it hard on you during your trial?" Maggie asks as she turns the key in the door of her room. "When you testified?"

"I was still a minor, so they weren't too tough on me," Orso says, following her inside. "The prosecutor did bring up premediated murder charges; he had to, since I brought my father's gun with me to my sister's house. I went there to kill him. But it was all very half-hearted. The prosecutor didn't fight too much when my attorney explained that I only did so to protect my sister who was in grave danger. Otherwise, I was a good kid and my brother-in-law was a known criminal, so no one thought he was a big loss to society."

"Buller won't be a big loss either, but I shot him, unpro-

voked," Maggie says softly, unbuttoning her coat. "Many years
after the abuse occurred. Do you think they'll make an issue out
of it?"

Orso considers his answer for some time. "You already
know what sort of a man Buller's lawyer is: an unprincipled liar,
a former member of the Nazi Party, which tells you all you need
to know about him. He will get behind anyone like Buller,
because in his eyes, men can't do wrong. If a wife is beaten
black and blue, she must have provoked the husband somehow.
If a child accuses their father of abuse, the child is certainly
lying because the mother taught the child what to say just to get
a divorce, muddy the father's name, and go on her merry, 'whor-
ing' way with half of the 'poor father's' money. So yes, expect
the worst from him tomorrow, but also rest assured, I'll call
objection each time he tries to overstep his boundaries. And so
will Harlow. He's a shark when it comes to his profession, he'll
go straight for the throat."

"Oh, you don't have to tell me. I've experienced it quite a
few times myself, back in the trenches."

They grin as their eyes meet, igniting with humor at their
shared past. They've been through literal war together. Buller
and his lawyer are just a minor hiccup compared to that.

The morning dawns crisp and bright, but not so bright as Orso's
smile as he nearly waltzes into Maggie's room, a fresh issue of
the *New York Times* in his hand.

"You ought to see this! Your girls, all your girls came
through!" He's pushing the paper into the hands of a
confused Maggie. Her hair's still in a towel turban after her
morning shower, she has to get ready, but he will hear nothing
before she reads the op-ed. It's titled simply "Our War," and
at first Maggie doesn't understand what it has to do with her
until the words, authored by six of her former fellow women

war correspondents, slowly come into focus in front of her eyes.

As women correspondents during the tumultuous time of war, we found ourselves not only on the frontlines of history but also navigating the treacherous waters of gender discrimination, harassment, and the daunting struggle for our voices to be heard. While the world was embroiled in chaos, the fight for our recognition was a battle of its own.

You almost always relegated us to the sidelines and dismissed our insights as trivial. I recall a particularly tense briefing where I raised questions about troop movements. A general, his voice booming, merely turned to me and said, "Sweetheart, stick to writing poetry." The laughter that followed was a sharp reminder of the uphill battle we faced.

You minimized our contributions, you questioned our presence, as if our very existence in the field was an affront to the status quo. You claimed that we—women—had it easy since we weren't conscripted, and yet when we asked to be sent to the frontlines, you outright prohibited it, arrested us, and stripped us of our credentials.

Harassment was another unspoken companion on our journeys. While we were under fire, we witnessed men treat us as if we were invisible. But when we reported on the air raids, quite a number of soldiers thought it was their right to invade our personal space, as if our mere presence was an invitation for their advances. It made us question whether our contributions mattered at all. We were not just reporting on the war, we were fighting our own battle for respect and recognition.

The war may have brought us to the forefront, but the struggle against sexual harassment and the systemic silencing of women was a pervasive issue that transcended the battlefield. Too often, we were met with disbelief when we spoke out —our voices drowned by the very systems designed to protect us. The justice system, in many cases, failed to hold perpetrators accountable, leaving us to grapple with our trauma in silence.

And now you fight against us speaking our truth? You try to silence the woman who was robbed of her innocent childhood? You try to silence the woman who dared to defend herself, when she saw the shadow of her abuser father in her own husband?

Maggie Sullivan is one of us and she speaks for all of us. If any of you went through a fraction of what she had to go through, you wouldn't just be quietly trying to give a voice to voiceless victims in occasional articles, you would scream from the rooftops, raising armies to avenge your suffering.

Maggie Sullivan is neither a dangerous women's rights crusader nor a man-hater—or whatever you've decided to call her. Neither is she mentally ill. Traumatized, yes, but if you want to institutionalize every single woman who is traumatized by a man, the streets of each city, of each tiny village will empty out.

Maggie Sullivan didn't hate her father. She didn't hate her husband. All she wanted was to love them and be loved, just like we want to love you, we want to share this life with you, but sometimes you make it so very difficult!

The days when we were forced to look on in silence when one of us was slandered and tortured are over. We will keep standing up for one another until every single one of us is free— from abuse, from violence, from laws that are still skewed against us.

Now it's up to you if you want to be on the right side of history, together with us, or walk alone.

Do better.

Sincerely, women

Maggie's eyes well up as she traces the names—Higgins, Miller, Stringer, Gellhorn, Vanderwert, Kirkpatrick—with her trembling fingers. Her war sisters. She swipes at her face and laughs and sniffles and laughs again, still at a loss for words, overwhelmed by profound emotion.

"I can't believe they wrote it," she whispers.

"I can't believe they printed it." Orso laughs as well, also in disbelief. "Your *Times* editor must be fending off phone calls from disgruntled advertisers as we speak. It can't have been an easy decision for him."

"He's always been one of the good ones." Maggie holds the paper to her chest, all smiles and tears of gratitude. "Like Lee's *Vogue* editor. Like you. Like my daddy. Like your daddy. I want to say like Harlow, but let's see how today goes first."

Orso laughs together with her and leaves the room to let her dress.

As Maggie pins her last wayward lock in place, she steals yet another glance at the newspaper left open on her bedspread and feels she isn't alone any longer. They have her back, her war sisters, like she had theirs, and with them by her side, even the Nuremberg courtroom doesn't seem so frightening.

THIRTY-FOUR

Minutes drag on like rusty nails across the skin as Maggie waits on the wooden bench outside the courtroom. From behind the closed door, the muted clatter of typewriters is incessant as reporters craft the narratives that will inform the world. The walls themselves seem to listen, ready to absorb the story of justice and accountability.

This Friday morning, the Palace of Justice has become more than just a building to Maggie; it has turned into a symbol, a beacon of hope that the world can hold those in power accountable for their actions. Funny how that notion grows from fathers and husbands to the highest-ranking Nazis as one begins to unravel this tangled ball of yarn.

When the MP serving as a bailiff calls her at long last, Maggie doesn't quite feel her feet. The courtroom hushes itself as she makes her way to the witness stand and raises her hand in an oath to speak the truth and only the truth.

On the prosecution team's table, stacks of legal documents are carefully organized, each page a silent testament to the horrors that demand justice. Translators, tasked with bridging language barriers, work with intense focus in this rehearsal for the main events to come.

From the defendant's bench, Buller stares at her as she takes her seat. Maggie stares right back until Harlow clears his throat as he steps before her, calling for her attention.

He walks her through her childhood, through the good, the bad, and the ugly. With professional coolness, he extracts the most painful memories with surgical precision for the court to hear. The audience murmurs audibly in disgust when Maggie recounts how exactly Buller expressed his fatherly love and why her mother had no other choice but to run in the middle of the night, leaving her other children in the hands of the man who had no business to be anywhere near children.

But then Oskar Henning, Buller's attorney, takes Harlow's place and the first thing he does is sneer at Maggie with all the contempt he can muster as he fixes headphones on his clean-shaven head. He shuffles through papers on his stand and chuckles lightly. The microphones pick it up with ease.

"Something amusing?" the American judge asks him.

There are four of them, representatives of Allied countries, presiding over the trial. The other three look bored. It isn't Göring who's on trial. They don't really care for Buller and his sick tendencies, even if they're true.

"Just thinking how amazing it is, the fact that she seems to remember so much of her early years."

Maggie doesn't wear headphones herself. She understands perfectly her mother tongue as it slips off Henning's reptilic lips.

"Do you remember yourself at three?" Henning continues with a vague gesture toward the panel of judges and the audience. "Let alone at one. I can barely remember myself at five."

"Are you here to cross-examine me or the witness?" The American judge gives the German attorney a look that inspires immediate hope in Maggie.

Chuckles echo around the audience. The air around Maggie feels a little less frigid.

"The witness, Your Honor."

"Well then, I advise you proceed with questioning her and not me."

"Yes, Your Honor." Henning doesn't smile any longer. Instead, he stares at Maggie with accusation, as if it was she who got him in trouble. "While I was going through your testimony, I found it to be quite particular, the fact that you seem to remember only instances with Herr Buller allegedly being inappropriate with you. Why would you say that is the case?"

"Same as with your memory as an adult," Maggie responds in a measured voice. Inside, the storm is raging, but Harlow and Orso instructed her well. Reacting to Henning's veiled insults and insinuations will only support his portrayal of her as someone unstable and hysterical. She needs to be in perfect possession of herself, no matter the dirt Henning drags her through. "If I asked you what you did on April 24, 1944, you likely wouldn't be able to recall. However, if I asked you what you did on Victory in Europe day, or on your birthday this year, you would easily tell me. Extraordinary events tend to stick in our minds, no matter how young or old we are. So, yes, I remember very well how unnatural my father's touch was to me as a one-year-old child when he would bathe me."

"How was it different from your mother's? Did she have a different bathing technique?" Another needle. Another revolting sneer, both predatory and dismissive at the same time.

"Have you ever asked your wife to scrub the spot on your back you can't quite reach when you bathe? Would you consider asking your male neighbor to do it next time, in case she's ill or traveling? It's just bathing, according to you." Maggie's voice is still perfectly level, but the audience catches the sarcasm at once, breaking into hushed snickers.

"Witness, answer the question," the judge reminds her, but even the skin around his eyes crinkles ever so slightly at the corners.

"I don't remember my mother bathing me at all so, my guess is, her 'technique,' as you call it, was very normal, not worth committing to my memory."

"If your father was abusing you for years, as you claim, why did you only tell your mother about it when you were nearly five?"

"Because she was pregnant again and hoping for another daughter. I could suffer through the abuse myself, but I wouldn't make my unborn sister go through it if I could help it."

"But you had no qualms about your mother abandoning your little twin brothers? The ones already born into this world, the ones needing their mother still?"

"I did, but it wasn't my choice to make. My mother couldn't take all of us. She still regrets it to this day. Had she been able to do so, I'm certain that both Ragnar and Hansjörg would have been raised to be good young men who would fight the Nazis on the Allied side instead of being turned into Nazis themselves."

Henning throws more accusations her way, vile taunts calling into question her account of events or dismissing her answers as conjecture. Maggie parries them with frankness and grace, but then he stoops so low, even the audience falls silent in quiet condemnation.

"Isn't it true that you killed an innocent man, Walther Beck, whose only crime was being Waldemar Buller's driver, and left your own wounded father lying in a pool of blood in front of his own family because you are incapable of feeling love or affection, just like your mother? Isn't it true that you two roped your innocent sister into your lies until you both drove her mad? Isn't it true that you are the true villain in this story and not Waldemar Buller, whose only crime was to be a good, caring father and an upstanding citizen, who didn't abandon his sons to their fate like Frau Buller did, but raised them, all alone, into defenders of their fatherland? They only followed orders when they shot at the enemy, Fräulein Sullivan. You have no such excuse. You acted of your own free will—"

Both Orso and Harlow are on their feet, screaming their objections; the judge is raising his gavel to call for order when a single woman's voice pierces through the pandemonium: "My rapist acted of his own free will too when I was nine years old, Mr. Henning. Like you're doing right now, standing up for the likes of him. I can't wait to hear how your own granddaughters will disown you and spit on your grave when they are big enough. And guess what? I'll fly across the ocean once again, with my cane and all, just to watch them do it."

The Military Policemen are already reaching for her to hustle her away on the judge's orders, but she's cackling like a witch of olden times, laughing at the grand inquisitor himself, her eyes fastened on Maggie with devilish mirth. Her baby sister Norma.

And Daddy, he's here too, the towering six feet three of his stocky Irish form, telling the MPs to keep their hands where they belong. His daughter was out of order, he understands, but he will walk her out himself.

The MPs step away. They want no quarrel with him.

Daddy still finds a chance to turn and nod at Maggie—the same curt but so profoundly powerful gesture that shaped her entire childhood in America. *You got this, girl. I believe in you.*

And then, only Mommy and Maggie are left: the former wiping her beautiful face with the back of her hand and Maggie holding her hand to her heart, mouthing, "I love you so much" across the courtroom. Flashes snap all around, catching the exchange that leaves not a single person in the audience untouched.

Under Buller's increasingly irate look, Henning tries a

couple more questions, but soon recedes altogether. Maggie's family has crossed the Atlantic to come here to support her. Buller has no one in the room: neither wife, nor children, not even a former comrade to testify to his defense. This tells the audience all they need to know.

When Maggie exits the courtroom, a very different crowd of reporters surrounds her. With Norma and her parents by her side, she smiles into Lee Miller's camera and pulls her namesake Higgins into a hug, reporter's pad and all.

"Do you have anything to say to the world, Miss Sullivan?" Higgins is her usual perky self, blonde curls, a thousand-watt smile, and a shark's mouth snapping at anyone coming too close to her story. Although, Maggie suspects, today it's more about them coming too close to her, Higgins', friend.

Maggie doesn't think over her answer too long. It comes out on its own, straight from the heart. "Waldemar Buller isn't an anomaly, unfortunately. There are plenty of such men around. Most ills in our world come from the image they want to project and protect by all means—of the protector, the provider, the man of the house. However, it's never about protection, it's only ever about control. What starts as 'I'm the man of the house and therefore I control all the money, what everyone eats, where everyone lives, what everyone wears,' gradually turns into outright abuse of immediate family members whenever they 'disobey the man of the house.' Wives and children get beaten, 'disciplined,' reminded of 'their place,' and the authority they are never to challenge. Said abuse eventually snowballs under any authoritarian, hierarchical system allowing such 'disciplining'; it escalates into segregation of all sorts, religious persecution, curtailing of rights, and eventually culminates in wars. Men like Buller start small, they push boundaries further and further, testing how much they can get away with and, given unlimited control, they end up complicit in literal genocide. In the early twenties, Buller was beating my mother and abusing me, because there were no laws to defend us. In the forties, he was inspecting concentration camps and deciding just how many inmates could afford to be fed and how many would have to be sent to the gas chambers, because there were no laws to defend them."

She looks around at the eager journalists capturing her every word. Her breath catches momentarily, but her beloved dad's here, his big warm palm on her shoulder, lending much-needed support.

"And our silence, our compliance, it will never help anyone," Maggie continues, recovering herself. "It didn't help the Native American population; it didn't help the enslaved Black population; it didn't help European Jews and it certainly never helped a single woman. You see, the system, in which at least one minority is oppressed, be it based on race, or gender, or religion, or disability, is a broken one. It's up to us to fix it. And I have enough people around me today to give me hope that we can. Buller took a lot from me, but not my hope for a better future. It won't come fast and it won't come easy, but it will come. And whoever doesn't want to share it with us may remain in the past, in the dark ages where they belong, until they die out like the relics they are."

Photographers' flashes light the way as Maggie, with her family by her side, leaves the Palace of Justice, closing that old, German chapter of her life for good. Her entire body feels weightless, darkness purged from it together with her testimony. She faced her monster and said her piece. Let them decide what to do with him. He's no longer her business.

"So proud of you." Norma's lips brush Maggie's cheek, warming her instantly with the infinite love for her baby sister.

"My brave, brave girl," her mother exhales in a shaky breath as she brushes a wayward lock of hair from Maggie's temple.

Only her dad, the one who's been a true father to her, doesn't say anything. He's never been a man of many words. He's simply always *been* there for her, her mother, and Norma. And now, as he wraps his arm around her shoulders, Maggie knows that he always will be, until his dying breath—the father every girl deserves.

EPILOGUE

Brooklyn, New York. November 1945

"The death sentence, eh?" James Sullivan folds the paper neatly in two and puts it down with a contented sigh. "Good riddance to bad rubbish."

Maggie grins at him across the breakfast table and the mountain of pancakes her mother is presently dividing into four equal parts. It's November and yet Norma is here instead of Bellevue and every Sunday is now a holiday in Alma Sullivan's eyes.

"Have they found out what happened to the boys?" she asks, almost drowning Norma's pancakes in syrup despite her youngest daughter's protests.

Maggie and her father exchange a quick glance, which doesn't escape Alma.

"It's all right, you can tell me. It tore my heart, leaving them there, with that monster, but after hearing all about the crimes they committed... I suspected it was only a matter of time before he corrupted them like he did everything he touched."

Alma's putting on a brave face, but Maggie knows how

much it torments her mother, having sons for war criminals. Of course, it's not Alma's fault that they were raised the way they were, but she still can't help replaying the past in her mind, wondering if she might have whisked them away together with Maggie, questioning if she tried hard enough... Blaming herself for what was her ex-husband's doing, and only his. Forgiving herself is something she needs to arrive at herself; in the meantime, Maggie will keep loving her as much as she can until she wipes the last trace of doubt from her mother's mind.

"Ragnar was killed in action during the Battle of Berlin," Maggie says, cutting into her pancake with a fork. "Hansjörg was apparently taken prisoner of war by the Soviets but died in captivity a few months later. Officially, heart failure, but Ricci says they likely killed him after they found out he was the SS."

"Oh, he's Ricci now." Norma regards everyone at the table meaningfully and even Alma smiles through the pain of the news she had grown to expect.

"You can still call him Orso, squirt," Maggie says, thankful for the lighthearted change of subject.

"One yourself."

Maggie catches her parents exchanging a look and in it, the unspoken prayer for all good things for their dear girls is written plain as day. They fear a relapse still; it's too good to be true, having their daughters jest so effortlessly with each other, to partake in a Sunday meal instead of secluding themselves in Norma's bedroom or Maggie's apartment and sharing the darkness they carried on their shoulders for much too long.

"When is he coming here?" James asks, trying to sound nonchalant and failing miserably.

"Dunno." Maggie pretends to shrug without care and also fails. "Still prosecuting the Nazis to the full extent of the law."

"A man after my own heart."

"I knew you'd approve."

"Better than that wannabe writer."

Maggie rolls her eyes and feigns annoyance, but then he reaches out and pinches her cheek like he used to do when she was a child and she laughs the same carefree laughter she only had when he was around.

Later that day, as the sun sets over Brooklyn, casting a warm golden hue across the bustling streets, Maggie sits on the stoop of their brownstone, a mug of tea sweetened with honey in her gloved hands, gazing out at the world that finally feels a little brighter. The weight that she has carried for so long feels lighter, as if the shadows of her past are slowly dissipating into the evening sky.

Somewhere in Germany, other people are answering for their sins. The very idea of the justice that shall soon be served to them as well makes the tea taste even sweeter.

Maggie turns at the creak of the door opening behind her and smiles at Norma descending the first two steps to join her on the stoop.

"I'm thinking of getting a job," Norma suddenly says, waving at the neighbor passing by with her dog on a leash. "I know I don't have much to offer in the formal education department—"

"Dr. Adler 3:15—'One shall not talk poorly about oneself,'" Maggie interrupts her with a raised mug.

"Nice verse," Norma acknowledges, deadpan. "Where's it from? Psychiatric New Testament?"

"The very same. Now say it right."

"I know I missed out on getting a formal education because I was trying to survive the depressive neurosis inflicted upon me by a lowlife rapist," Norma corrects her previous statement with the beginnings of a grin.

"That's better."

"But I thought, I'm not that bad an artist."

"The understatement of the century."

"So I thought, what if I bring my portfolio to the *Times*? You mentioned they were looking for illustrators."

"Wanna go tomorrow?"

"Can I?"

"Of course."

"OK."

They share a quiet moment, a silent understanding passing between them. The trial and the verdict have brought a sense of justice, a long-awaited closure that neither thought was possible. For the first time in years, Maggie feels a sense of peace, brought on by a simple morning newspaper. The knowledge that her birth father can no longer harm anyone else allows her to breathe deeply, to embrace the possibilities that life still holds.

Maggie moves to hug her sister with her free hand and lowers head atop Norma's that is now resting on her shoulder. Their bond, once fragile and strained by shared trauma, is now stronger than ever.

Norma looks up, her eyes reflecting the resilience and hope that have carried them through the darkest times. "Do you think we'll be all right, Mags?"

The stars begin to twinkle in the evening sky. Maggie knows that their journey is just beginning. There will still be challenges to face, but with all the people standing by their side, she feels ready to embrace whatever comes next. She'll write and speak and advocate for those who can't advocate for themselves. Brooklyn, with all its noise and chaos, is now a place where they can rebuild, where hope flourishes anew.

"I think we will, Norms. I think we will."

A LETTER FROM ELLIE

Dear reader,

I want to say a huge thank you for choosing to read *The Photographer's Secret*. If you did enjoy it, and want to keep up to date with all my latest releases, just sign up at the following link. Your email address will never be shared and you can unsubscribe at any time.

www.bookouture.com/ellie-midwood

I hope you loved *The Photographer's Secret* and if you did I would be very grateful if you could write a review. I'd love to hear what you think, and it makes such a difference helping new readers to discover one of my books for the first time.

I love hearing from my readers – you can get in touch through social media, or my website.

Thanks,

Ellie

www.elliemidwood.com

facebook.com/EllieMidwood
instagram.com/elliemidwood

A NOTE FROM THE AUTHOR

Dear reader!

Thank you so much for diving into Maggie's story and watching the justice she was owed being served. Even though Maggie is a fictional character, she's a collective image of real women correspondents, several of whom are mentioned in the novel. All the historical events surrounding those real women, such as Helen Kirkpatrick, Maggie Higgins, Lee Miller, and Ann Stringer, are based on true fact and experiences they lived through while reporting from the frontlines. I also chose not to fictionalize any of the publications they worked for, so the readers who love to dive deep into research (I am one of those!) wouldn't have any trouble finding their articles and seeing historical events unravel through these women-pioneers' eyes, told in their own words.

While mapping out Maggie's journey through war-torn Europe, I also generally stuck to history surrounding troop movements and major events, such as the Malmedy massacre and the Buchenwald liberation.

As for Maggie/Grete's childhood chapters, most of them are based on my recollections of my own abuse as a child. Unlike Grete, I wasn't fortunate enough to be saved from my monster as a little girl, no matter how much I dreamed of an escape. In the end, I saved myself, making the same trip as Grete did— from Europe to America, where I could start a new life.

Unfortunately, my abuser never had to face any consequences for his actions as the legal system failed me then as it still continues to fail far too many little girls (just as it does grown women) suffering from sexual and physical abuse. The change, brought on by the Me Too movement and the 4B movement, is gradually happening, but it's still nowhere close to serving survivors as it should. I never got the closure that I wrote for my Maggie. All I could do was sever all contact with my abuser as soon as I could do so safely and let karma take care of him. It did: he died in his early fifties from a stroke, alone in his apartment, where he remained undiscovered for weeks until the neighbors called the police to complain of the smell. At this stage of his life, he had no friends or family left who wanted anything to do with him.

Neither does this change, which is moving at a glacial pace, stop abuse from happening, still, in 2024 as I'm writing this. The name of Gisèle Pelicot comes to mind, whose own husband repeatedly drugged her and invited dozens of men to rape her while she was unconscious. Most of them lived within a fifty-mile radius from the Pelicots' residence. Gisèle's rapists' ages range from twenty-six to seventy-four. Their professions include: a firefighter, a journalist, a prison guard, municipal counselor, a nurse. Most of them have no criminal record. Many of them have families and children.

The horror of this latest case highlights the point I wanted to bring up when I only set out to write Maggie's story: most women know their abusers. They are our colleagues. Neighbors. Friends. Lovers. Husbands. Uncles. Brothers. Fathers. There is literally no safe place for us, not even in our own homes.

If you're a man reading this and your heart is aching for change, there's so much you can do for women in your lives: respect their boundaries and call your friends out if they don't do the same. Pass on the message that "no" means "no," instead of "you just have to keep trying." Don't have different sets of rules for your sons and daughters. Teach them that they're equal. Don't ask your daughter to cover up when a certain uncle comes over: if he looks at her in a suggestive way, don't invite him over. In fact, don't associate with him whatsoever. Don't ask the young women in your family (be they daughters, sisters, granddaughters, or nieces) to give you or anyone else a kiss or a hug. Teach them bodily anatomy early. It's better for a child not to hug someone if they don't feel comfortable than to teach them that they have no agency over their body or wishes—the agency that they will carry into their adult lives. Be their hero, like Maggie's adoptive father was. Like my grandfather was to me. Trust me, we don't put you all in the same basket and don't blame you for the actions of those other men. But we do need your help and support to change this world for the better for us and for the future generations of women to come. Also, let us not forget that patriarchy harms men as well. It shames male victims of sexual abuse and domestic violence into silence, into rejecting therapy and/or medication, into substance abuse and, in worst cases, into suicide. It teaches aggression as the only outlet for every emotion they experience and create more trauma for them, their families and communities around them. In the end, everyone suffers.

Remember, silence only helps the abuser, never the survivor. Start being loud together with us. Call them out. Fight them. Prosecute them. Exclude them from society. Let them die out like the cancer they are. So no little Grete shall have such a ghastly, disturbing story to tell, ever again.

ACKNOWLEDGMENTS

First and foremost, I want to thank my incredible editor, Ruth Jones, for helping me bring Maggie's story to light. She handled Grete's chapters with sensitivity and respect and truly helped me tell Grete/Maggie's story the way it needed to be told: to shed light on unspeakable abuse and at the same time honor women who went through hell and back and came out stronger in the end, and had quite a lot of stories to tell. I wouldn't have been able to do this without her unwavering support and encouragement.

To everyone in my lovely publishing family at Bookouture for working relentlessly to help my book babies reach the world. Jen Shannon, Mandy Kullar, Jade Craddock, Jane Donovan— thank you for shaping my ramblings into a coherent novel! Richard and Peta, you made it possible to have my babies translated into twenty(!) languages. I know I'm an author, but I honestly have no words to fully express my gratitude to you.

Huge thanks to Jess Readett and Sarah Hardy for organizing the best blog tours ever and securing the most interesting interviews for each new release. Even for an introvert like me, you make publicity a breeze. Working with you is a sheer delight!

Ronnie—thank you for all your support and for being the best husband ever! And for keeping all three dogs quiet when I work. I know it's not easy, given how crazy they are. I love being on this journey with you.

Vlada and Ana—my sisters from other misters—thank you

for all the adventures and the best memories we've already created and keep on creating. I don't know how I got so lucky to have you in my life.

Pupper, Joannie and Camille—thank you for all the doggie kisses and for not spilling coffee on Mommy's laptop even during your countless zoomies. You'll always be my best four-legged muses.

And, of course, the hugest thanks, from the bottom of my heart, to all of you, my wonderful readers. I can never explain how much it means to me, that not only have you taken time out of your busy schedules, but you chose one of my books to read out of millions of others. I write for you. Thank you so much for reading my stories. I love you all.

PUBLISHING TEAM

Turning a manuscript into a book requires the efforts of many people. The publishing team at Bookouture would like to acknowledge everyone who contributed to this publication.

Audio
Alba Proko
Sinead O'Connor
Melissa Tran

Commercial
Lauren Morrissette
Hannah Richmond
Imogen Allport

Cover design
Eileen Carey

Data and analysis
Mark Alder
Mohamed Bussuri

Editorial
Ruth Jones
Sinead O'Connor

Copyeditor
Jade Craddock

Proofreader
Jane Donovan

Marketing
Alex Crow
Melanie Price
Occy Carr
Cíara Rosney
Martyna Młynarska

Operations and distribution
Marina Valles
Stephanie Straub
Joe Morris

Production
Hannah Snetsinger
Mandy Kullar
Jen Shannon
Ria Clare

Publicity
Kim Nash
Noelle Holten
Jess Readett
Sarah Hardy

Rights and contracts
Peta Nightingale
Richard King
Saidah Graham

Printed in Great Britain
by Amazon

59072420R10158